BOTTLE-SHOCK

A Deadman Gulch Mystery

KIM FIELDING

Tin Box
—— PRESS ——

Bottle-Shock: A temporary condition, often caused when wine is bottled or when bottles are shaken or shipped, that interferes with a wine's flavors. It is "cured" with a few days of rest if shaken or shipped, or within a few weeks after bottling.

—WineRoad.com, Glossary of Terms

CHAPTER ONE

From Everett Vaughn's vantage point on the tall, rickety ladder, the bookstore's Grand Opening banner looked just fine.

"The right side needs to be a little higher."

He glared at his sister, standing below, her head tilted thoughtfully. "Charlotte, if I move my arm one more inch, I'm going to fall off this thing. I will hit your hundred-and-thirty-year-old floor with my forty-three-year-old body, and I will break."

"No problem. You can sue the ladder manufacturer and get rich."

"I can't sue anyone if I'm dead."

She flashed a grin. "I'll sue, then, for pain and suffering. The sheer trauma of seeing my beloved baby brother done in by their dangerous product. Then I'll get rich."

"You'd lose due to contributory negligence."

She made a dismissive sound, and Everett sighed before painfully stretching his arm to its limit and taping the end of the sign a little higher.

"Now it's a tad too high," she said.

Ignoring her, he carefully descended the rungs until his feet were back on terra firma. But when he looked up, he saw that she was right: the sign hung slightly crookedly inside the storefront window. He hoped it simply added to the charm. Besides, the bookshop's grand opening would be only a short-lived event and the banner would come down in a few days. A task that would likely be assigned to him.

Everett didn't mind helping her out; after all, that was why he'd come to Deadman Gulch in the first place. He also didn't mind that she had lots of things for him to do. Busy hands kept him from dwelling on what was absolutely not his midlife crisis. But between the not-crisis and the proximity of his older sister, he found himself regressing sometimes, acting more like a petulant kid than—God help him—a middle-aged man. He probably needed to improve his attitude.

Luckily, Charlotte was now distracted by the books in the window display and was rearranging them for the zillionth time. "Maybe I should pick a different theme," she mused.

"The natural environment is an appropriate theme. It's topical, and it's local. We're in the Sierra Nevada foothills, right at the outskirts of the Stanislaus National Forest. We're in the middle of a lot of nature."

"City boy," she muttered.

Everett thought she'd done a great job with the display. It included books for kids and adults, novels as well as nonfiction. The latter weren't just bland guidebooks, either. She'd chosen volumes focusing on environmental justice, on traditional land stewardship by Indigenous people, and on issues related to wildfires. One really interesting-looking book was about the long-term impact of local mining practices. Her final touches included a few appropriate props such as pinecones, a compass, several chunks of iron pyrite, and some old firefighting gear.

He was really proud of her for all the thought and work she'd put into the shop. He'd told her so, more than once. But it seemed that she wasn't satisfied.

"Hey, Jess?" she bellowed. "Do you think I ought to go with the famous-California-authors theme instead?"

Charlotte's best friend and business partner, Jessica Reyes—currently hidden behind the pastry case—yelled back from the other side of the vast room. "Too late. Do that one next. Everett, come here and taste this."

He eagerly abandoned his indecisive sister in favor of baked goods.

Charlotte didn't seem to notice. When he reached the pastry case, Jessica popped up like a stage magician and handed him a cookie. "I especially want your input on the size of the chocolate chunks and the quantity of sea salt."

"Aye-aye." He gave a little salute with one hand as he grasped the cookie with the other.

She watched him, narrow-eyed, as he nibbled. Jessica, like Charlotte, was in her early fifties. But unlike Charlotte—who tended toward jeans and T-shirts—Jess seemed to emulate the style of Endora from Bewitched. Today her hair was flaming orange, her eyeshadow sparkly blue, and her bell-sleeved dress purple and gold. "Well?" she prompted after he'd chewed and swallowed.

"I think I need a second sample. You know, just to make sure."

She rolled her eyes but handed over another. Although she didn't have an oven on-site, there was one at a relative's bakery-café, Rising Times, just down the street. Everett would have assumed that Jessica was in competition with the relative, but in fact the plan was for the bakery to supply many of her treats. The consensus was that it benefitted everyone to have an additional outlet for the bakery's goods.

"The salt is perfect," Everett said. "Those few flakes on top hit the tongue just right. But I'd reduce the chocolate chunk size a little so they're more evenly distributed. Tastes great, though."

She gave a businesslike nod. "Noted. I'm considering an oatmeal version too. But maybe offering two choc chip–based cookies is overkill. I'll ponder." She resumed lining the bottom shelf of the pastry case with doilies.

"And I'll be happy to taste-test anytime."

Charlotte had continued to dither over the window display, and Everett decided to hang back so his sister wouldn't catch sight of him and make him ascend the ladder again.

He took the opportunity to give the entire place a long look. The brick building stood on Main Street in the heart of the town's commercial district and had for many decades housed a general store founded around 1850, during the California gold rush, and rebuilt several times after nineteenth-century fires ravaged the town. Charlotte and Jess had preserved much of the original interior plasterwork and an old painted sign—Gentlemen's Clothing—was still faintly visible on one wall. Instead of clothing and household goods, books now filled two-thirds of the area, while the remaining space housed the pastry case, an array of coffee-making paraphernalia, and a dozen little tables with chairs. The air smelled of coffee and cinnamon and, just a bit, of old wood and paper. The overall effect was quaint and inviting, the sort of shop where locals and tourists might be tempted to linger over the shelves while sustaining themselves with cappuccino and lemon squares.

That was the plan, anyhow. For the sake of his sister and her best friend, he hoped that Gulch Pages & Pastries was a rousing success.

He also hoped he was done climbing that ladder.

Everett was just considering whether he ought to put the ladder away—maybe hide it behind other things in the storeroom—when the front door jingled merrily and a man, carrying a cup of coffee, stepped inside. He brought with him an overpowering scent of cologne that made Everett want to sneeze.

"Oh, sorry," said Charlotte with an unusual coolness in her tone. "We're closed. Grand opening is tomorrow." She pointed at the slightly crooked sign in support of her statement.

"I'm not here as a customer. I just wanted to have a chat." Dressed in an Armani suit and accessorized with large rings, he flashed a very white, very expensive smile. He was probably only in his thirties, but Everett would have bet big money that the nose and jawline were courtesy of a surgeon's scalpel and the smooth skin was thanks to Botox. Although the man was objectively attractive, he didn't rev Everett's motor in the least.

Charlotte also didn't look impressed. "I'm sorry, but we don't have time for that right now. We're busy getting ready for opening day."

"I'm sure you are." But instead of leaving, he walked closer to her, offering his right hand for a shake. "Allow me to introduce myself. I'm Blake Cannon." He paused as if that should mean something.

"Charlotte Tabor." She gave the hand a perfunctory shake. "But if you'll excuse us, Mr. Cannon, we're very—"

"Of Cannon Development," he said grandly.

Her expression didn't change. "I know."

Everett exchanged glances with Jessica, who was leaning atop the pastry case to watch. They were both familiar with that particular tone in Charlotte's voice, although of the two of them, Everett suspected that only he had borne the brunt of it. His sister had practically raised him, and as a kid he'd called it her Mister Voice. As in *You better explain yourself fast, mister, or you're toast.*

Of course Cannon didn't know that, and he kept up with that too-wide smile. "Well, as you may know, my firm is at the forefront of Gulch's renaissance. One part of those efforts involves polishing up our city's facade. You know—making sure we present an appealing image to visitors."

"I wasn't aware you were an elected official," Charlotte said coldly.

"I'm not. Although who knows, maybe someday." He turned his smile up a few watts. "Right now I'm simply a concerned businessman and community leader."

Jessica snorted, but if Cannon heard her from across the room, he ignored it.

Charlotte was clearly close to having had enough and crossed her arms. "As a businessman, I'm sure you appreciate how important it is to focus on work when there's a deadline. I have work now."

"Yes. I thought I might offer some tips, courtesy of my considerable experience. For example, there's your stock. Nobody buys books anymore. At least, not novels. They can get them so much cheaper electronically. I recommend you carry items such as upscale clothing and souvenirs, perhaps along with giftable coffee table books and the like."

"This is a bookstore." Charlotte's jaw was clenched. "And I don't need your tips."

Cannon made a sour face. "Well, I wanted to discuss your... display." He made a finger-waving motion toward the front window and, when she didn't respond, heaved a noisy sigh. "It's rather controversial, you see. And controversy isn't good for business, is it? We wouldn't want to offend potential customers. I suggest you remove those books in favor of more palatable titles. Perhaps some collections of pretty nature photos and some hiking guides. We just wouldn't want visitors to get the wrong idea about Gulch."

He set down his coffee on a nearby shelf, picked up a volume on climate change, flipped carelessly through the pages, and then—maybe by accident—dropped the book on the floor.

Hoo boy. If the guy wasn't such a colossal jerk, Everett would have felt sorry for him. The last time he recalled seeing that expression on his sister's face was when he was sixteen and, together with his stoner buddy Kush, snuck onto the golf course after hours, stole a cart, and went joyriding around the grounds until someone called the cops.

The room felt like a saloon scene in an old Western, right after some idiot had dissed the legendary gunslinger. A fair number of those showdowns had likely occurred in Gulch's early years, and now here they were again. Thank goodness Charlotte wasn't armed.

"Mr. Cannon." She enunciated it clearly, much as she must have done in her teaching days, facing a roomful of unruly middle-schoolers. "You are invited to take your ignorant, mansplaining self out my door, down the street, and back to Los Angeles or whatever miserable hole you crawled out of." She marched past him—close enough to make him flinch—yanked the door open, and waited.

He spent a moment or two trying to decide how to handle the affront. Then he straightened his back and retrieved his cup. "You'll regret this, Charlotte."

"That's Ms. Tabor to you."

He skulked past her, and as soon as he was gone, she slammed and locked the door. "What an ass," she said with feeling.

Always the younger brother, Everett couldn't resist. "You didn't find his tips helpful?"

She narrowed her eyes. "Climb the ladder and straighten that sign."

Two hours later, Charlotte was finally satisfied with the banner and the location of the paperback spinner rack. She'd set up tiny tables and chairs in the children's section and practiced with her point-of-sale system by making Everett pretend to buy things. At her direction, he'd installed a new sign on the gender-neutral restroom door, fixed the sticky drawer in the antique console table serving as the cashier counter, and evened out the slightly wobbly table that displayed a selection of classic novels.

Now he adjusted his tool belt and sat down in the café section with Charlotte and Jess, all three of them sipping coffee and munching on cookies. "You know how I'm theming the next window?" Charlotte paused. "Gender." She obviously still hadn't recovered from her encounter with Blake Cannon.

"And what does that mean?" asked Everett, because Jess was smart enough to keep her mouth shut.

"Gender identity. Gender in global politics. Feminism. Intersectionality between gender and marginalized identities. Heck, maybe I'll even include some materials on sexuality. Taddeo's *Three Women* would be an interesting choice."

Everett chuckled. "That doesn't sound very palatable, Ms. Tabor."

"Palatable my ass. I bet Blake Cannon doesn't read anything except the social media apps on his phone."

Jess nodded. "And even then, it's mostly photos and hashtags."

As the women cackled, Everett scrunched up his nose. "What kind of name is Blake Cannon anyway? Sounds like a soap opera character. What's his deal?"

"You're judging soap opera names, Everett Vaughn?" said Charlotte.

"Hey, I didn't name myself."

Jess held up a hand to quiet them. "Cannon's from Los Angeles," she said, as if that explained everything.

Although Everett had lived in California for less than two weeks, he'd already picked up on the certain amount of disdain that Deadman Gulch residents held for big city folks in general and those from Southern California especially. He wasn't steeped in the local lore enough to understand the source of these feelings. Maybe he'd ask Charlotte—sometime when she wasn't already in high dander.

He decided to change the subject. "What else needs to be done before tomorrow, Char?"

She looked around thoughtfully before shrugging. "Not a lot—just some probably unnecessary fussing on my part." She reached across the table and patted his hand. "I really appreciate all the hard work you've put in. Thank you."

"I enjoyed it," he said honestly. It had been mostly physical work like assembling shelves, painting, hauling boxes, and fixing squeaky doors and loose floorboards. Not only had using his hands and muscles been a great way to get himself out of the murky mess in his head, but he'd also liked Charlotte and Jessica's company, along with the knowledge that he was helping his sister's dream become reality.

"If you want a thrilling career in retail, you're welcome here," she said.

"Thanks, but it's maybe a little too people-y for me." That was true, but he also knew that his sister couldn't afford to pay another employee right now and wouldn't let him work for free. Besides, he was thinking that maybe manual labor—and being his own boss—was the way to go, at least for a while.

"Then your servitude is ended." She made a shooing motion. "Go off and find yourself. You are planning to stick around town, though, right?"

"I signed a six-month lease." And to reassure his landlady, since he wasn't employed, he'd paid the whole amount up front. That had taken a decent bite out of his dwindling savings. "Besides, I have the feeling you'll be finding little things for me to do for a while yet."

She gave the creaky, quirky old place a fond look. "Yeah, probably."

He stood, gathered the empty plates and cups, and carried them to the sink, where they joined several others. He'd check back later to see whether Jess wanted help with a final cleanup before the grand opening.

After saying his goodbye to both women, he headed outside. It was a fine early-autumn day, the sky bright blue and the trees along Main Street beginning to show yellow and red. The air remained warm, but not oppressively so, and by evening there would likely be a hint of crispness. The sidewalks were nearly deserted: most locals were at home, the day-trippers from the valley had left, and there weren't many overnight visitors midweek. The scene would probably be very different this weekend when the Gulch Grape Gala occurred, but in the meantime Charlotte and Jessica had some time to get the business running smoothly, and Everett had the downtown nearly to himself.

There wasn't really much to the downtown, simply a half-dozen blocks of shops and restaurants lining Main Street and extending a block or two down some of the side streets. Most of the buildings dated from the post–gold rush fire days and had remained intact since the late nineteenth century, lending Gulch an authentic Western feel. Smiling to himself, Everett swaggered a bit as he walked, pretending that the tool belt around his hips was a gun belt, and instead of a hammer and screwdrivers, he actually carried a pair of holstered Colts. Sheriff Vaughn, keeping an eye out for horse rustlers and bank robbers. He sort of wished he had a Stetson and boots with spurs.

One block down from the bookstore, he paused to gaze into a display window at Mother Lode Discoveries, a sprawling antique mall that took up most of the building. An oak icebox was on display. Although it was a little beat up, some TLC would make it into a really nice bar cabinet. And restoring it would keep him busy for a couple of days. That is, if he were the kind of guy who needed a bar cabinet, and planned to stick around longer than six months.

"Hey! Hey, handyman!"

Ordinarily, Everett would have ignored the shout. But since there were so few people out, he suspected it was directed at him. He turned to see Blake Cannon hurrying toward him from across the street, dashing into the empty street without looking. He came to a halt in front of Everett.

"You're the handyman from that bookstore." He sounded slightly accusatory.

Curious where this was going to lead, Everett nodded.

"Do you speak English?"

Taken aback, Everett said, "Passably."

"Okay, good. I need to hire you to do some work."

"I'm not—"

"Look, what are those women paying you? Be honest, now—I'll be verifying it. And I'll pay you a dollar an hour more." Cannon nodded once, as if that was going to cement the deal.

Everett hid a smile. "Exactly what work did you have in mind?"

"Handyman work, of course." Cannon rolled his eyes. "I bought a house and it needs some things done. The previous owner had atrocious taste. Minor repairs and installation, some painting, that sort of thing. I'd do it myself, but I'm far too busy. I've tried several times to hire people, but frankly, I find most of the locals to be... unreliable. It's totally unprofessional."

Although Everett knew he should probably inform Cannon that he was, in fact, the bookstore owner's brother and not Mr. Fix-It, he didn't. He found listening to this ass too amusing. Besides, maybe he could find a way to wreak some slight vengeance on Charlotte's behalf.

"Are you licensed and bonded?" Cannon asked.

"Nope."

"Didn't think so. Well, I'll have to make do, I suppose. I'll be paying you off the record, of course. That means you won't have to pay taxes on it, so it's like earning even more."

Everett added patronizing to Cannon's catalog of faults. "I don't know...."

"What are your rates? I'll reimburse for materials as well, although I'll need to approve purchases ahead of time and receive itemized receipts."

"Hmm." Everett considered his options. He wasn't officially a handyman, but he could handle most minor household projects, and hadn't he just been thinking how much he enjoyed working with his hands? This would keep him busy for a little while, which was good, and a few extra bucks wouldn't go amiss. Charlotte clearly detested this guy—for good reason, it seemed—but maybe Everett could dig up some dirt on him. His sister did enjoy good gossip.

"Fifty an hour," said Everett, a number he basically pulled out of his ass.

"Again, remember that I will be confirming this."

That would be interesting. "Go right ahead."

Cannon grimaced. But he must have been desperate, because after a moment he sighed. "All right. I'll expect you to be prompt and to clean up after yourself. And to follow my instructions carefully."

"Aye-aye, captain."

"Fine. I'm at the top of Winter Camp Road. Just follow the road until it ends—you can't miss it. Arrive promptly at eight tomorrow morning. Bring your own tools. I will give you instructions when you arrive. I expect you to use the highest standards of care."

"Okay."

Cannon gave another curt nod and turned to walk away. Then he stopped, and, clearly as an afterthought, asked, "What's your name?"

"Everett Vaughn."

"I'll see you at eight sharp, Everett." He marched back across the street, again without looking.

For a while, Everett stood there, bemused. He knew he should have come clean, but he had a hard time resisting a little minor mischief. He was honestly capable of the kind of work that Cannon wanted. Everett had been doing a lot of those things recently for Charlotte. He'd learned of necessity when he was a kid, since their house was practically falling down around them and nobody else had the time or inclination to fix things. And he'd always enjoyed a bit of tinkering. Using his hands to make broken things work and to improve physical spaces gave him deep satisfaction.

So... fine. He'd play handyman, at least for a day or two. Whistling happily, he made his way home.

CHAPTER TWO

Everett felt fortunate to have rented this house. It was only a couple of blocks uphill from Main Street, just around the corner from the old schoolhouse that now served as a community center. The little two-bedroom bungalow was over a hundred years old but in decent condition, and it had come fully furnished. It belonged to a friend of Charlotte's who'd relocated to Sacramento to care for an aging parent and who intended to move back to Deadman Gulch someday. She was willing to rent it for a reasonable price and on a six-month lease, so that was perfect.

It didn't feel like home, however. He'd arrived with only a couple of suitcases—the rest of his belongings in Chicago storage—and nothing in the house was his. He'd hoped that living like this would give him a sense of freedom, but instead it made him feel restless and a little disconnected.

Well, maybe that was what he needed right now. Maybe this stage of his life was like taking an old piece of machinery apart and cleaning it thoroughly before reassembling it.

With that optimistic thought, he made a salad and cooked some pasta for dinner. One advantage of moving to Gulch was that his eating habits had improved. There were a limited number of restaurants, none of which were open late, and neither of the two grocery stores was open late either. There was a weekly farmer's market, however, so he'd stocked up on apples, figs, avocados, and greens, all of which were much nicer than he was used to back home.

No, Deadman Gulch was home, at least for the time being. He needed to remember that.

He turned on the TV for company while he ate, but he didn't pay attention to the news show out of Sacramento. Instead he concentrated on updating his to-do list. One priority was finding a way to get regular workouts. There was a yoga studio in Gulch, but that didn't interest him. The nearest gym was almost thirty minutes away, and because he didn't especially enjoy exercising, he knew he'd rarely summon the willpower to manage that. But he couldn't do nothing. Now that he was well into his forties, he couldn't take fitness and good health for granted. Walking, running, and bicycling were all risky in Gulch, where locals and tourists tended to zoom around in enormous four-wheel-drive monstrosities and where Main Street was one of the few roads with sidewalks. Also, there were hills. He wasn't a fan.

It occurred to him that with the money Cannon would pay him, he could afford to buy some used exercise equipment and keep it in the spare bedroom. A stationary bike or elliptical and some hand weights, maybe. He spent a good chunk of the evening researching the possibilities. And then, mindful of his morning responsibilities, he went to bed early.

But he didn't fall asleep right away. He told himself it was because he wasn't yet used to Gulch's nighttime silence. Back in Chicago—even in the suburbs where he'd recently lived—there was noise at all hours. Vehicles rolling by, sirens and horns and car alarms, people shouting and dogs barking. Music blasting through open windows, neighbors slamming doors. So yes, it was odd to hear nothing but crickets chirping and the occasional unsettling rustle of some small creature outside.

The truth, however, was that what actually kept him awake was the emptiness of his bed. He had been accustomed to having his husband —now ex-husband—beside him, big and warm and familiar. Sometimes snuffling or snoring, sometimes accidentally kicking him or pushing an elbow into his ribs. And when he allowed himself to remember that another man might now be lying there in his place while Everett slept alone, well, that wasn't conducive to an easy rest.

Maybe taking up an exercise regimen would help.

Everett woke up early, showered and shaved, and then walked to Rising Times, the bakery two blocks down from the bookshop. While the rest of the stores remained dark, Rising Times was brightly lit and wafting delicious scents through the open door. They were primarily a takeout business, with only a couple of tiny tables inside, but their breads and pastries were good and they served a decent cup of coffee.

"Good morning!" chirped the tattooed and pierced young woman behind the counter. Xochi Reyes had recently taken over the business from her mother, who was somehow related to Jessica. Cousins, maybe. Everett hadn't quite caught the specifics. In addition to Xochi supplying many of the goodies for Jess's café, she had also offered the use of her ovens now and then, an arrangement that seemed to please everyone.

Everett smiled at Xochi. "Bake anything especially wonderful today?" Everything she created was wonderful, which was another reason why he needed to up his exercise game.

"How about a brown butter apple blondie?"

"Sold. And a gallon or so of coffee, please."

It took her only a few minutes to fill the order and for him to pay, but since there were no other customers at the moment, he loitered. He'd already learned that Xochi was an excellent source of local gossip, maybe because nearly everyone in town passed through her door regularly. Or maybe just because good pastries put people in a chatty mood.

"Hey, do you know anything about a guy named Blake Cannon?" A little background info on his new employer might be helpful, and he didn't want to ask his sister.

Xochi scrunched up her face as if she'd smelled rotten food. "Yeah."

"What's his deal? He didn't make a good impression on me yesterday."

"I shouldn't say anything bad about a customer." But then she shrugged. "He hardly ever comes here anyway, so he doesn't really count. You know, he walks around town with a Peet's cup, like he's trying to impress people. But the nearest Peet's is in Stockton, and I know he's not driving two hours round-trip every day to get his latte."

Everett nodded and took a sip of his own coffee, burning his tongue in the process. He always did, and he never learned. "He was trying to boss Charlotte around yesterday—telling her what to sell and what books to display."

"I bet that went over real well." She grinned.

"Yup. But who is he?"

"Some kinda developer, I guess. He showed up about six months ago and rented a little office space on Black Bart Road next to Orna-mentery."

"Ah." Everett had always wondered how Christmas-themed shops managed to stay in business year-round, but at the moment that was irrelevant. "What's he developing?"

"A resort and, like, gated community."

Everett blinked. Gulch was a nice enough town, but it wasn't espe-cially upscale, and aside from some successful wineries, there wasn't a lot of big money floating around. "Resort?"

"Fancy-schmancy. Like Napa. Expensive hotel, famous restaurant, golf course, shops full of stuff nobody around here wants or can afford."

So that was why he was so worried about the town's image. Everett couldn't imagine these plans were popular among the locals. Even if Cannon's resort was successful, not much of the money would trickle down to them, and some of the existing businesses would go under. Gulch currently boasted one gold rush–era hotel, one motel from the seventies, and a couple of bed and breakfasts. If wealthy people came from the Bay Area or SoCal, they would want to spend their money at the resort, not at the Snooze-Inn... or at Rising Times.

Xochi peered at him. "Why are you asking? Your sister didn't want to tell you all this?"

"I didn't want to ask her. I, uh, sort of agreed to do some work for him."

She jerked back. "You're going to be his lawyer? Look, if you're planning to help him ruin our town and—"

"Whoa! I'm not his lawyer. I've put away my legal shingle forever, and I'm not even licensed to practice in California." It was interesting, however, that Xochi knew about his former profession. Probably Jessica had told her. "I'm just going to do some home repairs for him."

She visibly relaxed and straightened the container of sugar packets. "I guess that's not so bad. I mean, that place is messed up. The guy who used to own it was, uh, eccentric. Cannon could use all the help he can get."

Everett might have continued the conversation, but Marian Fisker from the antique mall next door wandered in, her tiny dog clutched in her arms. Charlotte had introduced her to Everett shortly after he arrived in town, when Char bought an antique table from Marian to use in the shop. Everett wished both women a good day and headed home to finish his breakfast and get his truck.

———

Although the Toyota was a fairly new acquisition for Everett, it was nearly twenty years old. It had accumulated a lot of miles, a collection of dings and scratches, and—he was pretty sure—a distinct personality. He'd chosen it because it was cheap and able to haul things, a definite benefit while he was helping Charlotte ready her store. All-wheel drive also seemed wise in a location where ice and snow sometimes happened and plows could be slow to arrive. Plus, some of the roads were in rough shape even in good weather.

The truck was dark red on the outside, and its gray interior smelled like french fries. If it sat too long between uses, the engine tended to grumble when he started it up. The radio—no Bluetooth in this baby—worked when it wanted to. He felt very butch behind the wheel.

He'd named the truck Janet, after his mother. He'd never before named any of his vehicles, but with this one it seemed apt.

Everett and Janet bumped down Main Street, still mostly deserted.

The sky had lightened, but the sun wasn't yet visible; it had to get pretty high before it could be seen from the western slopes of the Sierras. Everett felt content, his belly full of blondie and a decent dose of caffeine zinging through his bloodstream. He wore old jeans and an NSYNC tee, the latter a joke gift from Sam that Everett couldn't quite bear to part with. This lifestyle was way better than the olden days, when he slogged through traffic on the Stevenson Expressway, clad in his lawyer costume. If he never had to wear a tie again, he'd be a happy man.

A couple of miles east of town, Everett turned left off the state highway onto Winter Camp Road. It zigged and zagged uphill, first past some modest houses and then a few small ranches before plunging into a thickly forested area dotted with what looked like little vacation cabins. Their steep mossy roofs, littered with branches and evergreen needles, and their vacant weedy driveways emanated a general air of neglect. Beyond the cabins, but still amid what might have been old-growth trees, the road took a sharp right turn, rose steeply, and then abruptly ended in front of a house that clung to the hillside.

Everett paused, engine idling, and stared. He'd never claimed any mastery of architectural design details, but this structure looked sorely out of place. It was shaped somewhat like a chalet, with a broad roof and wide eaves—fairly appropriate in a mountain community even if Switzerland was a long distance away. But this thing had a stone facing on the bottom floor, black metallic siding on the two stories above, and a roof made of red clay tile. "The architect must have been on 'shrooms," he muttered.

The only landscaping—if the term was used loosely—consisted of several enormous empty pots in abstract shapes, painted silver and placed near the entry door. A black BMW was parked in the driveway in front of the triple garage. Everett pulled in next to it and turned off the truck. When he got out, he stood for a moment, simply taking in the environment.

It was oddly quiet. No traffic or noisy neighbors, which was no surprise. But also no birds or chattering squirrels. Sure, it was still early, but Everett was sometimes awakened near dawn at his house by sparrows, jays, ravens, and a bunch of other feathered creatures he couldn't identify. He'd even complained about it to Charlotte, who'd rolled her eyes and called him City Boy. Here, though, there was nothing.

The clomp of his boots on the pavement seemed especially loud, and when he rang the electronic doorbell, the sound echoed. A moment later the door swung open so suddenly that Everett jerked back. Cannon stood there in dress slacks and a pale-blue dress shirt, a tie hanging from one hand. He smelled strongly of that nose-tickling cologne. "Oh, it's you," he said.

"You said eight sharp, and it's—"

"Yes, yes. I know. Come inside."

He led Everett at a swift pace through a foyer, down a hallway, and to a small half bath that appeared to have escaped from Versailles: marble floor, ornately papered walls and ceiling, and an atrocious amount of gilding. There was even a petite crystal chandelier hanging from the ceiling. Perhaps the designer had been aiming for whimsical, but the room gave Everett a headache.

"I bought this property in foreclosure. It suits my needs, but the previous owner was as poor at furnishing the place as he was at handling his finances. I'll require experts for some of the tasks, but I assume you can handle the simple ones."

Everett tried not to bristle. "Safe assumption."

"The faucet is dripping," Cannon announced. "I keep seeing water around the base of the toilet too. And I need a new mirror and new towel bars installed. Are you capable of these things?"

A plumber might have been a wiser choice for some of that, rather than a general handyman, but Everett had done all of these things in the past. "Sure."

"I expect top-quality workmanship. Also, no excess noise—I'll be working from here this morning. And clean up after yourself when you're finished. If I find you've done an acceptable job, I have several other tasks around the house."

"Let me go get my toolbox." Then a thought occurred to him and he paused. "We should write something up. A written contract."

Cannon pasted on an insincere smile. "Oh, that's really not necessary. It's just a few little fix-its."

Ordinarily Everett would have dug in his heels. His years as an attorney had taught him that everything gets put in writing, and besides, he could dash off a contract in a couple of minutes. But he wasn't in the mood to argue. So he smiled back, took out his phone, and opened the Voice Memos app. He pressed the Record button. "Just for the record, you know?" He stated the date, the location, and both of their names. "I agree to complete specified handyman projects in an acceptable manner and within reasonable time. You agree to pay me fifty dollars per hour, due upon completion. Agreed?"

Cannon frowned. "Wasn't it forty-five?"

"It was fifty."

After a brief hesitation, Cannon nodded and then reluctantly said, "I agree."

Everett stopped recording and pocketed the phone. It wasn't a great substitute for a written contract, but it was acceptable for now. He marched off to retrieve his tools.

It was a little tricky to work in the confined space of the powder room, and Everett's knees definitely weren't what they used to be. But he enjoyed himself nonetheless, just as he had while helping Charlotte at the bookshop. After spending months feeling aimless and unproductive, it felt good to be accomplishing something, even if all he was doing was stopping a couple of leaks. He imagined himself clad in patched coveralls and a porkpie hat, toiling through twelve-hour workdays and six-day workweeks under pre-OSHA conditions, but proud to bring food home to his adoring family.

Cannon stopped by a couple of times, allegedly to make sure he was doing okay, but more realistically to keep an eye on him. He probably wanted to make sure Everett wasn't lollygagging to pad his fees.

Just as Everett was making sure that the second towel bar was level, and his stomach began grumbling for lunch, his employer came by again. "I'm going in to the office. I have work to do there."

"Cool. I'm done here."

Everett stepped out of the bathroom so that Cannon could test the faucet, peer at the toilet and new mirror, and tug lightly at the towel bars. He did all of this with a degree of intensity that suggested the results were critical and he was skeptical. Finally, he scrunched up his mouth. "That mirror's not centered over the sink."

Instead of answering, Everett whipped out his tape measure and demonstrated that in fact the mirror was perfectly aligned.

Cannon seemed a little disappointed to have nothing to complain about. "All right. Now if you'll excuse me...."

"That was four hours and ten minutes. I'll round down to four even, which makes it two hundred bucks."

"Fine. I'll mail you a check."

"Payable on completion." Everett held up his phone again. "You can Venmo me."

With a certain degree of ill grace, Cannon sent payment.

Then, seeming to remember that he had more work which needed doing, his demeanor changed. "Eight tomorrow. I have to make a little trip, but I'll text you the access code for the lock and send a list of tasks."

"Okay." Working without this guy hovering over his shoulder would be infinitely more pleasant.

"I will warn you that I have security cameras installed throughout the house."

With some effort, Everett managed not to snarl. "Look. I'm not a liar, a cheat, or a thief. If you're going to continue to treat me as if I am, we can just end our business dealings right now." He crossed his arms. He was shorter than Cannon, and not particularly muscular, but his previous career had given him plenty of practice at letting his opponent know he meant business. He gave Cannon his well-practiced *that's my last best offer* stare.

Cannon sighed before nodding twice. "All right. Let's both assume good faith, shall we?"

After hesitating for a moment—just long enough to make Cannon wonder whether that statement had been adequate—Everett said, "Okay. I'll be waiting for your text." He finished gathering his tools, his mind already on the pulled pork sandwich he was going to order at Big Al's BBQ.

CHAPTER THREE

Later that afternoon, Everett strolled by the bookshop just to take a peek at the grand opening. It looked busy, and since Charlotte and Jessica didn't need him getting in the way, he decided to stay outside. He stared through the window of the little gem and mining shop next door, Miner's Stake, which never seemed to be open, and then browsed the racks at the Western-wear shop before buying a flannel shirt jacket in a blue-and-black buffalo check. On the one hand, he was supposed to be on a tight budget. But on the other, he had an extra two hundred sitting in his Venmo account right now, with more promised tomorrow. Plus, the weather would soon be chilly and he liked the idea of rocking the whole mountain-man look. Hell, maybe he should grow a beard.

After dropping off his parcel at home, he went back out and wandered around town for a bit, admiring what he assumed to be the last of the summer flowers adorning people's yards. He found himself entertained by the varieties of outdoor décor. Some people opted for wind chimes, little flags, or concrete birdbaths, while others embraced the whole Western/gold rush theme. Wagon wheels were common, as were horseshoes affixed to various objects. One house had a child-sized mining cart filled with rocks painted shiny gold. Another had succulents planted in old cowboy boots.

Eventually he found himself at a hilltop cemetery. Although many of the graves dated to the mid-nineteenth century, there were also plenty of recent ones decorated with flowers and trinkets, demonstrating that these dearly departed were still mourned. He wondered what had happened to his parents' remains after they died—he'd never asked—and then wondered whether he wanted to talk to Charlotte about it. Probably not. Let the dead rest in peace.

It was after six when he returned to Main Street. Some restaurant customers sat at outdoor tables, but the shops and wine-tasting rooms had closed. So had Gulch Pages & Pastries, but Charlotte caught sight of him hovering near the front door and let him in. Jessica had apparently left already.

He looked around and noted that while he couldn't tell how many books had been sold, it was clear that things had at least been moved around. "How'd it go?"

"Nobody complained about the window display."

So she was still rankled about that. Maybe best not to mention his work for Cannon just yet. "And sales? Everything was smooth?"

"As smooth as can be expected. I can't find where I put the giveaway bookmarks. A kid brought in an ice cream and promptly dropped it on the floor. Deja is convinced that the point-of-sale tablet is haunted."

Deja, who attended the nearby community college, was one of the six people that Charlotte and Jess had hired as part-time help. All of the staff had been in over the previous week for training, so Everett had been able to meet them. He liked Deja, who was especially enthusiastic about the history and biography sections, but who also tended to be a little too chatty when they should be working.

"Does Deja expect you to exorcise the tablet?"

"Not yet. They're waiting to determine whether the ghost is friendly. Oh, but when you get a sec, could you take a look at the knob on the door to the back room? It feels loose."

"I'll do it now." He wandered to the back while she continued to close out the cash register. Sure enough, the screws needed tightening, but since he didn't have his tools with him, he'd stop by tomorrow after finishing at Cannon's place.

For now, he meandered into the fiction section. It had been a long time since he'd done much pleasure reading, mostly because sitting for too long made him feel antsy. But it had occurred to him recently that he could try listening to audiobooks while he worked or exercised, so now he browsed to get ideas for what he might listen to. He made a mental note to ask Charlotte later if there was any way to buy audiobooks through her. Might as well send a little profit his sister's way.

"Want me to drive you home?" he asked when Charlotte was ready to go.

"No thanks. Actually, Rob's coming to pick me up and take me to dinner in Sonora. Want to join us? We're going to that steak place."

"You don't need a third wheel, but thanks."

"Rob and I have been married for almost thirty years. We've had plenty of just-us time." She fished a keyring out of her purse and switched off the lights, leaving only the streetlamps through the front windows for illumination. The shadows between the aisles seemed very deep.

Everett shook away a chill. "Thanks for the offer, but I think I'm going to eat a gummy tonight and watch stupid stuff on TV."

"And eat something healthy," she said sternly, as if he were still nine.

He grinned at her. "Don't I always?"

At the curb just outside the shop, Rob sat in his idling Jeep. He'd gone paunchy and bald, and he dressed exactly like a high school science teacher—because he was a high school science teacher—but he was also a genuinely good man who supported Charlotte in her retail venture. He and Everett waved at each other as Charlotte climbed into the SUV. Then Everett watched their tail lights recede before making his way home.

He did not eat something healthy. Instead he cooked pancakes and bacon, drowned the plate in syrup, and washed everything down with two bottles of IPA. That pretty much negated the need for any THC to get him into a mellow mood, so after dinner he skipped the edible, slumped on the couch, and blearily watched home-improvement videos on YouTube.

He used to own a home. Well, he'd co-owned one. The townhome was only a few years old, which meant there was nothing much for him to fix. Which had been just as well, considering he spent most of his waking hours at work or commuting in and out of the city. On the rare occasions when something had needed adjusting or repair, Sam had insisted on calling a handyman. It was one of the things they used to fight about.

"Not anymore," Everett reminded himself now. The townhome had been sold. Sam was living on Lake Shore Drive, renting an upscale apartment with a gym, a pool, and views of Lake Michigan. While Everett was here in Deadman Gulch with YouTube on the television and a spot of syrup on his T-shirt.

And a job, at least for the next day. That was something.

He was midway through learning how to install a garage door when his phone buzzed. He considered ignoring it, but concerned that Charlotte was experiencing a bookstore-related emergency, he glanced at the screen—and saw a text from Sam.

You doing okay?

Well, he'd never told Sam not to contact him. They'd agreed to stay on friendly terms, in fact. They'd both been remarkably mature and levelheaded about the whole thing. Nobody's fault, they agreed. They'd simply grown apart.

Still, Everett couldn't resist a slightly snotty reply.

Eaten by bears.

It took a while for the next text to arrive, although the three blinking dots indicated that Sam had started to type but likely hesitated. Finally, three images showed up in quick succession. First a GIF of a dancing cartoon bear; then a photo of a football player in a navy-and-orange uniform; and finally a picture of a very large, hairy, shirtless man. A single question mark appeared after that.

Everett snorted a laugh.

Hyperbole. I remain uneaten in any sense.

But are you doing okay?

Did an ex—even an amicable one—have any right to ask this?

Everett pictured Sam standing in front of the big window in his living room, watching the city lights reflected on the lake, feeling virtuous for worrying about Everett's welfare. Not that he should worry. Everett might not have his act together at the moment, but he wasn't doing anything more foolish or dangerous than eating too many carbs. He wasn't self-destructive. As far as midlife crises went, his was pretty low-key.

I'm good, he replied after a while.

I'm glad. A long pause, and then, *I miss you.*

Okay, that was a shitty thing to say, and Everett didn't answer.

Once upon a time, he'd thought that the two of them were going to work out. They'd met over ten years ago while representing opposing sides in an insurance dispute, and they'd clicked instantly. Neither client had been especially pleased with the settlement, but Everett and Sam had spun into a whirlwind romance that culminated six months later in vows before a Cook County judge. They'd had a brief honeymoon in Paris because Sam was a closet romantic. They bought the townhome because Sam insisted it was more practical than an old fixer-upper. And then they both went back to their jobs. Everything was great.

Until it wasn't.

In the end, it was probably the pandemic that doomed them. Before that, they'd both been too busy to notice if anything was lacking. Most of the time they spent together, they were asleep, and during the rest they were running errands or doing chores. Then they were locked up together, and surprisingly, that wasn't too bad either. It didn't feel right to complain when the entire planet was going through a miserable period and lots of people were far worse off than they were.

But as things started to transition back to some approximation of normal, the cracks widened. Everett felt stagnant. No, it was worse than that—like Alice and the Red Queen, he was running desperately and getting nowhere. He needed something else, something new, something worth living for. Sam, on the other hand, was determined to root himself even more firmly in place. After a lot of discussion, they had to accept that they were no longer on the same journey.

Nobody cheated. Nobody hated anyone. They hadn't even yelled that much. The divorce was quick and peaceful. The proceeds from their house went to finally pay off their student loans, and they split what was left over. Sam had used part of his to rent an apartment; Everett didn't know what he'd done with the rest. Everett had enough to support himself for a year or two. The first year was spent as a nomad, gifting himself with the travel he'd never been able to manage before. And now he'd landed in California—for the time being—to help his sister and to decide what he wanted to be when he grew up.

And now Sam was texting him.

Sorry. Kind of drunk. Being maudlin. Do miss you, though.

Wasn't that just like Sam to put a comma in a text for God's sake? Everett considered opening another bottle of beer but couldn't muster the energy. Instead, he replied *You don't really miss me. I'm like the shitty pizza at Lancini's. I was convenient and you were used to me and now I'm gone.* There was much, much better pizza to be found in Chicagoland, but Lancini's had been on the way home and was open late, so they'd gotten takeout from there often—until the health inspectors closed the place down.

You're not shitty.

Start dating. Find yourself the human equivalent of Pequod's.

I always did like deep dish. After a moment, Sam added *You finding good pizza there?*

You know California. It's all avocados and kale. Everett added an avocado emoji, because when would he next have the chance to use one?

Sam replied with a laughing emoji. Then Everett turned off his phone and hauled himself upright to fetch another beer.

CHAPTER FOUR

Since it was a downright chilly morning, Everett wore his new jacket on the walk to breakfast. The blue-checked flannel was lined with fleece, and he took satisfaction in the fact that he looked much more like a handyman than a corporate lawyer. He should probably get a hat soon, and some gloves. He'd owned both of those items in Chicago but before moving had donated them—along with his suits, ties, dress shoes, and the long wool overcoat that made him feel, on occasion, like a noir detective. He was happy to avoid another Chicago winter, but he'd need at least a few wardrobe additions to survive the coldest months in Gulch.

He bought coffee and a danish at Rising Times, but because Xochi was busy, he didn't stay to chat. Back outside, he gazed at window displays. He greeted three dog-walkers and the quartet of ancient codgers who congregated on the benches outside the library. He briefly scrolled through news headlines on his phone, immediately regretted it, and tucked the phone back in his pocket. He did not, thankfully, sit hunched in a car, hands tense on the steering wheel, watching the miles crawl by as he made his way into the law office.

But there was work to do today, so eventually he walked home, got into his truck, and drove to Winter Camp Road. Somehow the little cabins looked even more forlorn today, although he brightened slightly when he caught sight of some deer browsing among the underbrush. His window was rolled down, allowing foresty scents to waft in. He caught a hint of wood smoke and hoped it was someone's fireplace and not a wildfire.

He suddenly felt tempted to turn the truck around and drive deeper into the mountains so he could take a long hike in the woods. Not that he'd ever done anything like that—there hadn't been mountain opportunities in Illinois, even if he'd had the time—but the concept appealed. Maybe it was the influence of his shirt jacket. But he had promised Cannon he'd show up today, and Everett wasn't the type to break promises. Even when he made them to jerks.

There was no sign of the BMW at Cannon's house, which made sense since he'd said he wouldn't be there. Using the code he'd been provided, Everett let himself inside, then paused in the entryway. It was a little weird to be in someone's home when they weren't there, and Everett barely knew the guy. There were a few security cameras, and in case Cannon was watching, Everett waved at the one near the entry.

Cannon had texted a list of chores, which Everett scanned, deciding what to tackle first. There would be more than enough to keep him busy all day: painting a bedroom, installing new handles on the kitchen cabinets, replacing the ceiling fan in the living room, and assembling shelving in the garage. Because the empty house felt a little creepy, Everett decided to tackle the garage project first.

It took a while to figure out how to get to the garage from inside the house. The garage was built in, but the house had several floors due to the steep hillside, and the architect—if there had been one—had apparently tried to make the floor plan as confusing as possible. Also, the house was big, with way more square footage than a single man needed. Although that wasn't any of Everett's business.

When he finally found the garage, he whistled in amazement. It was much larger than it looked from the outside. One could easily fit four good-size vehicles in there and still have room for storage and a workshop. Right now it was mostly empty except for several long, flat boxes that contained the shelving pieces. The space also contained a healthy population of spiders. Everett didn't especially mind creepy-crawlies as long as they left him alone, and these seemed inclined to stick to their webs, so that was fine.

He popped in his earbuds, cued up music on his phone, and got to work.

By eleven o'clock, four heavy-duty steel-and-plywood shelving units were assembled and in place. That was a lot of storage space, which made him wonder what the hell Cannon intended to use them for. But again, none of Everett's business. He stretched a few times to work out the kinks in his muscles and debated whether to take a lunch break now or in an hour or two. He could definitely do with more coffee. But first, his bladder demanded attention.

Figuring there might be a bathroom down here, he opened some doors. The first led to a small room that contained the furnace, water heater, and electrical panel. The second was a closet holding only a few cans of paint. The third, however, revealed a narrow descending stairway. "Huh," he said out loud. "Yet another level."

He knew that some of the buildings downtown had very deep basements that connected to old mine shafts—the bookstore being one of them. Charlotte had joked that they should go down there and start digging in hopes of finding gold, but Everett was uneasy at the idea of unseen tunnels and lurking holes. Was there an old mine beneath Cannon's house too? The idea gave him a chill.

Cannon hadn't specifically forbidden him from poking around down there. Everett knew this was a technicality, but hell, he was an ex–corporate lawyer. He loved technicalities. And his curiosity was too strong to resist. So he grabbed a flashlight from his tool box and ventured down, an intrepid explorer venturing into the bowels of the earth—ew, that was an unpleasant phrase—in search of lost treasure.

The results were disappointing. The space was cool and a little damp, clearly dug out of the living rock, but there was no sign of gold ingots or anything else of particular interest. Instead, Cannon was apparently using the space as a wine cellar. Several dozen cases were stacked along the walls, most of them sealed, and the few that were open had a couple of bottles missing. Everett had always been a beer guy and knew very little about wine, so the vineyard names printed on the boxes didn't mean anything to him. Maybe he should learn more about the topic now that he lived in Deadman Gulch. The coming weekend's Grape Gala would likely provide a good opportunity.

Realizing that he still needed to pee, he climbed the stairs and resumed his bathroom search.

Everett cradled the phone against his shoulder as he tucked the last items into his toolbox. "It's five—I'm gonna call it a day." And go home and have good hot soak, maybe. His muscles ached.

There was a brief silence on the other end of the phone, followed by an annoyed-sounding tongue click. "Did you complete the chores?" Cannon asked.

"I did not. Shelves and cabinet handles are complete. New ceiling fan is up. The bedroom is taped but I haven't started painting yet."

"I would have thought you'd finish in nine hours."

"Eight. I took a lunch break."

"Hmm." Another tongue click. "Can you come back on Saturday? You can paint then, and I'll have a few other things."

Everett considered for a moment. "The Grape Gala is this weekend. Charlotte might need me."

"I need you. Look, I have a tight timeline, and I can't have you in the house again until Saturday. You'd be in my way. I'll pay you fifty-five an hour for Saturday."

Ooh, a whole five-buck-per-hour bonus. But it was true: a few more hours' worth of pay would go a long way toward stretching Everett's finances. And the bookshop wouldn't open until eleven. "I can do a few hours in the morning." Maybe he could even complete the bedroom paint job during that time. It was a small space.

"Fine. Eight."

"Okay. And you owe me four-hundred bucks for today, incidentally."

"I'm right in the middle of something, but I'll Venmo it to you when I'm done."

Although Everett was a little reluctant to wait, he agreed. They ended the call, and he hoisted his toolbox and headed for the door.

After dropping off his tools at home and then checking in at the bookstore—everything was fine, and apparently Deja had decided that the haunted tablet was benign—he took himself out for dinner at the Mexican place next door to the post office. Halfway through his third margarita, he remembered that Cannon hadn't paid him yet, so he texted: *Payment is due daily upon completion of services. Kindly remit $400 promptly.*

At first there was no answer, but then Cannon replied. *I'll pay after you finish the work on Saturday.*

Everett growled, which startled the family at the adjacent table, so he gave them an apologetic look before answering. *I was clear—payment due at the completion of EACH workday.* Dammit, he should have insisted on a written contract. He knew better.

Several minutes passed with no response from Cannon. Everett was sort of in the mood for a fight, but tussling via text wasn't nearly as fun as doing it in person, and besides, he was a wee bit tipsy. Not three sheets to the wind, but definitely one—okay, maybe two. This place mixed its drinks strong. He decided that sobriety was best at this point in the negotiations, so he'd take it up again with Cannon in the morning. It wasn't as if the guy was going to disappear on him; Everett knew where he lived.

Only a little unsteady on his feet, Everett wandered home. The air was chilly, which didn't bother him in his current state. The uneven pavement, however, was another matter, and he nearly fell several times. He wondered how many people had drunkenly stumbled through Deadman Gulch back in gold rush days and whether that might even be the source of the town's name. Some guy has a few too many shots of whiskey at a local saloon, falls into a ditch and drowns, and voila, eponym. Everett decided to ask his sister the next time he saw her.

The next morning, Everett vowed to never touch demon liquor again. Hangovers hadn't hit nearly this hard when he was in his twenties. But now that he was well into his forties, it seemed that all bets were off. It wasn't fair.

Instead of getting up early and walking to Rising Times, he downed some aspirin and lolled in bed until he felt strong enough for dry toast and tea. He still hadn't heard anything more from Cannon—or received payment—but his head pounded too much to deal with that at the moment. He puttered around the house, doing small chores. One of the kitchen drawers had been sticking, so he cleaned the tracks and sprayed them with a bit of lubricant.

In fact, quite a few things in the house needed repair. Nothing major, and nothing that threatened the structural integrity, but there were certainly things that could be done to improve the physical space and increase energy efficiency. Nothing had been updated since the seventies, as far as he could tell. He made a mental note to ask his landlady, Bev, whether she minded if he did a few small projects.

By midafternoon, after a shower and light lunch, Everett once again felt human. Good enough, in fact, that he ventured outside and walked to the bookshop. The place wasn't busy—not surprising for a Thursday —but a few people sat at tables in the café area and a few more meandered through the bookshelves. He watched Charlotte help a man pick out some picture books for his granddaughter. His sister was as animated as he'd ever seen her, clearly taking great joy in her work. This made him a little envious. He'd never felt that happy about his lawyer job, and now he had no career at all.

After Charlotte rang up the picture books, she walked over to where Everett lurked among the greeting cards. "I hear you had a good time at El Dorado last night," she said.

"I had dinner, yes."

"And margaritas."

"How did you—"

"It's a small town, baby brother. No secrets." She grinned smugly.

Great. "I'm a grown man. I can get inebriated if I choose, as long as I don't drive and don't become disorderly."

"Yes you can. Drinks are cheaper at the Oasis, though."

The Oasis was one of Gulch's three bars. Everett had never been inside, but judging from the outside, it was authentically... rustic. "Does the Oasis have chiles rellenos?"

"The Oasis doesn't serve food, which is probably a blessing. Cheap drinks, though." She scrunched up her face in a way that meant she was about to get serious. "Are you sure you're okay?"

"I'm not drinking my troubles away. I was just in the mood to get a little sloshed, and the margaritas were tasty. I don't need an intervention."

He tried not to sound angry because he knew she was worried about him and had never quite relinquished being his caregiver. But he wasn't one of her kids—her twin daughters were twenty-two—and if he wanted to do stupid things to himself, that was his prerogative. He decided to change the subject.

"Looks like the store's running well."

"So far. The big test will be this weekend."

"Will you need my help?" Then he remembered that he was supposed to go to Cannon's, assuming he received payment before then. "Saturday afternoon? All day Sunday?"

She looked slightly uncertain, an unusual state for her. "Could you maybe sort of... hang around? Just in case? I think I have everything covered, but Grape Gala crowds are big, so you never know. Is it too much to ask?"

"I'll be happy to," he said honestly. Maybe he'd commandeer one of Jessica's tables and keep watch in case disaster struck. "So the grape thing's a huge deal, huh?"

"About as huge as things get around here. Look, there are a lot of little towns in the foothills. This town relies heavily on tourist income, and we have two main draws—the caves and the wine."

He nodded. There were two caves nearby, Castle Caverns and Baskett Caverns, but he hadn't visited either. From what he understood, Baskett was named after a miner who'd discovered the cave by falling into it and dying, which only confirmed Everett's conviction that going into deep holes in the ground wasn't a great idea. Some people felt otherwise, however, and they happily paid for tours.

He'd stick to the other tourist attraction. "I'd like to learn some basics about wine. Do you have any good books on the subject?"

"Of course I do. But there are twenty tasting rooms in or near Gulch." She was using her school teacher voice. "Why don't you begin by speaking to some of the winemakers themselves? I suggest Granocchio to start. The owner there loves to educate people, and their tasting room is open into the evening."

That wasn't a bad idea. In fact, he should get right on it, especially since today was slow and things would likely start picking up tomorrow. He saluted her, waved to Jessica, and started for the door. But Charlotte stopped him with a yell: "Hey, Ev?"

He turned around, eyebrows raised. "Yes?"

"Are you free for an hour or so on Monday?"

He didn't need to consult his calendar. "Sure."

"Good, because I already volunteered you. My friend Carol Allen has a space at Mother Lode Discoveries. She always sells a lot during the Gala, and she wants to move some new items in on Monday. But she's in her seventies and had knee surgery not long ago. I figured you have that truck and a strong back, so...."

"So I'm helping Carol Allen schlep her antiques on Monday."

"If you don't mind. She'll pay you." Charlotte dropped her voice. "She's got plenty of money, so don't feel bad for taking some."

Everett shrugged. "Sounds good to me." He saluted again and then left in search of a wine education.

It wasn't easy to choose a tasting room. As Charlotte had pointed out, there were a lot of them—over a dozen within easy walking distance. He didn't know what differentiated them and, honestly, didn't understand why there were so damned many. How many ways were there to ferment grape juice?

After wandering up the street for a couple of blocks, he ended up in the one that Charlotte had suggested: Granocchio Cellars. The dim interior was narrow and deep, with stone walls, a bar running along most of the left-hand side, and a wooden floor that was probably original to the building. The right-hand wall sported a large world map and a dozen framed wine labels. A few shelves near the entrance offered fancy wine glasses; packets of crackers and nuts; and kitchen towels, coasters, and bottle openers with the Granocchio logo. The entire place smelled pleasantly of wine.

"Welcome in," called the woman behind the bar. She seemed to be the only person in the place. She was tall and thin and wore denim overalls with a maroon long-sleeved tee, her long gray hair held back by a tie-dye headband.

Everett sauntered over and slid onto one of the barstools. "Thanks."

"You here for a tasting?"

"I guess so. I mean, yes. Except I know pretty much zilch about wine."

She grinned. "You don't need to be an expert to enjoy it. But if you want a lesson, I'm happy to give you one. Learning about wine can open up a whole new world for you."

They exchanged brief introductions—her name was Willow—and she set a glass in front of him before grabbing a bottle from the rack along the wall. "Where are you visiting from?" she asked.

"Up the street. I live here—for the time being, anyway."

She looked pensive for a moment and then wagged her finger. "I knew I'd seen you. You've been working over at the new bookshop."

While she removed the cork and poured some white wine, he replied. "I'm Charlotte Tabor's brother. I'm here to help her set up and get things running smoothly."

"Well, helping out like that's real nice. My husband and our younger daughter run the production end of things, and during the busy season, our older daughter and nephew chip in. Family's not always the easiest to work with, but they can be the most rewarding. Now, let me tell you about this pinot grigio I just poured."

Over the course of the next two hours, Everett drank a fair amount while getting a crash course on wines. A few other customers stopped in, tried some varieties, and left clutching their purchases. But Everett remained, and Willow didn't seem to mind. In fact, she had an endless store of knowledge and seemed delighted to share it.

"So do you grow all of these different grapes?" he asked, swirling a glass of red called barbera.

She laughed. "We don't grow any at all. Growing grapes is a whole different enterprise from making wine. Now, some winemakers do both, especially the bigger ones. But a lot of us contract with vineyards instead. That allows us access to a bigger variety of grapes, and it allows small growers to concentrate on one or two types."

That made sense. He took a sip. He didn't taste all of the things that a more experienced connoisseur would, but he could make out a sort of spicy blackberry flavor along with a hint of oak. "How do you decide which growers to work with?"

"It depends." She leaned her elbows on the bar comfortably. "We prefer certain varietals, and we get to know the people who've planted them. You know, mostly all of us in the business get along, but things have grown more competitive lately. There's more money in it than there used to be. Sometimes we'll think we're all set, and then another winemaker will come along and swoop up a particular harvest we had our eyes on."

"Don't you have contracts?"

"Sometimes."

What was the deal with the lack of contracts around this place? Were the locals allergic to lawyers or paperwork?

As if she'd read his mind, Willow shook her head. "We're small potatoes. Well, small grapes, I guess. We're not like the big producers in Napa-Sonoma, and certainly not like the megacorps in the Central Valley. Winemaking is more than a business to us—it's our life. Most of us still think of it as a family thing. Families don't need contracts."

Everett begged to differ. Things like prenuptial agreements saved a lot of aggravation later, and while those hadn't been within his bailiwick, he had worked on plenty of trusts, articles of incorporation, and the like, all of which set out specific roles and responsibilities of family members. "I guess not everyone appreciates legal frameworks as much as I do."

Willow heaved a sigh. "I just wish they weren't necessary. Humans should treat each other with respect. Some people just don't get that."

He nodded his agreement. "I should probably get something in my stomach besides popcorn and fermented grapes," he said, dismounting the stool carefully. He wasn't drunk, but he also wasn't completely sober, and he'd been sitting a long time.

Before he left, he bought four bottles. As he carried them home, glass clanking softy inside the tote bag, he considered whether he'd enjoy a career in winemaking. Probably not, he concluded. Too much science, too many temperamental variables. Viniculture might be more his speed, since he liked gardening. Well, he liked the idea of gardening, but his actual experience had been limited to a few window boxes at the condo. Probably he should just stick to drinking wine rather than creating it.

It was depressing to be in a midlife crisis. Honestly, wasn't he far too old to be asking himself what he wanted to be when he grew up?

No, he decided as he fumbled with the lock on his front door, what he was actually doing was finding himself. That was a much more positive spin. For his entire life, he'd taken the most logical path, the most sensible one, and he'd never truly asked himself whether he liked that path. Now all he had to do was find a path that brought him joy. And that was no small quest.

CHAPTER FIVE

By Friday afternoon, the downtown had grown crowded. Parking spaces on or near Main Street were all taken, and the two public lots were full. Visitors wandered between shops and tasting rooms, some clutching ice cream cones and others carrying tote bags full of wine bottles. It was almost impossible to walk down the sidewalk due to the roadblocks created by folks peering in windows or stopping to chat.

The festivities didn't even start until the next morning, but Charlotte had said a lot of people arrived a day early and spent the night at one of the two hotels or in an Airbnb.

Jessica had chimed in. "My Aunt Olivia stays with a friend during the Gala and rents out her house, just for the weekend. She makes enough money to cover a month's mortgage." That had made Everett thankful that his landlady hadn't tried to gouge him by charging extra this month. It probably helped that he'd paid the entire six months up front.

He found himself irritated by the crowds. He knew in principle that local businesses depended on them, but in practice they were annoying as hell. He gave up on eating lunch out since all the restaurants were full, and he instead decided to walk up to the cemetery where, presumably, the company would be more peaceful.

Along the way he passed only a few people, exchanging nods with them before moving on. As he'd hoped, the cemetery itself was nearly deserted, with just a middle-aged couple standing at the far end, gazing at headstones. Everett climbed to the highest point and sat on a mossy stone bench, thoughtfully placed there long ago. The view here looked away from town and toward the east, where thick woods eventually gave way to some pastures, a scattering of houses, and the highway.

In fact, he realized, he was looking down over Winter Camp Road. He couldn't make out Cannon's house due to the trees, but he had a fairly good idea where it was. He scowled when he remembered that he still hadn't been paid, but when he readied himself to send a text, he found that cell service was almost nonexistent in this spot. He turned to face the opposite direction, watched some birds circling in the thermals and heard others calling from trees, and felt almost at one with nature.

He pictured himself clad in hiking boots and layers of old clothes, living in a tiny off-grid cabin, fishing and gardening to feed himself, spending his days communing with nature. He would catalog every local species of bird, discover a plant previously unknown to humans, and rescue an injured mountain lion that would become his best friend. There would be folktales told in Gulch about the mysterious wild man in the forest, but nobody would ever catch more than a glimpse of him.

No central heat or indoor plumbing, however. So never mind.

But could he do something outdoorsy for a living? He wasn't sure what the career options were. Park ranger felt too much like law enforcement, and he didn't want that. Lumberjack? Was that still a thing? He imagined himself bearded, wearing red flannel and boots, hefting an axe, and it didn't compute. Besides, he'd feel guilty about cutting down trees and, most likely, displacing all sorts of wild creatures.

He noticed that the nearest grave was for Achilles Curnow, who'd died in 1856 when he was only twenty-two years old. The stone was in poor shape, the engraved letters hard to read, and it stood slightly apart from any other graves. Somebody must have cared about Achilles enough to pay for the stone, but there wasn't any indication that he had family buried nearby. Maybe he'd come alone to Gulch, in search of a fortune, leaving his relatives back East or overseas. Maybe they never knew what had happened to him.

"Morbid much?" Everett grumbled aloud. He rose with a theatrical groan, slowly made his way to the cemetery gate, and then started down the curvy road that led to the center of town. For the first time since he'd climbed up here, he heard voices, and when he rounded a corner, he nearly collided with two men.

One was Blake Cannon, looking out of place in dress slacks and a pale blue button-up shirt. His fiftyish companion, attired in khakis, a red polo shirt, and a baseball cap, looked as though he'd just stepped off a golf course.

"What are you doing here?" Cannon demanded, as if he had the right to know.

Everett replied as mildly as he was able. "Walking. It's allowed."

Cannon paused a moment, frowning as if he were trying to think of some way to complain about Everett's presence. But apparently he couldn't, because after huffing once, he continued up the road at a rapid clip. The other man, who looked slightly puzzled, hurried to keep up.

"Hey!" Everett yelled at the retreating backs. "You still owe—"

Cannon spun around with a snarl. "It's all taken care of. I don't have access to my phone this very second."

That first sentence was certainly a lie, but Everett didn't want to make a scene in front of the stranger. "I'll follow up very soon."

"Come tomorrow, as you've agreed to. We'll settle it then." Cannon spun on his heel and marched away.

Everett was almost back to his house when his phone buzzed.

"How much do you love me?" Charlotte asked as soon as he answered the call.

Uh-oh. He stopped in front of his neighbor's display of gnomes pulling miniature carts of fake gold. "What is it?" he asked warily.

"A crisis. You know the Olive Branch?"

Of course he did; it was directly across the street from the book-shop. Everett hadn't been inside, but he'd looked in the windows and knew it carried kitchenware and gourmet foods, as well as fancy olive oils and vinegars that people could taste before buying. It had been some time since he'd cooked anything more than the basics, in part because his rented house was equipped with minimal equipment. He liked to cook, though, and had been considering a visit to the Olive Branch to pick up a few things.

"What's wrong with the Olive Branch?" he asked.

"Broken sink. Gary and Tom—those are the owners—haven't been able to find a plumber, which means they're going to have to close early today. And who knows when, or if, they'll be able to open tomorrow." She paused as if to let the import of that sink in.

"I'll swing by and see if I can help."

"You are an angel, baby brother."

Right, he thought as he hung up. We'll see if she still thinks so when she learns I'm working for Cannon.

He popped home long enough to grab his toolbox and then, knowing parking would be impossible, headed toward Main Street on foot.

The door at the Olive Branch was locked, with a hastily written sign taped on the other side of the glass: *We sprung a leak! Closed until we fix it.* He knocked, and a moment later a tall, gray-haired man in a plaid apron let him in. "Are you the angel?" he asked.

"Um, I'm—"

"I mean Charlotte's brother. Sorry. We're a little flustered right now." He looked it, with spots of high color on his cheeks and tight lines at the corners of his mouth, even when he tried to smile.

Everett stuck out a hand. "Everett Vaughn."

"Gary Rollins-Ross. And I am so glad you're here."

"I have to warn you, I'm not a licensed plumber. But I can—"

"Charlotte told us about you. Said you know your way around a toolbox. We could definitely use some of that right now."

"I'll do my best."

Gary led him through the store, which was bigger than Everett had realized and crowded with shelves and tables. They walked past displays of fancy kitchen towels, whimsical teapots, and themed salt and pepper shakers; between shelves laden with crackers, pastas, and jars of preserves; and to a section where stainless steel vats perched on tables. Each urn had a spigot and a label that specified the variety of oil or vinegar. There were also stacks of tiny plastic cups, presumably for tasting purposes, and a scattering of waste baskets for the used cups.

On one wall was a commercial-size metal sink, under which a second man crouched, plastic bucket in his hands. "Help!" he said when he saw Everett. A steady stream of water flowed from the pipe into a second bucket that was almost full. Puddles and wet footprints dotted the vinyl floor.

"We've been doing a sort of bucket brigade," said Gary. "As soon as one of them fills, I've been carrying it out back and dumping it. Tom's in charge of switching the full ones for empties."

Everett nodded. "Have you tried turning off the water?"

"The taps are off," said Tom, who looked close to panic. "This is the cold water line coming into the sink."

"Right. But usually— Hang on." He gently urged Tom out of the way, then performed the bucket switch. Gary grabbed the full one and, water sloshing over the edges, hurried it toward the back of the store. That taken care of, Everett reached over and turned the shut-off valve.

The rush of water stopped immediately.

"Oh my God, you fixed it!" exclaimed Tom. His panicked expression was replaced with delight.

"Not exactly." Everett peered closely at the pipe. "There's a plastic nut that connects the supply line to the valve, and it's broken. You're going to need to replace it before you can turn the water back on. Actually, the line itself is in pretty rough shape, so you're probably going to want to replace that too." He stood, groaning a little because getting off the floor wasn't as easy as it used to be, and stared mournfully at his wet knees.

Tom was nodding eagerly. "Is that something you can do?"

"I could if I had the right parts. But the nearest hardware store is in Angels Camp, and"—he glanced at his watch—"they'll be closed by the time I get there." Thanks to his projects at the bookstore, he was well acquainted with the hardware store's hours of operation.

Gary rejoined them with the emptied bucket, grinning when he saw that there was no longer a flood danger. When Tom quickly updated him, Gary seemed relieved. "So it's not going to cost us a fortune to take care of this?"

"Less than a hundred bucks for the parts—assuming you replace the hot water line too, which you should—and less than an hour of work. I don't know what plumbers' rates are around here, but—"

"Can you do it?"

Everett considered briefly. "Sure, if you can wait until Sunday."

Gary and Tom exchanged looks the way that longstanding couples did when wanting to have a silent conversation. It was Gary who answered. "We can manage without the sink this weekend—we use it for in-house cooking demos, and we're not doing any of those. Could you come Monday? We're closed then, so...."

"So I wouldn't be in customers' way. No problem. I have another appointment Monday, but it won't take all day."

The two men breathed tandem sighs of relief. Aside from their age and matching aprons, they didn't look much alike. Gary was tall, thin, and dark, whereas Tom was short, plump, and pale. Their body language, however, made it clear they weren't just business partners. "How long have you been married?" asked Everett, slightly envious.

Tom reached over to pat his husband's arm. "Depends how you measure it. We had a commitment ceremony in 1991. In 2004 we flew to Massachusetts and got legally wed there. We tied the knot in California in 2008, and then we did it again in 2013."

Although that made Everett even more envious, it also made him happy. "Which anniversary do you celebrate?"

"All of them!" they said in unison before Gary leaned down to give Tom a quick peck on the lips. They were frigging adorable, damn them.

Everett knelt in the puddle again to snap some photos of the underside of the sink and take a few measurements. He wanted to make sure he bought the right parts. Then, knees once again creaking, he stood. "Okay, so if you give me your number, I'll text and let you know when I can come by on Monday."

"Do you want payment now?" Gary asked.

They were the antithesis of Blake Cannon. Excellent. "No, Monday is fine. I'll just charge you parts plus twenty-five bucks." It really should be a quick job.

"And how much do we owe you for today?"

Everett laughed. "I didn't do anything but turn a knob. It's on the house." At this point, he mostly wanted to go home, change out of his wet jeans, and dig up something to eat. Standing among all the kitchenware made him hungry.

"Nope!" Tom clapped his hands briskly. "You saved us. The Grape Gala and the Holiday Fest are our two biggest sales weekends of the year."

Before Everett could argue that there were probably lots of people who would have known how to shut off the water, Tom and Gary scurried away. Everett grabbed his toolbox and headed toward the front door but was waylaid by Tom, who was clutching a cellophane-wrapped basket that appeared to be full of small items. "Here," he said, pressing it into Everett's chest. "Local goodies. Honey, jam, crackers, a lovely tapenade, cookies, dried fruits, chocolates.... Oh! Dan Lowman's peach salsa. It's to die for."

"That's... a lot."

"It's our nicest selection. I curate the baskets myself. Take it."

Since refusing didn't seem to be an option, Everett cradled the basket in the arm that wasn't holding the tool box. It was heavy, and the enormous violet bow tickled his chin. "Thanks. That's really generous of you."

"You saved our skins," Gary intoned, and Tom nodded. They walked him to the door and bade him cheery good-byes.

It wasn't easy to dodge pedestrians while carrying his dual burdens, and Everett almost tripped over a too-long flexi leash with a labradoodle on one end and a stylishly dressed twenty-something woman on the other, but he eventually managed to make it home with toolbox, basket, and body intact.

He set the toolbox in its usual place near the front door and plopped the basket onto the kitchen table, greedily eyeing its contents. Tonight's dinner was going to be unconventional but tasty. Maybe he'd turn in early tonight. He had the expectation that tomorrow was going to be a long day, and he assiduously turned his thoughts away from Blake Cannon.

CHAPTER SIX

The morning line at Rising Times snaked out the door and down the sidewalk. Everett took one look, sighed, and turned tail for his house, which was equipped with an ancient Mr. Coffee. Not an ideal way to begin the morning, but it would have to do.

As he leaned against the kitchen counter, steaming mug clutched in one hand, an idea struck. He found his phone and texted Charlotte, who he knew would be up despite the early hour. She was probably sitting with a coffee cup of her own and vibrating with nervous energy. *I'll be at the bookshop noonish. Want me to bring you something for lunch?* Maybe she'd have a chance to grab something from Jess's café, but she might want something more substantial than a pastry.

She responded quickly. *This is why you're my favorite brother.*

I'm your only brother.

She replied with a shrugging emoji.

Should I bring something for Jess too?

This time she sent several hearts, which he took to mean yes.

Knock 'em dead, big sis.

He tucked the phone away and finished his coffee.

The short drive to Cannon's house took longer than usual. Downtown was already getting congested, especially near City Park where,

Charlotte had informed him, a grape stomp would take place later this afternoon. People were setting up for that, and at one end of the park, horses were being harnessed onto a pair of reproduction stagecoaches that would offer rides up and down Main Street. Above the street itself, bright grape-themed banners fluttered in the morning breeze. Restaurant staff members set up outdoor seating, and uniformed police put out orange cones, presumably reinforcing no-parking areas. The lights weren't yet on in Gulch Pages & Pastries, but Charlotte and Jess would likely be arriving soon.

Winter Camp Road looked especially forlorn in contrast to the bustle downtown. Horses grazed in pastures, none of them bothering to look up as Everett rolled by. The cabins remained empty, which was too bad; had they been in decent shape, they all probably would have been rented out this weekend. And up at the top of the road, Cannon's BMW sat in the driveway. Everett pulled in next to it.

Although it was 7:58, nobody answered the doorbell, even after Everett rang a second time. A knock didn't bring a response either, and when he sent a text—*I'm here*—there was no text in return.

Maybe Cannon was avoiding him. Or maybe he expected Everett to let himself in, like last time. After a moment of dithering, Everett punched in the door code. He wasn't a criminal law expert, but he was fairly certain this didn't constitute trespassing or breaking and entering. A jury would agree that it was a reasonable assumption that he should go on in and begin work. Probably.

"Hello!" he called as soon as he stepped inside. But there was only silence in response, and the house had that particular echoey quality that happened when nobody else was there. Where the hell was Cannon? As far as Everett knew, the BMW was his only car, but it was possible somebody had picked him up and provided a ride. Or maybe he'd gone for a walk, although—despite their encounter near the cemetery—he hadn't struck Everett as the going-for-a-stroll type.

Not only hadn't Cannon payed for the previous work, but he also hadn't texted any instructions, so Everett had no idea what he was expected to do aside from painting the room he'd already taped off. If he hadn't been owed money, he would have given up and returned home. But this felt like another of Cannon's ploys, and Everett wasn't quite ready to throw in the towel. He'd been accused on more than one occasion of a certain, er, single-mindedness about things. This was a trait that had served him well in his previous career. Today he was feeling single-minded about Cannon.

For lack of any better course of action, Everett wandered toward the kitchen, which he hadn't previously seen. It was up a flight of stairs. Everything in this damn house was up or down a flight of stairs, as if M.C. Escher had been the architect.

When he reached the kitchen, Everett heaved a sigh. The space was large, and when the house was built a couple decades earlier, someone had put in a top-end kitchen. He would have had a great time cooking there. But now half of it was ripped out and a sleek stainless-steel island had been installed in the center. The island was fine per se and had probably been expensive, but it didn't fit the style of the house or anything in it. Oh well, it wasn't his place to judge other people's decorating choices.

It didn't appear that the kitchen was currently usable for much cooking, but the island was covered in papers and blueprints that hadn't been there during his last visit. Curious, Everett took a closer look. He didn't need to touch anything since one of the blueprints was unrolled, its corners held in place with empty coffee mugs.

It showed a swath of land. After a few moments of squinting and tilting his head—dammit, it was time for him to get reading glasses—he recognized the main highway and Winter Camp Road. The pastures and forest were gone, however. This layout showed a golf course in their place, as well as a hotel with outdoor pool and tennis courts, and a separate building labeled Events Venue. There was also a cluster of structures labeled Retail, and, off to one side, a small vineyard. Another section looked as if it included townhomes.

The top of the blueprint announced the name of the project: Il Vigneto Resort.

Now Everett fully understood why some locals might be resentful of Cannon's plans. If successful, a resort like this would attract a clientele very different from what Deadman Gulch was accustomed to. Wealthier and perhaps more sophisticated. Unlikely to be interested in browsing at Mother Lode Discoveries or Ornamentary. Averse to eating at Big Al's or drinking at the Oasis. A rustic little tasting room such as Granocchio Cellars wouldn't appeal to them. They'd likely spend little time in town. It was too far to walk, and they would want glitz and glamour. The resort would cater to all their whims and indulgences.

Cannon's project might make him and his investors rich, but it would do very little to benefit the locals. And the town's sweet, low-key ambience would be endangered.

It wasn't Everett's place to judge any of this. Hell, he wasn't even a local, although his sister and her family had lived here for years. These plans made him angry, however. What gave people like Blake Cannon the right to come in and screw up a perfectly nice place, all in the name of profits?

Now Everett was more determined than ever to find Cannon. Not just to get paid but also so Everett could tell him to go screw himself. Then Everett would march off in a foot-stomping, door-slamming huff. It would be great.

Unfortunately, there was still no sign of the man himself.

Then Everett's eye caught something he'd overlooked in the general chaos of the kitchen. Two items sat on the counter next to the sink: a Peet's Coffee cup and a phone.

Cannon definitely didn't seem like the type to go anywhere without his phone.

Everett approached it. When he tentatively tapped the screen, it displayed a string of text notifications, which would imply that the phone's owner hadn't checked it in some time. Also, the charge indicator was red and showed the battery at six percent. That was a little odd, especially this early in the morning. Didn't most people charge overnight?

This whole situation felt... weird. Everett possessed a reasonable share of intuition, and at the moment it was starting to set off alarms. Okay then, what to do? Simply leaving wouldn't sit right with him; it would leave too many loose ends and unanswered questions. He could call the cops, but had no idea what he'd tell them. Besides, they might not take too kindly to him being in the house without express permission.

Time to snoop in earnest, then.

He started on the upper level of the house, where there were several bedrooms, each with an en suite bathroom. Two contained nothing but haphazardly stacked cardboard boxes; one of them had been painted recently, based on the lingering scent. Another bedroom was set up as an office, but no papers or office supplies were in sight, and the desk, bookshelves, and filing cabinet showed a film of dust. The fourth bedroom had all the personality of a mid-grade hotel: a dresser, nightstand, and bed with a bare mattress, all pushed to the center of the room. This was the space he'd taped off, and the tape remained untouched.

Finally Everett reached what must have been Cannon's bedroom, enormous and with a view all the way to the highway. Cannon could stand here, a king surveying his domain. The furniture here looked to be of good quality but was too sleek for Everett's taste. On the wall hung a wedding photo of Cannon with a pretty woman who looked vaguely familiar, although Everett couldn't place her. The king-size bed was made, albeit carelessly.

On the floor below, Everett checked out the living room, dining room, and bathroom, along with an empty space that might have been intended as a den or family room. The next floor had the powder room he'd worked on and a room containing an impressive collection of exercise equipment. Everett ran longing eyes over an elaborate elliptical machine. One level down and he was in the garage, which held nothing but the shelves he'd assembled. They remained empty.

The only spot he hadn't yet searched was the cellar. As soon as he opened the door, a strong odor of wine assailed him. During his previous visit, he'd smelled nothing but a hint of damp. He moved cautiously down the stairs and turned the corner.

A body lay sprawled on the floor.

Even though Everett was not a detective, he understood a few things very quickly.

First, the body was that of Blake Cannon. Although he was belly-down, his head was turned enough for Everett to identify him.

His horribly mottled face was one of the clues about the second thing: Cannon was dead—very dead. His corpse was stiff with rigor mortis.

And third, Cannon had likely not died by accident. Beneath him was a large stain comprised of dried blood and wine. Shards of broken glass were scattered over and around him. It looked an awful lot like someone had bashed him in the back of the head with a wine bottle.

Well, shit.

CHAPTER SEVEN

Sergeant Cole McBeth twisted in the driver's seat to face Everett more directly. "You want me to find you a bagel? Might help settle your stomach."

Everett clutched a disposable coffee cup—from Rising Times, he noticed—and shook his head. "I'm fine."

"You sure? You were looking a little green around the gills for a while there."

"I'm fine," Everett repeated.

In fact, Sergeant McBeth was doing a good job distracting Everett from what he'd recently witnessed. Mostly because McBeth looked how Everett imagined a Western deputy sheriff ought to look: tall, well-built, and ruggedly handsome, with a square jaw and crinkles at the outer corners of his brown eyes. Everett could imagine him on horseback pursuing cattle rustlers. Or swaggering down Main Street with hands on his holsters, ready to outdraw bank robbers. Everett didn't have a uniform kink, but McBeth certainly filled his out very well. And his—

"Mr. Vaughn?"

Everett cleared his head with a small shake. "Sorry. I was just...." He let the sentence trail away for lack of a good way to end it.

"I understand. Seeing something like this can be very traumatic. If it helps to know, you did an excellent job describing what you experienced here this morning. You're very detail-oriented."

The words, said in McBeth's soothing tones, struck Everett as patronizing. He scowled. "Practicing law does that to a guy."

McBeth looked surprised. "You're a lawyer? I thought you were a handyman."

"I was a lawyer. I quit last year."

"Did you practice around here?"

"Chicago."

Everett stared through the windshield of the squad car at the cluster of vehicles parked in front of Cannon's house. Some were marked police cars, but not all. Deputies and crime-scene techs scurried around. One woman looked suspiciously like a reporter, but nobody was talking to her right now; she simply leaned against the grille of her SUV and watched.

As far as Everett could tell, McBeth was in charge. He had the annoyingly confident air of someone accustomed to telling other people what to do. One of the first to show up after Everett called 911, he had rousted Everett from his perch outside the front door, directed him into the passenger seat of the squad car, and taken copious notes while Everett tried to recall everything he'd done since arriving this morning. Sometimes other deputies interrupted McBeth with questions, but he always turned his full attention back to Everett.

"How did you go from being a lawyer in Chicago to fixin' up houses in Deadman Gulch?"

McBeth really said it like that—fixin'—as if Central Casting had made sure he sounded folksy. He had one of those warm voices, deep but not too deep. Perfect for conveying a sense of trust and security. Maybe he practiced it, along with the lifted eyebrow thing he was doing right now.

"I got burned out. I came out here to help my sister—she just opened the new bookshop. The old building needed a lot of work, and I'm pretty good with a hammer, so...." Everett was going to shrug, but it didn't seem worth the effort.

"I'm missing a step, Mr. Vaughn. You were helping your sister, but you were also helping Mr. Cannon? Is he a relative too?"

Thankfully, no was probably not the right thing to say about the recently deceased. "I just met him the other day. He saw me working in the bookstore, assumed I was Charlotte's hired handyman, and offered me some work. I've pretty much finished up in the shop and could use a few extra bucks, so I said yes." He didn't add that he'd also been motivated by curiosity about the man who'd acted like such a jerk.

McBeth looked slightly skeptical. "Still, that's quite a career change."

"Lots of lawyers get burned out. I'm not sure what my next chapter's going to be, but I do like working with my hands, so why not? There's no shame in manual labor." He hoped he didn't sound too defensive.

"Of course not." McBeth's voice was soothing. "I worked my way through college loading and delivering furniture and appliances. But I'm just trying to get a full understanding of your relationship with Mr. Cannon."

It now occurred to Everett that the sergeant might suspect that he had been providing Cannon with much more personal services than just hanging his ceiling fan. He shuddered at the idea. "I assure you that when I say I was fixing his plumbing, I mean it literally and not metaphorically. We did not have sex. I have no clue whether he was into men."

It looked as if McBeth was struggling to suppress a smile. "My conjecture hadn't actually gone in that direction, but thank you for the clarification. Your relationship was entirely professional—noted." He wrote something in his notebook; Everett couldn't see what.

An impossibly young-looking deputy with a blonde ponytail approached the car and spoke through the open driver's window. "Sergeant, we haven't found any next of kin yet. Maybe on his phone, once we can get into it, but...."

"But that'll take time. Yeah. Why don't you have a chat with Rossi? Maybe she knows something helpful."

The deputy shot an unhappy look in the direction of the reporter. "Ugh."

"C'mon, it's not so bad. I know you'll do a good job of extracting anything helpful from her without giving away anything we'd rather not share right now."

The compliment visibly perked her up. She nodded and hurried away, and McBeth returned his attention to Everett. "So where were we? Ah, you and Mr. Cannon were not an item. When did you first meet him?"

"Tuesday evening. I did some work for him Wednesday morning and all day Thursday. We didn't talk much. In fact, he wasn't even there on Thursday. He gave me the lock code and a list."

"So I take it you don't know who may be responsible for his death?"

"No idea." Everett paused a moment, took a breath, and decided he might as well be up-front about things that would eventually be revealed anyway. "He owed me money. He paid me for Wednesday but not Thursday, so he owed me four hundred bucks, and I wasn't happy about it. But that didn't make me homicidal."

McBeth's scrutiny was sharp. "He didn't pay you for your work, yet you returned?"

"I intended to persuade him to pay me this morning. And before you get any ideas, I mean only legal persuasion. In my experience, simply throwing around a few well-chosen legal words works wonders."

"Is that how you kept criminals out of jail?"

Everett rolled his eyes so hard he almost sprained something. "I practiced corporate law. No criminals for me." That wasn't precisely true. Some of the companies his firm had represented hadn't always skated on the right side of the law, although generally when they were doing something questionable, the only ones affected were other companies—who were also doing something questionable. At least that was what Everett had told himself. He'd eventually found himself less convincing, which was one of the reasons he'd quit.

"Ah," said McBeth. "So you don't necessarily know much about homicide."

Homicide. Now, that was an ugly word. It had occurred to Everett that he would be an obvious suspect, and that he should have lawyered up before talking to law enforcement. But at first he'd been in too much shock to think clearly. And besides, he'd spent more than enough time in the company of attorneys and didn't fancy the idea of spending more. Plus, he didn't know a single local lawyer. Charlotte might, but he was reluctant to ask her.

Oh, crap. Charlotte. Now she was definitely going to find out he'd been working for Cannon. Maybe Everett would be better off in jail.

"Sergeant McBeth, the only things I know about homicide are what I learned in Crim Law a long time ago. And the fact that I have no interest in committing it."

"Most folks have no interest in killing someone—until the right circumstances fall into their laps. Maybe the victim sorta has it coming."

Irritation, which had been simmering barely beneath the surface even before Everett discovered a corpse, flared hotly. "If you're expecting me to confess, not gonna happen because it wasn't me. And I certainly don't think anyone deserves to die over a few hundred bucks."

McBeth seemed more amused than annoyed at the outburst. "If I'm aiming to interrogate you, I guess I'll have to try harder. I'll keep that in mind."

Why did this guy have to be so obnoxiously smug and handsome? It wasn't fair. Everett glared at him.

After a long pause, McBeth sighed. "Okay. Unless you have anything to add, you can go. You're staying with your sister?"

"No, renting a place."

"All right. Just stick around town for a while, please. I'll likely be asking you more questions as the investigation continues."

"Am I a suspect?"

"Right now, just a material witness, counselor." McBeth clicked his pen a few times before tucking it into a pocket.

Although Everett didn't have any intention of leaving town until his lease was up—or until he decided what the hell to do with himself—he felt some resentment over being tied down like this. In addition, he wasn't exactly comfortable with the possibility of being accused of murder. What if McBeth decided to pin it on the outsider? Then another unwelcome thought struck: what if the cops turned their suspicions toward Charlotte?

"Are you going to get the Gulch PD to spy on me?" Everett tried to keep his voice even.

McBeth answered with a broad smile. "I *am* the Gulch PD. So to speak. Gulch contracts with the sheriff's department for law enforcement services."

Everett wasn't thrilled to be under police scrutiny in general, and particularly not with this man, but there wasn't much he could do about it now. Maybe McBeth would quickly get bored with him. And hopefully they'd find the murderer promptly and then leave him alone.

"I'll be happy to help however I can," Everett said, mostly honestly. He opened the car door and got out. "Thanks for the coffee."

"Here's my card. Call if anything relevant occurs to you." McBeth reached across the passenger seat and handed him the card. "And Mr. Vaughn? Welcome to Deadman Gulch."

CHAPTER EIGHT

Gulch Pages & Pastries was hopping. Every one of Jess's tables was occupied, and there was a line at her counter. The book aisles were so crowded that it was hard to get through, and Charlotte, Deja, and the other part-time staff looked slightly frazzled. It probably didn't help that a goodly number of customers were well into their wine-tasting adventures, which meant they were more raucous than bookshop patrons tended to be.

"Everett!" Charlotte bellowed from the cashier counter as soon as she caught sight of him. "Broken toilet. Burned out light. Weird noises in the storeroom."

He waved cheerily. "On it! Lunch is in back when you're ready for it."

He spent the remainder of the afternoon repairing things, cleaning up spills and crumbs, and tracking down the weird noise—a cat, which he decided to deal with later. He enjoyed being busy, especially since it kept his mind off the morning's events. And it meant he could postpone his little discussion with Charlotte as well.

Around five o'clock, Everett had a small fright when Sergeant McBeth wandered into the store. But the sheriff just took a long look at the activity, tipped his hat at Everett, and left. Everett let out a breath and continued tidying books on a display table that had been jostled by a customer with an oversize stroller. Who brought a toddler wine-tasting anyway?

Jess ran out of pastries soon after and closed up the café, but the bookshop remained open until eight without significant lulls in traffic. When Charlotte gently ushered out the last customers and locked the door, she and all the employees exclaimed in relief and then stampeded to the back room, where pizzas awaited. She'd arranged ahead of time for Lazzari's to deliver them—a wise decision since Lazzari's was probably slammed right now.

Deja reached for their third slice. "Oh my God, my feet are gonna fall off."

Charlotte, perched on a stack of cardboard boxes, shrugged. "Go home and soak 'em. You'll need them again tomorrow by noon."

"Why are people so... peoply?" Trini used to work at the same school as Charlotte and had retired a few years ago. She'd been happy for this part-time job, although she might be regretting that decision right now.

"They really are," replied Charlotte. She looked utterly exhausted but also happy. Her grand opening hadn't been a bust.

Deja chimed in. "I caught one guy taking photos of, like, half our books. I asked him about it and he said it's 'cause he can get them cheaper online. Like, he wasn't even trying to hide what he was doing."

But Charlotte didn't seem upset. "A lot of people did buy from us. That's what matters. And you guys were great. We're a good team. And we had an amazing day."

That brought a round of genuine, if somewhat sleepy cheers, and then the party broke up. Charlotte sent leftover pizza home with everyone, and Everett tidied up while Charlotte closed out the cash drawer and made sure the lights were off and the alarms set.

Everett suddenly remembered the weird-noise issue. "There's a cat in the basement," he announced.

"What?"

"That's what was making the noise earlier. I tried to catch it but I couldn't. I left some water down there, though. And, um, some of the sausage from the pizza." He didn't know if cats ate sausage or whether it was good for them, but it was all he'd had available at the time. He also wasn't sure that the cat was actually trapped down there. These old buildings had lots of little crawl spaces that a small animal could squeeze through, and there was also the mysterious and slightly sinister network of mines.

Charlotte frowned. "Great. Well, I guess it'll be fine overnight. I'll find a trap or something tomorrow. For now, I'm going to run the deposit to the bank."

"Want me to go with you?"

"Thanks, but my knight in shining armor has appeared." She waved toward the front door, where Rob stood on the other side of the glass, smiling. "He promised he'd stay away during open hours because this is my baby, but he still gets to play bodyguard."

The outside air smelled of wine and grilled meats, and voices carried from the Oasis and from the beer garden at Deadman Gulch Inn.

"Well, how'd it go?" asked Rob after giving Charlotte a kiss on the forehead.

"Swamped all day. I need to go home and have a good soak."

"That can be arranged, madame." Rob made a courtly gesture toward his car but then paused to look at Everett. "Want a ride home?"

"Thanks, but I think I can manage six blocks."

"I'm sure you can, but until they find the murderer...."

Charlotte, who'd been heading toward the car, froze. "Murderer?"

"Oh, I guess you were too busy today to hear the news. Someone killed that Blake Cannon guy."

"Oh!" Her hand flew to her mouth, and to her credit, she looked genuinely distressed. As much of a jerk as Cannon was, she still didn't want him dead. "What happened?"

"Nobody knows yet. His handyman discovered the body in Cannon's house."

"His handym—"

Oh no. Charlotte was a smart woman, and Everett could see the gears turn and click into place. When she swiveled her head to stare at him, he knew all was lost. "His handyman, Everett William Vaughn?" Her voice was artificially sweet.

He could deny everything; and for a moment, he nearly did. But she'd find out the truth soon enough—the truth she clearly already knew. Besides, he was a man in his forties, not a child. He could make his own choices about who to work for.

"Um, yeah," he mumbled, rubbing the back of his neck.

"Care to explain?"

Wisely, Rob was staying out of it, although he certainly looked intrigued—possibly entertained, in fact.

Everett could just walk home, right? It wasn't as if his sister would tackle him right here on the sidewalk and hold him captive until he confessed.

He sighed. "I was going to tell you. But you've been really busy, and, um...."

She opened her mouth to say something—no doubt something not very complimentary—but Rob surprised both of them by holding up a hand. "Honey? Ev stumbled upon a murder scene today, which must have been traumatic, and he still showed up to lend you a hand. Maybe cut him a break?"

Charlotte's jaw worked for a moment... and then her expression softened and she set a hand on Everett's shoulder. "Are you okay?"

"Yeah. It was... not pleasant and I almost puked and the cop was obnoxious, but I'm okay now. Thanks. And I'm sorry I went behind your back like that." He truly was.

"Do you need money that badly?"

Well, damn. He didn't deserve her sympathy and care. "Not really. Which is good since he stiffed me for—" Realizing his poor choice of words, he winced. "I know we're not supposed to speak ill of the dead, but I saw him treat you badly, and as far as I can tell, he was an asshat in general. But I was kind of curious about him, so I figured this would give me a chance to be sort of nosy."

"You discovered a lot more than you intended." Her voice didn't lack sympathy.

He shuddered. "And how."

"So what did you see this morning? Who killed him? Do you—"

"Charlie." Rob again. "You're dead on your feet. Remember that bath you wanted? And maybe a nice glass of nebbiolo?"

She wavered visibly, and Everett made a mental note to get the world's best brother-in-law something wonderful for his birthday. Then Charlotte pointed a finger at Everett. "Come to the shop tomorrow at ten. Be prepared to tell me everything."

Years of wayward middle-schoolers had quailed before this woman, and Everett wasn't about to break that tradition. "Will Jess be there that early? If not, I'll bring breakfast."

"Make it something good. And don't forget the coffee."

She got into the car, Rob gave Everett a wave before following suit, and they drove off. Everett, thinking that a bath and wine didn't sound bad at all, trudged home.

The next morning, by the time he stopped at El Dorado for two orders of huevos rancheros to go, word of the murder had spread. The restaurant staffers were talking about it, as were the customers in line at Rising Times. "Hey, wow, did you hear?" Xochi asked as she handed him his two large coffees.

"Yeah."

"We don't get much murder around here. It's not like Chicago."

"There wasn't much of it in my suburb either." He left money in the tip jar, took the cup carrier in one hand as he carried the bag of food in the other, and squeezed his way through the throng and back onto the street.

The fortunate thing was that neither the tourists nor the locals seemed to know that Everett had been the one who'd found the body. Also, the news didn't seem to dim the festive mood, which was a little sad, he supposed.

Charlotte saw him approach the bookshop and let him in without a word. It felt weird, just the two of them in the large space, most of the shop lights still off. He could almost imagine ghosts skulking in corners. In fact.... "There are glowing eyes behind the reading-glasses rack."

She didn't even look. "It's your cat."

"I don't have a cat."

"Well, you saw it first. A big orange one, right? When I got here this morning, it was napping in the middle of my window display, but then it ran off into the history section."

"Do you want me to—"

"Not now. Into the back room with you."

They sat at the previous night's pizza station: a battered wooden table that might have been lying around since the gold rush. Charlotte dug into her eggs at once, attacking them ferociously with her plastic fork, while Everett took a more reserved approach.

"Okay," she said after several mouthfuls, pointing the fork at him accusingly. "Give me the details."

He did, beginning with Cannon accosting him on the street and ending with Everett entering the basement room and finding the body. Somewhere along the line, the orange cat appeared, twined around Everett's legs, and stared until he shared the parts of his eggs that didn't have salsa on them. Afterward it gave itself a quick bath, then sashayed into the depths of the back room.

When he got to the end of the saga, Charlotte looked thoughtful. "Are you sure he was murdered? It wasn't an accident?"

"He had pieces of broken wine bottle on his head. Like, glass on him. I can't envision how he'd manage that on his own."

She shrugged in acceptance of that. "He must have security cameras, right? So the cops will be able to see who entered his house. Aside from you, I mean."

That was a heartening idea, and it meant it wouldn't take long for Everett to be crossed off the suspects list. Then he'd be free to leave town whenever he wanted to. Unless he needed to stick around to be a witness at trial. Ugh. A homicide case could take years to go to court. He'd have to see whether he could simply give a deposition instead.

Charlotte drained the last of her coffee. "I'm not angry at you anymore about working for him, but I do wish you'd said something from the start. I would've found out eventually even if he hadn't been killed. It's hard to keep secrets in a town this size."

"I can see that. And I'm sorry."

She stood and gathered the empty containers but remained by the table. "I'm going to give you some advice. You didn't ask for it, and I'm aware that you're a grown—nay, a middle-aged man—"

"Hey!" he protested.

"—but I will always be your big sister, which entitles me to give advice in perpetuity. It's in the contract."

He grinned at her. "Now you're sounding like a lawyer."

"No insults, young man. Here's my advice: be careful where you stick your nose. You said you accepted Cannon's job offer because you wanted to snoop around a little, and look where that got you. Remember all the other times you dug into things that were none of your business and ended up getting yourself into trouble."

Although he scowled, he couldn't exactly disagree. There had been multiple occasions during his youth and adulthood when his inquisitiveness—the more positive term he preferred—had resulted in injuries, disciplinary actions, or hurt feelings. Like when he became curious about what Sam had been doing on his phone and, through semi-nefarious means, discovered that his husband had been browsing on Scruff. A huge fight ensued. Sam was eventually but reluctantly able to provide evidence that the app had been relevant to one of his cases and that he hadn't been looking for a hookup. But by then their mutual trust had suffered a heavy blow. It was only one of the things that had come between them, but it was definitely a factor.

"I'll keep my nose clean," he promised.

"No, you won't. But at least next time you get yourself in trouble, I'll be able to say I told you so." Apparently satisfied with getting in the final word, she tossed the trash into a bin and marched to the front of the store.

CHAPTER NINE

Sunday was less frantic than Saturday. It was also a much shorter day, with the bookshop open from only noon to five. But everyone had carried over their exhaustion from the previous day, so by the time Charlotte locked the door after the final customer and Everett set out fried chicken from Big Al's, all the staff could do was grunt and moan… and stuff their faces.

The orange cat made its second appearance of the day, marching straight up to Everett and meowing until he gave it some of his drumstick.

"If you keep feeding it, it's never going to leave," Jess said through a yawn.

Charlotte snorted. "That ship has sailed. Maybe the cat belongs to someone in the neighborhood. It doesn't look neglected."

"He," said Trini as she wiped her hands on a paper napkin. "Most ginger cats are male. It's possible that this cat could be female—female gingers aren't as rare as male calicoes—but male is a pretty safe bet. And it seems pretty rude to keep saying *it*."

The cat finished the chicken and, apparently satisfied, started a bath. Everett had always envied cats' flexibility.

Deja looked at Everett. "What are you going to name them? Ooh, I know! Pick a locally significant author."

"I'm not naming them," Everett protested. "They are not my cat."

As if on cue, the cat rubbed against Everett's shin and then, ears pricked forward, rocketed into the darkness at the back of the room.

Groaning, Jessica stood. "Might be rodents. Having a cat around could be handy. But you need to get them a litter box, Ev."

"They're not my cat! I don't even like cats."

Nobody paid him any attention.

Rob couldn't pick up Charlotte tonight, so Everett walked along with her to make the bank deposit. Gulch was much quieter now that most of the tourists had gone home. There was still evidence of the gala—banners over Main Street and the scent of fermented grapes—but those would be gone soon and things would return to normal. At least until Holiday Fest, the week after Thanksgiving.

The deposit completed, they headed in the direction of Everett's house. She'd parked in his driveway this morning so she wouldn't take up one of the coveted spots closer to Main Street. It was a pleasant evening, and Everett liked the echo of their footsteps and the sound of a few early autumn leaves crunching beneath them. Chicago had never had this quality of silence, not even in the burbs.

"Are you happy with your first weekend?" he asked.

"Yeah. Sales were strong. I told everyone that even when they're not in town, they can order from me and I'll ship. Maybe one or two will even do it."

"Retail's a hard gig."

"So's teaching, and I did that for a long time. So's practicing law."

Everett made a face, which she didn't notice since she wasn't looking at him. "I don't do that anymore."

"No, but you did. And now it's okay to move on and do something else."

They were nice words, but he had trouble taking them to heart. If it wasn't for the divorce and house sale, he'd still be paying off student loans. "When I went to law school, it was because I wanted to change the world. Fight for justice and all of that. Only, it turns out that kind of law doesn't pay well, so I went over to the dark side."

"It covered your bills."

"Yep. And I did nothing that mattered. Soulless paper-pushing. It wasn't fun and I didn't make anyone's life better." That came out sounding more desolate than he'd intended.

By now they were standing in the driveway, their shadows long in the light over the garage door. Both of them were tired, yet neither made a move to part. They spoke in soft voices, although the hour wasn't yet late.

Charlotte set her hand on top of her car. "The way I look at it, we're wherever we are because of choices we made. If we're happy where we are, then those previous choices were good ones even if they didn't seem so at the time. If we're unhappy, well, we can't change the past. So all we can do is make different choices now and in the future."

"Wise commentary, sis. But it doesn't tell me what I should do."

"You'll figure it out. In the meantime, Carol Allen is expecting you at ten tomorrow morning. I'll text you her address."

He'd almost forgotten about that commitment. And the fact that he had to drive to Angels Camp to pick up plumbing parts for Gary and Tom's sink. At least both of those were tasks he could do with a clear conscience.

Charlotte started to say something else but paused when a car rolled to a stop in front of the house. The car was marked with the Milagro County Sheriff logo, so Everett wasn't surprised when Sergeant McBeth got out and ambled over.

"Evenin', Ms. Tabor, Mr. Vaughn. I hear the weekend was a success for the stores on Main Street."

The folksiness had to be an act, right? But Charlotte smiled at him. "It was. How's Sophie doing?"

"She's disappointed she can't have you for English this year."

"Well, she'll do fine with Mr. Schiedler. But tell her to stop by the shop when she has time—there's an author whose books I'd love to introduce her to."

Everett shouldn't have been surprised that these two knew each other, but he wasn't sure what to make of it. It sounded as if McBeth's kid had been one of Charlotte's students. Would that make Everett a less likely suspect in McBeth's eyes? Or at least clear Charlotte off his list?

After another minute or two of chitchat between his sister and the sergeant, Everett couldn't contain himself any longer. "Are you stalking my house to make sure I didn't skip town?"

"No, I wanted to ask Ms. Tabor a few questions and I saw she was parked here. I figured I'd catch her after things slowed down today." If McBeth was offended by Everett's rudeness, he didn't show it. If anything, he seemed slightly amused.

Charlotte ignored Everett. "I'm happy to talk to you, but can it wait until morning? I'm dead on my feet. Um, sorry—not the best phrase under the circumstances."

McBeth chuckled. "Sure, it can wait. I guess Cannon's not going anywhere."

"Thanks. Come by the shop around ten, if you like." She shrugged. "I don't know if I have anything helpful to tell you, but I'll be available then."

"In an investigation, you never know what information is going to prove useful. I prefer to spread my net wide at the outset."

"Am I in that net?" Everett demanded. Because he was bad at keeping his mouth shut.

"Mr. Vaughn, at this point, everyone is."

It wasn't clear whether that should be reassuring or worrying. "Can't you just look at his security cameras? Sounds pretty open-and-shut, unless he had a whole crowd traipsing through his house Friday night."

For the first time, McBeth looked irritated, although possibly not at Everett. "Unfortunately, no. That would be too easy, and the Fates are not smiling on me right now."

Charlotte patted his arm sympathetically. "That's what you get for being named McBeth."

"So foul and fair a day I have not seen," he recited. "Well, hopefully things will work out better for me than they did for the Thane of

Glamis." Then he tipped his hat, got back in the cruiser, and drove away.

Everett glared after him. "I don't understand any of what he just said."

"It wouldn't hurt you to gain a little culture, you know. He was quoting from the Scottish Play and referring to the title character, with whom he shares a name, albeit differently spelled."

"Did you just use albeit in conversation?"

She swatted him. "Go inside. Get some rest. Consider furthering your education."

Everett obeyed some of those instructions. He went into the house, grabbed a beer from the fridge, and collapsed into the ugly but supremely comfortable armchair. It felt good to put his feet up.

Yet he couldn't fully relax, thanks to McBeth, who'd said the security camera footage wasn't available. That meant that Everett couldn't yet be ruled out as a suspect and also that the actual murderer wouldn't be caught right away. And it piqued Everett's curiosity. Why couldn't McBeth see the footage? A technical glitch, maybe. Or perhaps it was because he lacked the password; but if that were the case, surely the security company could assist.

And then there was the sergeant himself. Everett couldn't figure him out. It was unclear whether he actually believed that Everett was the culprit. And what kind of sheriff's deputy recited Shakespeare?

For a good chunk of Everett's life, he'd discussed any thorny problems with Sam. Who hadn't necessarily had a solution, but sometimes just talking it out helped. So did receiving a dollop of sympathy.

Now Everett had only himself, and that sucked.

CHAPTER TEN

Rising Times was closed this Monday, so after Everett got up, he drove straight to Angels Camp, where he visited a Starbucks. There was nothing wrong with the Venti Americano he ordered. In fact, he got it for free with loyalty points—a result of his morning routine in Chicago. Although the pastry was also perfectly acceptable, none of it had the charm of Rising Times, and the barista, unlike Xochi, didn't attempt to catch him up on the latest gossip.

He took his time at the hardware store. After selecting the plumbing supplies, a new cordless drill caught his eye, much nicer than his old one. Then a stainless-steel colander for the kitchen, along with a new set of hand towels. Somehow a cat litter box also made its way into his cart, along with a bag of kitty litter and a set of pet dishes. And once he had loaded all of those things into Janet, his truck, well, it just sort of made sense to detour to the feed store and pick up a bag of cat food. Maybe if the orange cat showed up again, they wouldn't beg for whatever Everett was eating.

Janet seemed pleased to be hauling a load, however modest, and she rattled less than usual on the drive back to Deadman Gulch. Everett was getting used to driving through the hills, and he enjoyed the way it felt. There was always a sort of mystery, even when he was familiar with the road, because you never knew exactly what you'd see over the next rise or around the next curve.

Back in Gulch, he dropped off everything at his house and drove over to Carol Allen's place. It was a neat ranch-style home not far from his place, with a big front yard that housed an impressive collection of outdoor furniture. The front door had an oversize wreath in autumn colors, but he didn't get a good look because the door opened before he was halfway across the lawn and a tall woman with gray braids came outside. She wore jeans and a flannel shirt and, aside from the brace on one knee, looked as if she were fully capable of hopping on a horse and rounding up some dogies. Whatever those were.

"Hi, Ms. Allen, I'm—"

"It's Carol, and my, aren't you a handsome one. You're going to have all the single women in Gulch beating at your door."

Dammit, he was blushing. "I'm gay," he mumbled.

"All the single gay men," she corrected without missing a beat. "Although unfortunately there aren't many, not in this town. Let's see... there's the Evers boy, but he's away at college and probably too young for you anyway. Then there's—"

"I'm not looking for, uh, romance. Thanks."

"Doesn't matter. Sometimes it comes looking for you."

He was relieved at her lack of homophobia but absolutely didn't want to discuss his love life—or lack thereof—with her or anyone else. "Charlotte says you have furniture to move?"

"I can't tell you how annoying it is to need help. My arms are still strong, but my knees have betrayed me." She glared at the brace.

"Well, I'm happy to help."

"Go ahead and back into the driveway. I'll open the garage."

The interior space, big enough for three cars, was filled with neatly arranged furniture and shelves with labeled boxes. "An impressive collection," he commented.

"Well, it's a hobby of sorts. I haunt estate sales and encourage people to poke around in their attics and barns. Sometimes it's easier for people to part with things if they know they'll go to someone who appreciates them. And it's fun for me, like treasure hunting—and full of surprises. Just last month a nice young couple contacted me because they found an entire horse skeleton in a shed on some property they'd inherited. I don't handle that sort of thing myself, but I put them in touch with someone who does."

"Why was there a horse skeleton in a shed?"

Her eyes sparkled. "Oh, there's a story! Come on inside and I'll tell you."

Since he couldn't think of a graceful way to refuse—and she didn't really give him a chance—he ended up sitting in her nice kitchen, drinking coffee and eating cookies while she told him about the horse. And about several other hunter-gatherer adventures, as she liked to call them. He hadn't planned on socializing, but she was entertaining and he wasn't in a rush.

Almost an hour had passed when she mentioned Blake Cannon. "Can't say I'll be shedding any tears over that one."

"Did you know him?"

She narrowed her eyes, and her words came out almost in a growl. "That lying bastard? You bet I did."

Everett wasn't supposed to nose around. But it shouldn't really count as nosing around when someone left such a wide opening. Heck, he'd be rude if he didn't ask. "What did he lie about?"

Instead of answering, she got up—with some difficulty, favoring the knee—and left the kitchen. When she returned a few moments later, she held a large photo album, which she set on the table before sitting down again. She opened the cover to reveal a black-and-white photo of a man and woman standing in front of a rustic cabin. "These were my mother's parents. This picture was taken in the early twenties, when Mom was a baby."

Everett peered at them and saw their resemblance to Carol. "Nice-looking couple."

"Wasn't Granddad a looker? They owned the Miracle Creek Campground, back when folks were just starting to drive up into the mountains for nature getaways."

She flipped the pages, showing him more photos, postcards, and brochures. One particular image made him exclaim, "Hey! I know where this is!"

"Just outside of town. The campground barely survived the Depression, but things really picked up in the fifties. Some of my earliest and happiest memories are of that place. My grandparents built almost everything themselves, later with help from Mom and her brothers. It wasn't fancy, but it was my little corner of heaven, you know?"

He could imagine it—campfire stories, roasted marshmallows, visits with woodland creatures—although he'd never done much outdoorsy stuff himself. "It sounds really nice."

"It was." She sighed. "After my grandparents died, my Uncle Otis took over the place. Mom was busy raising kids, because that's what a woman was expected to do back then, and her other brother moved away. Unfortunately, Uncle Otis was an idiot, and his son—my cousin Junior—isn't any better. Neither of them could run it properly and they wouldn't listen to advice. After Uncle Otis died, Junior finally threw in the towel and shut it down. He still owned the property, but he wasn't doing anything with it. All those tidy little cabins rotting away. Do you want more coffee, Everett?"

The non sequitur temporarily threw him. "Um, I don't— No thanks. I've had a lot today."

"I'm sure you have other things to do besides listening to an old lady yack."

"You're not old, and I'm enjoying your company. But what does this"—he gestured at the album—"have to do with Cannon?" Having seen the blueprints, he had an inkling, but he wanted to hear the whole story.

"Well, early this year Cannon rode into town and started sweet-talking Junior. Cannon said he'd buy the campground—made it sound as if he was doing Junior a favor. Said he'd restore everything to its original condition and reopen the campground. And my idiot cousin believed him. Sold it for a song. Come to find out, though, that Cannon intended to obliterate the whole place and stick a golf course there instead. A golf course! Bunch of rich people overpaying to hit little balls with sticks. All that natural habitat gone. All that water wasted. You don't golf, do you?"

"Nope." That was the truth, and he was glad of it. "That must be heartbreaking, to lose something so important to your family."

She gave a wide grin. "Maybe that won't happen, now that he's croaked."

Everett tried to swallow a laugh but ended up snorting instead. "Silver linings, I guess." He glanced at his watch. "I really should get moving, though. I have a sink to fix at the Olive Branch."

"Ah, Gary and Tom. They charge tourist prices, but everything they carry is good quality. And they're such nice fellows. They've bought several of my pieces for their home."

They stood, and Everett helped her carry the dishes to the sink. Returning to the garage, she pointed out a curio cabinet, a small table with elegantly bowed legs, and an oak hall tree. "That should all fit in your truck. Can you wrestle them yourself?"

He eyed them carefully. "I think so."

"I have some larger pieces I'd love to move as well. Look at that secretary, for instance. And that lovely sideboard. If you can recruit a couple of strong helpers, I'd be happy to pay all of you."

"You do know I'm not a professional mover, right?"

Her only answer was a smile.

The table and hall tree moved relatively easily into the truck bed, wrapped in old blankets provided by Carol. But the curio cabinet was more difficult. Not only was it heavy, but its sheer bulk and lack of handholds made it difficult to grasp, and the glass front made it extra fragile. It didn't help that Carol kept trying to give advice and even offered to help lift it.

"Your knees!" Everett protested.

"Stupid old things. Definitely a design flaw in humans."

Just then, a familiar-looking police car rolled to a stop in front of the house, and a moment later, a familiar-looking sheriff's deputy got out. "Need a hand?" McBeth called as he sauntered closer.

"We surely could," Carol replied.

Everett, who was less than thrilled to see McBeth again, frowned. "Are you stalking me?"

McBeth got that amused expression. "That's my house," he said, pointing across the street. "And if I did want to stalk you, you're not that hard to find."

"I thought you were interrogating my sister."

"All done. My thumbscrew and rack are all tucked away for now." Why did he have to be so smug?

"And is furniture-moving part of your job?"

"Our motto is Serving the Community. There are a lot of ways to serve, Mr. Vaughn."

Annoyingly, McBeth turned out to be both strong and skilled at maneuvering furniture. Which made sense since, Everett recalled, McBeth had done this professionally while in college. Not only did he help lift the cabinet, but when it didn't fit well in the truck bed with the other items, he moved everything around until it did.

"There we go." He hopped out and patted the side of the truck.

Carol had briefly disappeared during the maneuvering. Now she handed McBeth a baggie full of cookies. "Save some for Sophie, now," she warned.

"Oh man, but it's your snickerdoodles. They're the best."

That was just a lie. Though Everett didn't think that they were bad cookies, they were too dry and the cinnamon overpowered the other flavors. Not that he would have said so to Carol, of course. And anyway now she was pressing a wad of bills into his hand.

"Carol, you really don't have to—"

"Of course I do. This is my livelihood and I cover my business expenses. I'd pay Cole too but he won't take it."

"You know I can't, Carol."

She clucked her tongue. "Silly rules. I'm just an old lady trying to pay people for honest work."

Seemingly unperturbed, McBeth turned to Everett. "I bet you need help getting those out of the truck too. I'll meet you there." Before Everett could mount a protest, McBeth was already walking away. During the entire short drive to the store, Everett grumbled to Janet about deputies who were way too self-assured and annoyingly competent.

Mother Lode Discoveries was closed on Mondays, but Marian Fisker must have known that Everett was on the way. As he parked in front of the store, she stood in the open doorway with a handcart steadied in one hand. "I'll show you where to put them," she called as he climbed out of the truck.

McBeth arrived, trotted over to retrieve the cart, and hopped into the bed of Everett's truck. Which was awfully presumptuous of him. He did make it a lot easier to unload the furniture, though, and to maneuver it through the crowded store to Carol's space. Once the pieces were delivered, Marian instructed Everett and McBeth on how to arrange them.

Finally the two men were on the sidewalk outside. "Thanks for your help," Everett said with as much good grace as he could muster.

"It's my pleasure to serve." McBeth cocked his head. "You do seem to have quite a few odd jobs, for a lawyer."

"Ex-lawyer. And Charlotte asked me to give Carol a hand."

"I see."

Not knowing what McBeth meant by that, Everett changed the subject. "Does Carol's cousin Junior live around here? I think you might want to investigate him."

"For what?"

Everett rolled his eyes. "Murder, of course. He sold some land to Cannon and might not have been pleased with Cannon's plans for it. That's a motive, right?"

"Are you adding private investigator to your résumé?"

"No, but I'm—"

"You do know you're a suspect, right? And that you look even more suspicious when you go around trying to cast blame on other people?" McBeth seemed more amused than accusatory, but maybe he always looked like that before throwing someone in jail. Maybe it was a new police tactic: Good Cop, Bad Cop, Amused Cop.

After a few calming breaths, Everett managed a response. "Just look at the security camera footage, why don't you? What do you need? A warrant? A tech person?"

"I need a time machine so I can go back and make sure that Cannon pays his bill so the security company doesn't discontinue his service."

Everett's stomach dropped. "There is no footage?" Although disappointing, that seemed par for the course for a guy who weaseled out of his debts. Speaking of which, how had Cannon planned to build a golf course if he couldn't afford to pay a handyman and security company? Or maybe he could afford it just fine but was one of those rich jerks who thought he was above paying for goods and services.

McBeth was scrutinizing Everett closely. "You honestly thought we'd be able to see what went on inside that house."

"Of course I did. There were cameras. He made a point of mentioning them, and I saw them myself."

"Interesting. There was no camera in the room where you found the body and where, presumably, he was attacked."

Everett shrugged. "I didn't notice that. I'd been there only briefly before."

"Why were you in there previously?"

"I was working in the garage, building some shelves, and I had to take a leak. I went in search of a bathroom." He might as well be completely honest. "And also I was being a little nosy. It's a weird-ass house."

"Hmm."

"What does that mean?" Everett crossed his arms, realized it made him look defensive, and uncrossed them. But that made his arms feel awkward. What was an innocent way to stand? And why had he gotten himself into this conversation in the first place?

McBeth heaved a heavy sigh. "You know something? About fifty percent of good police work is intuition. A hunch or a feeling won't stand up in court, but it'll often help steer an investigation in the right direction. And Mr. Vaughn, my intuition says you are not the person who's responsible for Blake Cannon's death."

Everett didn't know whether to be relieved or to assume that McBeth was lying and this was another ploy to get Everett to incriminate himself. His curiosity got the best of him. "Why?"

"Dunno exactly. Charlotte's a nice woman, an upstanding member of the community, but that doesn't mean her brother isn't the worst kind of miscreant. But you don't seem especially sinister, and you did seem to truly want me to see camera footage. You're not off the hook yet, however."

"I'm guilty until proven innocent, you mean? Crim law may not be my thing, but I'm pretty sure that's not how it goes."

McBeth flashed another confident grin. "But you're in my town now, pardner. I make the law in these here parts." He winked, tipped his hat, and got back into his car.

Everett glared after him until the car was out of sight.

CHAPTER ELEVEN

"Try this one now. What do you think?" Tom Rollins-Ross handed Everett another little plastic cup holding a sample of olive oil.

Everett dutifully dipped a hunk of french bread, ate it, and considered. "Basil-infused. It's tasty, and I bet it would be amazing on pasta. Ooh, or pizza. But the herbiness sort of drowns out the olive oil flavor, so I wouldn't use it if I was going for something more purist."

"Uh-huh," said Tom and gave his husband a look that suggested they'd fought about this and Tom had just scored a point.

Gary, however, wasn't ready to concede. "But you don't always want something purist."

"No. I guess it would depend on how much storage I had, and how much money. If I was limited on either, I'd rather just buy a single bottle of really good uninfused oil—like that one I tasted a minute ago—and add additional flavoring layers separately."

"Fine. But you do admit that even with a tiny kitchen and limited budget, you'd try to own at least a few varieties of vinegar, right? White, balsamic, rice...." He gave Everett another little cup, this one aromatic with the scent of apple cider vinegar.

"You bet." Everett dipped another chunk of bread and chewed

happily. "But I like to experiment in the kitchen. Not everyone else does—some like tried and true."

"Well, there is something to be said for that." Gary grabbed Tom's hand and kissed the back of it.

Everett had repaired the sink quickly and without mishap, and then Gary and Tom, learning that he'd missed lunch, had insisted on sitting him at a bistro table at the back of the store and feeding him tidbits from the gourmet food section. Somehow this had further morphed into an oil- and vinegar-tasting experience, in which they'd questioned him thoroughly on his impressions.

"How'd you learn to cook?" asked Gary.

"Trial and error. And self-defense. Otherwise I would have been stuck eating my sister's cooking, and, well, I'm not sure I would've survived to adulthood." He knew that she'd done her best to keep him fed despite severely limited funds and time; she'd also worked and attended school full-time. He also knew, however, that her culinary skills hadn't improved. Rob was the designated cook in that marriage.

In any case, Everett enjoyed puttering around in the kitchen. It was like doing a home-repair job: it kept his hands and mind suitably occupied, and he ended up with something useful.

"Your parents didn't cook much?" Gary handed Everett a plate of cheese and crackers. "Have some of that. Were you a latchkey kid?"

"Something like that. Mom died when I was three and Char was thirteen. And Dad... well, he tried to hold down the fort for a while. But I'm sure losing your spouse is rough, and single-parenting is also rough, and finances were tight even when Mom was around. He didn't handle it well." When Everett was younger, he'd been furious with his father. But later on, therapy had helped him realize that Dad wasn't entirely to blame. Not only had he been in a difficult situation, but he came from a generation of men taught to suck it up and not show emotion. And he hadn't had any friends or adult relatives who he could depend on for moral support.

"I'm sorry," said Tom gently. "It's so painful to not have supportive parents. I came out to mine when I was sixteen—well, to be honest, I was never all that in. They couldn't accept it. Kicked me out. I ended up getting emancipated, supporting myself, going to college... and eventually meeting the most wonderful man in the world." He smiled at Gary, who kissed his hand again.

At least Everett had been spared that kind of heartbreak. Charlotte had never minded that he was gay. "Did you ever reconcile with them?"

"No. There was... a very cold-war sort of détente, but that's all. Gary's folks, however, embraced me fully, so I gained a wonderful family."

With effort, Everett suppressed a wistful sigh. Sam's parents and siblings had always been cordial to him, but never truly warm. They didn't mind that Sam had married a man, but they clearly wished it had been a different man. Oh well—maybe that had made the divorce easier. Less trauma all around.

The three of them nibbled quietly for a few minutes, then Tom made a funny little *hm* noise and hurried off to the back room. When he returned, he held a wine bottle and three glasses. "None of us are working this afternoon, right? Might as well imbibe."

"When in Rome," Everett agreed.

After Tom poured, they all took a moment to savor. "What do you think?" he asked Everett.

"It's nice. I like it. But that's about all I can tell you because I don't know wine."

"Oh honey, you've come to the right place to learn! And you know, it doesn't have to be complicated. You just get to know some varieties and pay attention to the flavors. Then just go with what you like. Snobs who have more money than sense will shell out big bucks just because they've heard a particular label is the thing. It's like buying designer clothing just because of the name. Smart connoisseurs figure out what they enjoy, regardless of price. There are plenty of moderately-priced wines around here that are excellent. Like this syrah." He raised his glass, swirled it a bit, and took a satisfied sip.

Gary had been rolling his eyes. "Sorry about my husband. He has a pet peeve."

Everett was really enjoying this couple. And Tom was right—the wine was really nice. "Tastes like... berries? And chocolate."

Tom nodded as if Everett was his star pupil. "Excellent, yes. The flavor profile for syrah changes quite a bit depending on climate—heat gives the grape more licorice and coffee notes. One benefit of Milagro County is that we have a lot of microclimates. A grower can sometimes get varying results with the same grape on different parts of their land."

Another swallow of wine followed by some salty white goat cheese and Everett's world was improved appreciably. "You clearly have a passion for the subject. So how come you run this store instead of a tasting room? Not that your shop isn't great, but—"

"I get it," said Tom. "We thought about it at one point. But Gary's first love is food, not wine, and—"

"My first love is you," corrected Gary.

"Second love, then. Besides, the wine business can be awfully cutthroat sometimes, and that's not our kind of thing."

"Cutthroat? Like... organized crime? Government corruption?"

Both of his hosts laughed. "You've spent too much time in Chicago," said Gary. "We're talking competition. It didn't used to be like that, but a few of the newcomers.... Like Cannon, for example." His expression had soured.

Everett's ears pricked up. "What about him?"

Tom refilled the glasses, fetched a box of shortbread from a shelf, and distributed the cookies. Then he winked and dipped one into his glass before taking a bite. "Cannon's one of those snobs I mentioned. Sorry—he *was* one. Pretended he knew more about the subject than he actually did. Went around boasting that guests would be shelling out a hundred bucks or more for a bottle of wine with his resort label."

This didn't surprise Everett. He could easily picture the guy standing there in a designer suit, rubbing his hands with glee while patsies overpaid. "Was his wine any good?"

"He didn't have any! Not yet, anyway. But I heard that he was creeping around and trying to buy up entire harvests that had been promised to established winemakers. And instead of decent payments, he was offering a share of resort profits plus 'exposure.'" Tom made finger quotes for the last word.

That also sounded entirely on-brand for the guy. "Did any growers take him up on the offer?"

Tom shrugged. "No idea. My guess is that if they did, they wouldn't exactly advertise the fact."

Everett wondered whether McBeth knew about this. If not, he should. Everett dipped a cookie in wine and decided it wasn't bad.

Subsequent conversation turned to tales from each man's slightly misspent youth. Well, Everett's and Tom's misspent youth. Gary, by all accounts, had been a choirboy. A second bottle of wine was opened and emptied, and by the time darkness fell, a third. After more gourmet snacks, Everett was both tipsy and full, and the three of them were giggling like teenagers over their mutual admiration for Pedro Pascal.

"I should probably go," Everett said finally. "I've eaten half your stock already."

Tom, who'd imbibed considerably more than his husband, gave Everett a friendly pat on the arm. "We helped. And it was totally worth it for the company. But we still need to pay you, don't we?" He started to get up.

Everett gestured him back to his seat. "I think I've consumed more than my fee already."

"No, that was our treat for saving our necks over the weekend—and because we like you. We still owe you for parts."

Now that Tom and Gary felt like friends, Everett was hesitant to charge them anything. After all, he wasn't a professional plumber and wasn't yet desperate for cash, despite the fact that he'd never see the four hundred bucks that Cannon owed him. And the fix-it job hadn't taken long. "Maybe I could have a store credit? My rented kitchen's not very well equipped, and I—"

"Yes!" Tom leapt from his chair, raced over to a display of dutch ovens, and waved an arm as if he were a game show host revealing the grand prize. "Which color would you like?"

Everett's heart gave a greedy little ta-thump. They were Le Creusets and that beautiful cerise-hued baby likely cost four or five hundred bucks. He used to eye them in cookware stores, but Sam had always pointed out that Everett probably wouldn't use one often enough to justify the cost. Everett had hinted strongly that he'd like one as a birthday or Christmas gift, but Sam had never complied.

But now Everett shook his head. "Those are way too expensive. I didn't—"

"Which color?"

Gary laughed. "You might as well give up now, Everett. There's no winning when he gets that stubborn look."

Well. If they were going to insist.... "Red. But on one condition. I'm going to make a batch of my killer minestrone, and you're going to come over and share it with me." He hadn't prepared that recipe in over a year.

Tom grabbed the red dutch oven. "It's a deal." He beamed as he passed it to Everett.

<hr>

It was slightly hazardous to carry a heavy piece of cookware on uneven streets in the dark after having indulged in too much wine. Fortunately, Everett and the pot made it home safely, and if McBeth was lurking somewhere, he hid successfully.

The pot looked good on the stove, and Everett spent some time admiring it and patting its cast iron lid. He felt the same, regarding expensive power tools and cookware, as some people feel about fancy sport cars—although, as he used to point out to Sam, a DeWalt cordless drill or a Zwilling knife was a lot less pricy than a Corvette.

As if on cue, Everett's phone buzzed with a text from Sam: *How are the bears?*

Hibernating.

The three little dots hung there for a moment, taunting him. Then the next message arrived. *So there's this guy....*

Sighing heavily, Everett slumped into a kitchen chair. *Can u just spit it out? Im tired.* He deliberately used the u and skipped the apostrophe, knowing that both would annoy Sam.

Fine. I'm dating someone. We've gone out five times now. We're sleeping together.

At first Everett thought the pang was jealousy, but then he realized it was that close cousin, envy. He wasn't upset that his ex was seeing someone, but it did make his own solitude a little more bitter.

Why r u telling me this? Divorce is final. He doubted that Sam was boasting or trying to make Everett feel bad; Sam simply wasn't that kind of jerk.

I didn't want you to hear it secondhand.

Everett wasn't sure how Sam thought that would happen, being half a continent apart. What's more, Everett had more or less granted Sam their mutual friends in the divorce, which seemed only fair since Sam was staying put in Chicago and Everett wasn't. But all of this was far too much to discuss via text, and it didn't particularly matter anyway.

Thnx for the consideration. Wish u luck with him. Sincerely. He added that last word so that Sam wouldn't think he was being sarcastic.

Thank you.

Is he a lawyer?

Sam responded with a laughing emoji. *He's a boating instructor.*

That made Everett blink a few times. It had never occurred to him that such a career existed in Chicago, although upon reflection it made sense. But Sam didn't like boats and had steadfastly refused to do even one of the Chicago River architecture tours that tourists enjoyed so much. So how had he ended up with this guy?

Well, whatever. After a moment's search, he sent the pirate flag and sailing ship emojis. *Ahoy matey*, he typed. And then, because he truly did want Sam to be happy, he added, *I hope it works out for you.*

Thank you.

Everett put the phone on silent and set it facedown on the table. Didn't he have a bottle of wine somewhere?

CHAPTER TWELVE

The rest of the week passed quietly. Everett did a few little chores for Charlotte, who was happy with how things were going at the shop. He dutifully taste-tested more of Jess's cookies and suggested she consider autumn-themed sugar cookies now that the season was beginning to settle in. People seemed to love things shaped like pumpkins. He left out food and water for the cat and emptied the litter box, but only once caught a glimpse of an orange tail as the creature disappeared around a corner.

On Thursday he went for a walk in the woods, discovered after about a mile that his shoes were not going to cut it, and returned to Janet. Maybe he should invest in some hiking boots.

On Friday he stopped in at the Olive Branch and formally invited Tom and Gary over for Sunday night dinner. The idea of entertaining was unexpectedly exciting. It had been a long time.

He saw McBeth twice. Once they passed on the highway, heading in opposite directions, and once McBeth was coming out of Rising Times just as Everett was going in. That time, they exchanged quick hellos and nothing more. It was unclear whether the apparent lack of interest meant that Everett was truly off the hook as a suspect, or if McBeth was simply being circumspect about the investigation.

In either case, the residents of Deadman Gulch were much more inquisitive, especially once word got around that Everett had discovered the body. He became instantly more popular, with locals stopping him in shops and on the street and attempting, with varying degrees of subtlety, to extract details. But Everett could keep his mouth shut when he had to, and so he told them that he was too traumatized to discuss the matter. They were disappointed but let him be.

On Saturday he went grocery shopping and then stopped by Charlotte's house to get a jar of sourdough starter from Rob.

"Lactic acid bacteria," Rob had said fondly as he handed over the jar. "Such useful little guys. When I taught AP chem last year, we did a module on them. We baked bread and made kombucha."

"I bet that kept the kids interested."

Rob shrugged. "I do what I can."

Back home, Everett was juggling an armful of grocery bags while trying to unlock the door when an SUV parked in front of the house. The woman who hopped out looked familiar, although he couldn't quite place her.

"Mr. Vaughn!" she called, just as he fumbled but caught the keys. "Do you have a few minutes?"

"For what?" He knew he sounded irritable, but in his experience, when people asked whether you had a few minutes, nothing good ever followed.

"I just want to ask you a few questions."

"About what?"

He'd managed to get the door open, and she reached him just in time to catch the bag that contained the sourdough jar. He stood in the doorway and waited for her to respond. She was about his age, he guessed, short and sturdy, with a determined set to her jaw that reminded him of Charlotte. Suddenly he remembered where he'd seen her before—at the crime scene. "You're a reporter," he accused.

"Which is why I want to ask you questions."

They stared at each other for a moment, and when she didn't relent, he sighed. "Fine. Come on in."

She followed him to the kitchen and set the jar of starter on the counter while he put away the groceries. "How long have you lived here, Mr. Vaughn?" she asked as he tucked veggies into the fridge.

"Everett, and a few weeks."

"I see. And you're a handyman, yes?"

He glanced over his shoulder and saw that she was already scribbling in a notebook. "Sort of. Hang on and I'll make us some tea." He wasn't a frequent tea drinker, but offering seemed like a civilized thing to do. Also, it had occurred to him that while she was prying info from him, he might be able to get some out of her. Very quid pro quo, a la Hannibal Lecter. Too bad he hadn't purchased any fava beans.

She didn't wait patiently, choosing instead to wander around the kitchen and peer at things while he finished with the groceries. He let her. It wasn't as if she would gain anything useful from staring at his landlady's chicken-and-cow-themed clock or at the laminate countertop that was probably older than Everett.

Finally he faced her across the equally vintage oak-and-brass kitchen table, each of them cradling a warm mug. "I didn't catch your name."

"Jo Rossi. I write for the Milagro Daily Dispatch. Which hasn't been daily for almost a decade now, but tradition dies hard." She leaned back in her chair and grinned. "Now, tell me what it means to be a 'sort of' handyman."

He decided to give her a condensed version. "I'm in Gulch temporarily to help out my sister. She owns the bookshop. I'm earning a few extra bucks doing some odd jobs."

"Got it. And Cannon hired you to do what?"

"Fix up some stuff in his house. Look, I'm undoubtedly a suspect, and the last thing I want is to piss off the local constabulary. So tell me what you want to know and I'll decide whether I want to tell you." He took a sip of tea and regretted it when he burned his tongue.

She was apparently wiser and hadn't yet sampled hers. "You don't have to worry. If Cole really thought you were the murderer, he would have let you know by now."

It took a moment before Everett realized that she was referring to Sergeant McBeth, and then he scowled. "Maybe he's lying low until he gathers more evidence."

"Cole McBeth has some fine qualities, but subtlety isn't one of them. Never has been. I've known him since grade school."

That was interesting. Although Everett knew he should drop the subject entirely—why let this nosy person suspect that he had any special interest in the deputy—he couldn't resist. "All that folksiness—is it just an act with him?"

She laughed. "He's like a character in a movie, isn't he? But he's for real. His family has been here since the nineteenth century and they own a lot of land around here. He grew up on a ranch about ten miles away. He was one of those handsome boys who knows he's handsome but doesn't let it go to his head too much and who didn't mind showing up for school with manure and hay stuck to his boots. But Everett, I'm here to ask about Blake Cannon, remember?" She blew gently on her tea.

"Fine. What do you want to know?"

"Do you have any idea who killed him?"

"Nope. Someone strong, I guess."

Her eyebrows raised. "What makes you say that?"

"I've heard that skulls are fairly hard. Someone hit him with a wine bottle hard enough to kill him."

"The blow to his head didn't kill him," she said smugly, clearly pleased to know something that he didn't.

"How do you know?"

"I had a chat with the medical examiner, who overshares a lot more than the sheriff would like. But MEs are hard to find, so the sheriff tolerates it. And it turns out that Blake Cannon died primarily from blood loss. The blow with the wine bottle knocked him forward, he hit his head on the floor and lost consciousness, and then he bled out." She shrugged. "He also had benzodiazepine in his system—Xanax—along with alcohol, which might have thrown off his balance and made him more susceptible to blacking out."

Everett considered this. It was a shame for anyone to die, especially so young, but at least it sounded as if it had been a relatively painless way to go. It also created additional suspects, since nearly anyone could have swung that bottle with enough oomph to unbalance him.

Jo had another question. "Everett, did Cannon say anything to you about why someone would want to harm him?"

"I wasn't exactly a close confidante. I'm just a guy he hired to do some things around the house. We didn't talk much, and when we did, it was about the work."

"Hmm." Finally she sipped some of her tea. "Did he pay you on time?"

"What does that have to do with anything?"

That produced a dramatic hand wave from her. "Everything's connected, and when you gather information, you gather everything and sort through it later."

"That doesn't sound efficient or sustainable."

Another hand wave. "He owed a lot of people money, which makes it harder to narrow down the list. I was just curious whether he'd followed his usual habits with you."

"I don't know about anyone else. He did pay me a portion of what he owed, but not all. But even if I were the homicidal type—which I'm not—it'd take more than four hundred bucks to set me off."

"You might be surprised, Everett, how little money it can take to set some people off."

No, he wouldn't. Too many years as a lawyer had taught him that lesson. But he didn't bother to say that to Jo. "So do you have any working theories?"

Her expression turned evasive. "Not... no. Not really. Nothing worth mentioning."

"Do you think Sergeant McBeth and his colleagues will find the killer soon?"

"Dunno. We may be rural, but we're not ignorant or backwards. And Cole isn't stupid. He was class valedictorian, in fact."

Everett managed to not roll his eyes or say something rude, but it took considerable effort. He wasn't sure why McBeth irritated him so much. It wasn't as if the guy could be blamed for doing his job and trying to catch a murderer. And he hadn't treated Everett badly. There was just something annoying about him. He was too... perfect.

"Maybe McBeth did it."

Jo blinked owlishly. "Why on earth would he do that?"

"I don't know. Maybe they were engaged in a criminal enterprise of some kind. Maybe McBeth doesn't like it when outsiders mess around in his town. Maybe they had some kind of secret grudge going back for years. Ooh! Maybe they are actually half brothers who were vying for a family inheritance."

"Someone's dead. He might not have been popular, but we still need to take it seriously."

Everett stood and collected the cups, hers still mostly full. "It's been a lovely chat, but I have things to do." Yes, he was being rude, but she'd lectured him right here in his own damn kitchen. And he *was* taking it seriously. He was a suspect, after all. Also, he was the one who'd found the body, and that hadn't exactly been the highpoint of his week.

She stood but didn't seem inclined to leave quite yet. "This is my community, and I want it to be safe. People don't always appreciate journalists, but our work is important. In a case like this, sometimes we can uncover information that police are unable or unwilling to obtain themselves."

Now he felt slightly guilty for being a jerk. He carried the cups to the sink and set them inside, wiped his hands on one of his landlady's cow-printed towels, and faced Jo. "I get it, and I'm sorry. But I honestly know very little about Cannon or his death, and I wish I hadn't gotten mixed up in it. I really just want to mind my own business."

After a pause, her face softened. "This is Deadman Gulch, Everett. Nobody minds their own business."

CHAPTER THIRTEEN

Everett's vague plan, after Jo Rossi left, had been to relax with a book. He used to read as a kid, but he hadn't had time for pleasure reading as a young adult and had lost the habit. But now that he was related to a bookstore owner and had tons of free time, he figured he should take it up again.

The problem was, now he couldn't settle. He had three books sitting beside the floral-patterned recliner in the living room. One was a nonfiction account of a serial killer at the 1893 Chicago World's Fair. He'd chosen it because he thought the setting would be interesting and because Charlotte said it was very well written. But the theme was just a little too close to the recent event in Gulch, so he set it aside. The second, a murder mystery set in a rural manor house, was even worse. And the third was a gay romance novel that he didn't even remember buying and which made him frown because happily-ever-afters were nonsense.

"I could head to the shop and get something else." But then he realized that the store would be closing in about half an hour, and Charlotte probably didn't want him underfoot.

Still muttering, he hauled himself out of the chair, put on his shoes and flannel shirt jacket, and headed outside. He passed a few people who were walking up from Main Street, most likely tourists on their way to see the schoolhouse. The building wouldn't be open since there were no events happening today, but the exterior was worth a look too. It would probably be even more scenic in a few weeks when the trees were in full fall colors.

Main Street wasn't anywhere near as crowded as it had been the previous weekend, but a fair number of visitors strolled along, peering in windows and eating ice cream from Dairy Heaven. When Everett passed the Olive Branch, Tom happened to be holding the door open for a customer whose hands were full of brown paper bags. Tom waved merrily, making Everett smile. He felt almost like a local.

On a whim, he ducked into the Miracle Hills tasting room. It turned out to be more sophisticated than Granocchio Cellars, with polished concrete floors, strings of fairy lights near the ceiling, and smooth jazz playing on the speaker system. The man and woman behind the bar, both in their thirties, were attractive and expensively dressed. A display on one wall highlighted all the awards their wines had won.

"Welcome in!" called the man almost as soon as Everett stepped inside. The woman was busy pouring for a small group perched on barstools.

Everett approached the man and eyed the bottles arrayed behind him. There were a lot, and most of the names still meant nothing to him. Was it truly necessary to have so many varieties? They were all just fermented grapes, after all.

"Would you like to do a tasting?" the man asked smoothly. "We also have some nice charcuterie boards, if you want to pair the wine with food."

In Everett's early years—his mother dead, his father off Lord knew where, and Charlotte juggling school and jobs—his meals had often been haphazard. He learned to prepare his own pretty quickly, but sometimes there wasn't much food in the house. On those occasions, he'd often prepared a makeshift dinner consisting of government cheese, generic-brand saltines, and, if he was lucky, hot dogs or what-ever lunch meat had been on clearance. He used to arrange the compo-nents artistically on a plate and munch on them while he did homework or watched TV. Nowadays, places like Miracle Hills were using more upscale ingredients for the same thing—and charging twenty bucks.

"Just wine," he said.

The man explained that they had three different samplers to choose from, and he also explained the difference between them, but Everett didn't understand and stopped listening until the guy paused. "Look," Everett said, "I'm a wine newbie. Just pick one for me, okay?"

"Sure."

Everett ended up with a wooden tray holding five glasses, each containing a small amount of red liquid. Every shade of red was different, and he spent a few moments wondering whether wine connoisseurs graded their drinks on hue as well as flavor. Oh, and nose, which he guessed was a wine-snob way to say smell. But honestly, as a former member of the legal profession, he really couldn't judge others for using jargon. At least wine jargon wasn't in Latin. As far as he knew. Maybe it was in French or Italian instead.

"This will help," said the wine barista—or whatever they were called—who placed a laminated card beside the tray. He pointed to a particular section of the card. "This is what you're drinking, in order."

Everett squinted to read the small print. Clearly he was going to have to give in soon and buy reading glasses—probably from Charlotte's shop—but not today. He could just barely see that the card contained a list. There was an entry for each of his wine glasses, showing the name of the wine, its vintage and place name, and a brief description of what the wine was supposed to taste like. The merlot, for example, allegedly had notes of currant, vanilla, cardamom, and leather.

He took a sip. It was nice, but it just tasted like wine to him—not spices or BDSM equipment.

The wine guy had been helping another customer, but now he sailed over. "What do you think?"

"Um, I like it? Hey, how come the list says Lodi after the name?"

"That's where the grapes are from. We get a lot from the San Joaquin Valley."

Everett knew where that was—basically due west of Gulch,

between the Sierras and the coast ranges. "I thought they came from around here."

The man didn't look offended by the blunt statement. "Some do. We own a couple of vineyards In Milagro and Calaveras counties, and we contract with some growers nearby. But we also contract with growers elsewhere. Very few of the winemakers grow all of their own grapes."

That was consistent with what Willow at Granocchio Cellars had told him. "Doesn't dealing with other growers make things more complicated?"

"It can. But there are good reasons to do it that way." He rested his elbows on the bar and leaned forward, dropping his voice as if imparting secrets. "For one, land is expensive, and it's not cheap to grow grapes. So unless you have a whole lot of cash or you're not planning to produce many bottles, it makes sense to outsource. You also have access to more varieties that way, and more diversity in taste within a single variety."

Oh, right. Willow had talked about that too. "Because the same grape tastes different when grown in varying microclimates."

The man gave him a wide smile, as if Everett were his star pupil. "Precisely. And the other thing: viniculture, winemaking, and marketing are three distinct skillsets. The bigger producers can afford to hire specialists to do each of those things, but the smaller mom-and-pop operations can't. Do you like that pinot noir?"

Everett was momentarily confused before realizing that, while the man was talking, he'd finished the merlot and had drunk the next glass too. He really should be paying more attention to his alcohol consumption. He peered at the card. "Um, cherry and forest floor?" Why did anyone want to savor forest floor?

His host's professional demeanor didn't dim. "That's what some people taste. But go ahead and enjoy, and let me know if I can offer more help." He sailed to the other end of the bar, where the customers were probably less clueless. Or more clueful, if that was a thing.

For a while, Everett eavesdropped on nearby conversations, but none of them proved particularly interesting. One young couple discussed whether to get a dog, and if so, what kind. A cluster of middle-aged women planned a group trip to Mexico. Four people had a lively argument about football. Pretty soon he stopped paying attention and instead composed imaginary wine flavor profiles in his head. Hibiscus, pepper, and wet wool. Peaches, fennel, and cardboard. Pineapple, garlic powder, and bicycle tire.

He'd moved on to considering how to describe his favorite beers, when a couple in their sixties occupied the table nearest him and started talking about the murder. As they nibbled on their brie and green olives, they seemed to take a morbid delight in the topic. They didn't know any more details than Everett did, and some of what they said was wrong. He didn't correct them, but his thoughts naturally returned to Blake Cannon.

What, aside from the obvious, could Everett conclude about the murder?

Well, as Jo had pointed out, the guy owed people money. That was a perennial favorite motive. He was also abrasive as hell, and his resort plans had pissed off a lot of locals. That wasn't super helpful at narrowing things down.

But then Everett realized two things. First, whoever did it was probably invited to Cannon's house and had a reason to visit the basement with him. And second, given the seemingly improvised weapon, the killing might have been spontaneous rather than planned. In fact, maybe the person hadn't intended to kill him at all—maybe there had been an altercation of some kind and the killer had simply swung at him. With a wine bottle.

This ought to reduce the number of suspects. He just needed a list of everyone—aside from him—who'd gone to the house. Well, Sergeant McBeth needed that list. Everett was supposed to be staying out of it.

It was a puzzle, though. And he'd never been all that great at minding his own business. Based on Jo Rossi's closing comment, he was evidently a good fit for Deadman Gulch.

CHAPTER FOURTEEN

"You really don't mind if I have thirds?" Tom eyed the dutch oven longingly.

Everett stood, grabbed Tom's bowl, and walked to the stove. "Have all you like," he said as he spooned out more. "I made a lot. I'm really glad you're enjoying." He returned the bowl to Tom and raised his eyebrows questioningly at Gary.

But Gary shook his head. "I'm going to eat all your bread instead."

"Good." Pleased with himself, Everett sat back down.

It was a delicious meal, if he said so himself. Influenced against his will by the charcuterie boards at Miracle Hills, he'd begun with an antipasto platter containing prosciutto, peperoncini, and artichoke hearts. The main course included a sourdough loaf he'd baked in the dutch oven first thing in the morning, along with a hearty minestrone prepared later in the same pot with root vegetables and angel-hair pasta. None of it was especially complicated, but his guests didn't seem to mind. They'd brought the wine.

"Did you really learn all this on your own?" Tom gestured to indicate the food.

"Mmm, sort of. On my own I learned how to make something edible on a limited budget. But later I worked in restaurants. No

Michelin stars or anything, just diners, little hole-in-the-wall family-run spots. I picked up some things."

"You learned well."

Everett felt his cheeks heat. He hadn't collected much praise in his life, especially for things that were important to him, and it was really nice to know that his new friends appreciated the meal he'd prepared. He poured everyone a little more wine. "I'm glad to have time for it now. When I was practicing law, we left the house early and came home late. We ate a lot of takeout." Which was more expensive than home cooking—another reason why their finances had never been particularly strong.

"I know what you mean." Gary sounded contemplative. "Tom and I own a food-related specialty store, but ironically, we hardly ever cook. We're too tired for it most nights."

Tom nodded his agreement. "Once a month Gary drives down to Trader Joe's in Stockton and fills a big cooler with frozen meals. They're tasty, and it's not as expensive as eating out, but.... Other than that, we eat a lot of sandwiches."

"And salads," Gary pointed out.

"And salads," Tom echoed sadly. Then his eyes widened and he clapped and broke into a wide smile. "I know!"

"Oh no," Gary groaned. It seemed that he was accustomed to his husband's brainstorms.

But Tom just waved a dismissal and leaned toward Everett. "I have a proposition. A business proposition, that is. I'm a married man. What if you prepared a couple of dinners for us each week? Prepped them ahead of time, I mean. We'd pay for the ingredients and whatever you think is a fair hourly wage."

Everett was going to protest that he wasn't a chef or caterer. But then he also wasn't a plumber or painter or carpenter, and that hadn't stopped him recently. He still needed some extra cash, and he enjoyed puttering around in the kitchen. And Gary wasn't protesting the notion—in fact, he looked as if he liked it.

"You've only had one meal from me," Everett pointed out. "What if this is all I'm capable of making?"

Tom chuckled. "I'd happily eat this once a week. Is this too much to ask, though? You can say no and I won't be offended."

In fact, Everett was feeling enthusiastic about the idea. He liked cooking for others and rarely had the chance. This would give him a captive audience, so to speak. "Let's... let's give it a try. See if it works out."

Tom clapped again, Gary grinned, and Everett started mulling over potential recipes.

After dinner they had tea in the living room, and Everett took notes on the Rollins-Rosses' food aversions. There were only a few, and they were all things that were easy to avoid, like anchovies and dill pickles.

"This is a comfortable house," Gary observed, looking around. "Could use some updating, but...."

Everett patted the recliner arm. "Yeah, it's a little too 1970s for my taste, but I guess some of that's back in style nowadays."

Somehow the conversation turned from that to old music and TV shows, which led to Everett's admission that when he was a kid, he loved watching *L.A. Law*. "Is that what inspired you to become an attorney?" Gary asked.

"Not really. Not directly, anyway. I wasn't much of a student, so I never really considered it as a career. After high school, Charlotte offered to help me pay for college, but she'd already done so much for me and she needed to get on with her own life." They'd argued about it a bit, but she ended up following her heart and moving to California, while he stuck around Chicago and took on whatever job would pay the rent. Faced with that sort of responsibility, he'd grown up a lot.

"So what was it?" Gary's voice was gentle, as if he didn't want to startle Everett from his brief reverie. And he truly seemed interested in the answer.

"A shitty boss," Everett answered with a chuckle. "I was part of a construction crew working for him. It was all under the table—no taxes that way, right?—and that would have been okay with me. Except sometimes he didn't pay us what we were owed. He especially cheated the Mexican guys because they weren't comfortable complaining to anyone about it. Then this one guy, Eduardo, got hurt on the job, and of course it turned out the boss wasn't paying for worker's comp. No health insurance either. The bastard basically said too bad."

Although that had happened a long time ago, the memory still angered him. Eduardo was a nice person and had two little kids. Everyone on the crew had pitched in to help, but none of them had much extra money.

"Anyway, I got it into my head that I was going to fight injustice. Ta-dah! I enrolled in a community college, worked my ass off, transferred to Northern Illinois University, worked my ass off some more, and got into Northwestern Law. Where I racked up a huge student loan debt and realized—too late—that I could never afford to take the kind of jobs I'd once dreamed of. No justice battles for me. I ended up writing contracts and researching obscure regulations on behalf of soulless corporations." He couldn't resist a deep, self-pitying sigh.

After a sympathetic pause, Gary spoke up. "There are lots of ways to help folks. Like saving a couple of old men when their plumbing goes awry."

That was a really nice thought. Sure, Everett hadn't rescued multitudes, but he'd helped out a few people recently. Hell, he'd even done some good work for Cannon.

Tom and Gary stayed for another hour, until they started yawning. Everett sent them home with leftovers.

Unless there was a three-day holiday to draw in tourists, some of the Main Street shops and restaurants were closed on Monday. The businesses that catered mostly to locals, such as the grocery stores, were busy, as some residents took advantage of their day off to do errands. Main Street itself, however, was slow. There was barely a line at Rising Times, nobody clustered outside the tasting rooms, and many of the parking spots remained empty.

Gulch Books and Treats, however, was open. Charlotte and Jessica said this was experimental, to see whether there were enough sales on Monday to justify staying open. If there were, they might eventually take Mondays off themselves and let the employees run things. For now, however, they were both working seven days a week.

When Everett wandered into the shop on Monday afternoon, he wasn't surprised to find Jess—dressed flamboyantly, as usual—wiping down the pastry case and Charlotte standing behind the cashier counter, leafing through a magazine.

"Día de los Muertos," Char said by way of greeting.

"Uh, hi?"

"The theme for the next window display. At first I thought Halloween—and that would be fun. But then Jess suggested Día de los Muertos instead, and that's better. Unless you think it's insensitive, considering the recent murder."

Before Everett could respond, Jess blew a raspberry. "There are going to be skeletons and ghosts all over town. The high school drama and art clubs will have a haunted house at the community center as a fundraiser. Kovacs Wines is going to have their annual Blood Suck. So you can—"

"Blood suck?" Everett repeated.

Jess flapped a hand impatiently. "They do it over a couple of weekends. People pay a bunch of money to dress up like vampires, eat snacks shaped like bones and eyeballs and brains, and pretend that the red wines they're drinking are blood."

"That sounds kind of fun." He'd consider going, if he had a date. Which he wouldn't, because clearly his romantic life had withered and turned to dust, like Dracula exposed to sunlight.

"My point," Jess said, "is that nobody's going to suspend those activities just because some jerk got himself murdered. And it certainly shouldn't stand in the way of a nice window display."

That made sense to Everett. "What would the display involve?"

Charlotte answered with enthusiasm. "Sugar skulls, of course. Marigolds. Papel picado banners."

"I'll sell pan de muerto," said Jessica. "And Mexican hot chocolate."

Everett nodded. "And you'll highlight books about the holiday?"

"There are some really charming children's books I'd love to display," said Charlotte. "But I'd also include books for adults, like Mexican–Californian history and global celebrations of the dead."

Jessica suddenly raced over, still clutching her dusting cloth. "Oh, I know what we should do! We should have a contest for writing calaveras literarias. We could give out books and treats as prizes."

Charlotte pointed a finger at her. "Yes! I bet I can rope in some of my friends at the school and encourage them to have their students enter. It would be a really fun writing exercise."

"What's—" Everett stopped as something crashed into his shin. He looked down to discover the orange cat winding in and out between his legs, occasionally head-bonking him. The cat looked considerably better fed than it had originally. "What are calaveras literarias? Aren't calaveras skulls?" He didn't speak Spanish, but he'd learned that word because it was the name of the neighboring county.

"They are," replied Jessica. "But in this case, they're little poems that make fun of friends, politicians, famous people. You write them as if the subject were dead, like an epitaph, but satirical."

Everett was going to ask more questions, but he realized that somehow the cat had ended up cradled in his arms. He didn't recall picking it up—had it teleported there magically? And now it was purring and doing that kneading thing with its paws, which was criminally endearing.

"Go for it," he said, addressing both women. "It sounds fun. And screw Cannon. Nobody liked him anyway."

As if on cue, Sergeant McBeth stepped through the open door. He and Everett stared at each other, McBeth with his usual amused smirk. "Is that your official statement on the matter?" he asked.

Everett, trying not to bristle too visibly, settled for a glare. "It's true. I haven't heard one person say anything good about the guy."

"But, at least as far as we know, he wasn't a murderer."

McBeth sauntered closer and started rubbing the cat's ears and chin, which made the creature purr twice as loud, dammit. And which also gave Everett a closeup view of warm brown eyes and a rather dashing, almost roguish amount of stubble. Also, he smelled nice, like leather and maple syrup. Which would be interesting wine-tasting notes, now that Everett thought of it. McBeth simply returned Everett's stare, as if he could read every unwelcome and inappropriate thought.

Everett set the cat onto the floor, where it gave a reproachful meow before wandering off between the bookshelves.

"Still stalking me?" Everett asked.

"Should I be?"

"Of course not!"

McBeth laughed and turned to Charlotte. "Sophie's home with a cold. When I was a kid, that meant canned alphabet soup and *The Price is Right*, but I'm afraid nowadays it probably means hours of TikTok instead. I thought I'd intervene by picking her up something to read. You mentioned an author she'd like?"

"Yes! Hang on."

Charlotte disappeared behind some bookshelves and Jessica returned to her pastry case, which left Everett and McBeth alone with McBeth still standing close. Uncomfortably close, probably employing a sinister interrogation method even without saying anything.

Everett should have kept quiet too, except he was constitutionally incapable. "Caught the bad guy yet?"

"Working on it."

"Shouldn't there be fingerprints?"

McBeth smiled. "Someone's been watching too much *CSI*."

"I do not!"

That only made McBeth chuckle. It was a sexy laugh—of course— the kind that made Everett's skin prickle in delicious and absolutely unwanted ways. When was the last time he'd felt that kind of frisson? Scowling, he stepped a few feet away.

Charlotte saved him by bustling back with three paperbacks clutched in her hands. "Sophie's going to love these." She handed them to McBeth. "A young woman accidentally ends up captaining a spaceship full of misfits in search of a home. They have adventures and, along the way, each learns the value of their own particular characteristics. But it's not preachy at all. The writing sparkles and it's full of humor. The fourth book is due out next year."

McBeth tucked the books under one arm and pulled a phone out of a pocket. "Sounds perfect for her. Thanks. Can I pay with this thing?"

"No charge."

He shook his head ruefully. "Aw, Ms. Tabor, that's kind of you, but you know I can't accept gifts."

Everett almost huffed out loud at the gratuitous display of honesty. Actually, maybe he did huff out loud: Charlotte shot him a glare before answering McBeth. "It's not a gift for you; it's for Sophie. And in fact, it's not a gift at all—it's an opportunity. I'm wondering if she'd be interested in writing book reviews for my newsletter. I'll have a section on young-adult titles, and some commentary from a genuine young adult would be wonderful. Sophie's such a strong writer. I can't pay, but any book she wants to review, she can have for free."

Was Charlotte making this up on the spot, and if so, why? Did she think she needed to get on the sergeant's good side? Oh God, did she think that Everett really was the killer?

McBeth and Charlotte exchanged some departure pleasantries, but Everett didn't much notice, too horrified at the idea that his closest flesh-and-blood relative might think he was a murderer. Sure, he'd been a little wild as a kid and unfocused in his early twenties. And okay, he was sort of unfocused again. But that didn't mean he was going around bashing people's noggins with wine bottles.

As soon as McBeth stepped out of the shop, Everett announced, "I didn't do it!"

Charlotte frowned in confusion. "What didn't you do?"

"Murder Cannon." Then he added, "Or anyone else," in case she was questioning that as well.

"Of course you didn't." She had worn a similar expression when he was six and had declared that after his next birthday he was going to quit school and become a fireman. It was her *isn't he cute, let's humor him* face.

He frowned, now slightly offended that she didn't think he was a murderer. Did she assume he was too weak or scared? That wasn't it at all. He had a moral code, dammit, just like Sergeant Do-Right.

And he probably needed to stop acting like a teenager.

"If you weren't trying to suck up to McBeth so he wouldn't arrest me, why did you do that whole"—Everett waved his hands—"free books for your kid thing?"

"Exactly what I said. Because I think it would be a good idea to have a young reviewer, and because Sophie's a bookworm with excellent writing skills. And she's a great kid. She's growing up without a mother, just like we did, but she has a much steadier father than we ever had."

Steady was definitely not a term anybody would have used for their dad. "What happened to her mom?"

"Divorce, when Sophie was a baby. Cole got custody and Sophie's mother ended up moving overseas—Portugal, I think—for her work. I heard it was supposed to be a temporary thing, but she never came back."

Huh. Everett grudgingly upped his estimation of McBeth. From everything he'd seen and heard, parenting was always a challenge, even more so for a single parent.

Everett and Sam had discussed having a kid, but with their demanding jobs, the timing had never seemed right. Also, he had the impression that Sam was less enthusiastic about the idea than Everett was, although Sam had never admitted that. Everett was pleased to be an uncle to Charlotte and Rob's daughters, who'd been whirlwinds of energy when they were little and had grown into delightful young women. But he did slightly regret never having become a dad. Oh well. Maybe he would have been bad at it.

"Hey, Char? I've been thinking about something. Can I run it by you?"

"Any time, little brother."

"Hang on!" called Jessica, who'd been watching silently from behind her pastry case. From what Everett understood, Jess often had family drama going on, in part because she was part of a big family. She might enjoy seeing her bestie have a bit of it for a change. In any case, she brought over two Americanos, one with cream and sugar like Char preferred, and one black. "Advice tastes better with coffee. Do you need cookies too?"

They demurred and she returned to her café, although she was undoubtedly listening in. Everett didn't mind. In fact, she could throw in her two cents, if she felt like it.

"So... here's the thing," he began. Then he paused, trying to decide how to word it. To her credit, Charlotte waited patiently, although she looked slightly pained as if expecting bad news.

He cleared his throat. "So you know how when I was younger, I was all gung-ho about fighting for justice, right? Only that didn't quite work out as planned. And now... well, I'm sort of stalled, and the only thing I do know is that I never want to practice law again. But I'd still like to make a... a positive contribution, even if only in some small way."

"Okay," she said slowly. "I understand so far. And by the way, Ev, there's nothing wrong with switching plans mid-career. Look at me and Jess, after all."

He didn't point out the difference, which was that they'd both put in long years at their original jobs before retiring and starting new things. That particular point wasn't important at the moment. "Okay, right. And I'll figure out something eventually, don't worry. But in the meantime, what if I fight for justice by helping find Cannon's murderer?"

Charlotte opened her mouth and closed it again, clearly making herself pause before responding. "That's what the police are for, honey."

"I know. But that could take time, and meanwhile it's sort of hanging over me and everyone else who had a grudge against the guy. Which is apparently half of Gulch. There are limits to what police can do. Little details like the Fourth Amendment, for example. But I'm not limited by those things. Maybe I can access info that the cops can't." Journalists like Jo Rossi weren't the only ones who could poke around.

She didn't answer right away, so he sipped his coffee and burned his tongue. Which reminded him of that famous case in which a woman sued a fast food chain after being severely burned by spilled coffee. Early in his legal career, he'd assisted in a similar case involving a man who cracked a tooth while eating ribs at a corporate-owned casual dining spot. Everett's firm had represented the corporation, which won, and he'd always felt a little bad about it. Yes, tooth damage was a risk when eating food with bones. But the law firm's client had been rich and the plaintiff poor, and the corporation had probably spent more on legal fees than if they'd just paid his dental bill plus a bit for his pain and suffering.

"I know you told me to mind my own business," he said to Charlotte unhappily.

"Indeed I did. But you're a grown man capable of making his own decisions. Look, I think it's a bad idea. You might even be putting yourself in danger. It's probably a symptom of having too much time on your hands. But if it's important to you...." She shrugged. "Go for it."

"Thanks, Char." He smiled warmly at her, then turned to face the café. "Anything to add, Jess?"

"Yeah. Keep us in the loop on what you dig up!"

CHAPTER FIFTEEN

The Deadman Gulch Inn, built of stone in the late 1850s, had survived the several fires that had destroyed much of the downtown. It was a large two-story structure with tall iron-shuttered windows and a long second-floor balcony. Each guestroom was named after someone famous who'd once stayed there, and it was a popular place for tourists despite—or maybe because of—rumors that it was haunted. It also boasted a nice restaurant with indoor seating, an outdoor beer-and-wine garden, and a saloon that looked as if it hadn't changed much since the place was built.

The saloon was where Everett found himself on Monday night. He'd eaten at home and had intended to stay in for the evening, but the weather was pleasantly autumnal and he felt restless. So he'd wandered, and his feet had brought him here.

It was a good place to be. About half the tables were occupied by a mix of out-of-towners and locals, and the conversational hum was pleasant without being distracting. Dark wood and warm yellow lighting gave the space a cozy ambience. The air smelled of beer and popcorn, the old wooden floor creaked when people walked over it, and the tables all wobbled a bit on the uneven floor. Everett didn't even have to squint to imagine prospectors bellied up to the bar alongside ranchers and stagecoach drivers. Mark Twain might be sitting at a table, spinning yarns. Maybe a few travelers from back East were there too, having recently arrived via the new transcontinental railroad. Surely Black Bart and his fellow outlaws were also likely; after all, Gulch had named a street after him. Everett pictured some of these colorful figures pausing to welcome him to town.

He sat alone at a small table in the corner with a pint of a tasty local ale. A pen and yellow legal pad lay on the table in front of him, but he hadn't yet written anything. He was trying to devise a strategy before committing anything to paper, because once things were written down, they always seemed more obligatory.

"Sticking to grains instead of grapes?"

The question pulled Everett from his reverie. He realized that two people stood in front of him, neither of them Mark Twain. He recognized the woman in the harem pants and crocheted top—Willow, the owner of Granocchio Cellars—and presumed the man was her husband. He wore jeans and a tie-dyed Grateful Dead tee, and his long hair was in a ponytail.

Everett smiled at them both. "I like to give equal time to all the alcohol-producing plants."

"Wine is better for you," she said with conviction. "It's a living thing, tied to the earth that grew it and shaped by the love and labor of the people who produced it. Beer is just beer."

"You'll have to excuse her," said the man, setting a hand on Willow's shoulder. "She gets passionate."

"Oh, I get it. Wine's complicated. A lot of people feel strongly about it."

Willow nodded. "This is my husband, Tim. Honey, this is Charlotte Tabor's brother."

Tim's eyebrows lifted. "The fellow who found the dead man!"

Involuntarily, Everett flinched. He wasn't used to living in a place where anonymity didn't exist, and he wasn't happy that his claim to fame was discovering a corpse. "Uh, hi," he said weakly. "I'm Everett."

"Hey man," said Tim. "What was it like? Did you freak out? Was he—"

Willow interrupted him with an unsubtle elbow to his chest. "He doesn't want to talk about it. I'm sure he was traumatized. Drink a few glasses of wine, Everett, and clear your head of toxic thoughts. Just let them float away." She demonstrated with wavy fingers near her forehead.

"Thanks."

They both gave a little wave before wandering through the doorway to the outdoor area where, Everett presumed, they would order wine instead of beer. After they were gone, he looked at the menu to see whether the saloon carried Granocchio wines, but it didn't. With so many local wineries, they probably had to be selective.

Still slightly disturbed over his notoriety, he picked up his pen and focused on the task at hand. He was under the general impression— maybe an inaccurate one—that detective work relied heavily on inductive reasoning. An investigator gathered clues and used those clues to build a hypothesis about the identity of the culprit.

But legal arguments, as he'd learned in the first year of law school, worked the other way around. You started with a general conclusion, such as "Your client owes my client twenty-million bucks for breach of contract," and then you found information to support that conclusion. Or, if you were a judge, you looked for both supportive and negating information.

Everett was comfortable with this, so why not use it now? He'd start with a working theory about who'd done it and then search for evidence that supported or disproved that theory. All he needed to begin, then, was to generate a list of the most likely killers.

He tapped his chin with the pen a few times before writing *Junior*. And then, after a brief hesitation, *Carol Allen*. In the spirit of fairness, even though he knew he'd soon be crossing this one out, he wrote *Charlotte*. He felt like a traitor, but he was aiming for comprehensiveness and objectivity here. She had to have an alibi, and when he found out what it was, he could eliminate her from the list and feel as if he'd accomplished something. In fact, just to prove he was being fair, he also wrote Everett and then, immediately and with conviction, drew a line through his name.

There. Progress already.

He was mulling over whether to include Jessica when someone approached his table. "Excuse me. Can I join you?" she asked.

She was a very attractive woman in her twenties, with a mane of balayaged hair and an outfit that looked too fashionable and too expensive for Gulch: white wide-leg jeans, a textured cardigan with a single button holding it closed, no visible blouse, and a lot of bling on her neck and fingers.

Everett glanced around and saw that several tables were unoccupied, so why did she want his? As far as he was aware, the saloon was not a hot pickup spot, and even if it were, no way that she'd be interested in him, even if she thought he was straight.

Although he was still hesitating, she sat in the other chair. "You're Everett Vaughn, right?"

Oh, dammit. "Look, I'm not going to talk about the murder. It was really—"

"I'm Blake Cannon's wife. Ex-wife. Widow?"

With a start, he realized he'd seen her in the wedding photo in Cannon's house. "Oh. I'm so sorry for your loss."

"Let's face it—it's not that big of a loss. Blake was a dick." She sighed deeply. "Not that I wanted him dead or anything, but.... We were about to divorce. I'd just talked to my lawyer that morning."

Everett had no clue what words were appropriate in a situation like this. Condolences? Congratulations for avoiding expensive and stressful divorce proceedings? Sharing that he, too, had recently split from his husband? Agreement that yes, Cannon was a dick? "Um, if you want me to tell you what happened, I don't think I can—"

"I want to hire you."

"Pardon me?"

She leaned back in her chair and settled her hands on the table. She had long nails, all perfectly shaped and elaborately decorated with a leopard-print design. "Blake hired you to fix things up, right?"

"Yeah, I was doing some handyman stuff for him."

"And I bet he owed you money." She rolled her eyes and didn't wait for a response. "That house is still a mess. God, I hate that place. He bought it without telling me and then expected me to move here to Podunk. Like, what am I supposed to do in this place? Learn to milk cows? That was one of the reasons I left him. Not the only one, but it was a biggie. Also he was mean to Bella."

His confusion must have been clear, because she tapped at her phone and then turned the screen so he could see a photo of a white labradoodle. "Bella," she explained.

Wait. Everett had seen this woman—and her dog—before, walking on Main Street. He'd almost tripped over the leash. Was that before or after he found Cannon's body? He couldn't recall.

"Okay, Mrs. Cannon, I understand—"

"God, no. I'm Izzy, all right? Izzy Kincaid."

Everett realized he was still clutching his pen. He set it down and picked up his glass instead, then drained it. "I still don't understand what you want from me," he said.

"I told you. I want you to finish fixing up the place. The deed's in my name too, and hell if I'm gonna continue paying the mortgage on that dump. You're gonna get it in good enough shape so I can sell it. Oh, and don't worry. The crime-scene people are done."

For several moments, he simply stared at her, waiting for her to say that this was a joke—although humor in this situation seemed highly unlikely. She scrunched up her lips and sighed. "So, can you do it?"

God, she was serious. "You know I'm the one who found, uh, your ex, right?"

"Duh."

"Then why the hell do you want to hire me?"

Judging from her expression, he was the dumbest and most annoying human on the planet. "'Cause at least I know you can do... whatever needs doing. I'm not gonna waste my time digging around Yeehawville to find a new handyman, when probably all I'd find are meth heads and old creeps."

Everett was beginning to get the sense that, despite the impending divorce, Blake and Izzy had been a pretty good match. She might not be quite as pompous as he was, but she was every bit as demeaning and obnoxious. He didn't want her as a boss any more than he'd wanted Cannon, but.... If he had access to the house, he might be able to dig up some clues. Things that Sergeant McBeth might not have seen.

He wished he had more ale.

"Ms. Kincaid," he said carefully. "Can you sell the house so soon? Legally, I mean?" He didn't know much about real estate law or probate law in general—and zilch about it in California—and he preferred to keep it that way, thanks very much. But he couldn't help asking.

She was going to sprain her eyes with all the rolling. "I don't know. I better be able to, and fast. That's my money tied up in it. Anyway, I have my lawyer working on it."

Everett would have been willing to bet that she was a nightmare client, although of course he didn't say so. Instead, he pondered. And then pondered some more, while Izzy tapped her nails impatiently on the table.

"How'd you know you'd find me here?" The question had suddenly hit him.

"I asked around. And I'd appreciate an answer quickly. I have a long drive tonight."

He frowned. "Where to?"

"San Fran, of course! Did you think I was going to spend the night in this armpit?" She tossed her hair behind her shoulder.

Everett had recently been informed in no uncertain terms that nobody in San Francisco referred to their city as San Fran, and they'd all rather jump in the Bay than call it Frisco. It was simply San Francisco or, more familiarly, The City. Apparently nobody had shared this with Izzy, or she simply didn't care. "Isn't that a hundred-fifty miles from here?"

"Yes!" she snapped. "That's how far we are from civilization. So are you going to do it?"

He was badly torn. He knew he should probably refuse, yet there was the benefit of getting access. Also, some money would be nice.

"I will do it on three conditions," he said, half hoping she'd refuse.

"What?"

"First off, I need to talk to the police first and make sure this won't piss them off. Technically I'm still a suspect, I think, although I can assure you that—"

"I don't care who did it. Blake probably deserved it. And fine, go ahead and ask the cops."

Wow, she was cold. Everett and Sam hadn't always seen eye-to-eye and their marriage had dissolved, but if Everett were murdered, Sam would not be this indifferent. For some illogical reason, that knowledge made Everett feel slightly better about his own situation.

"Number two, I'll want a written contract specifying the exact work to be done, my fees, deadlines, and... and all the other pertinent details." Which he could think of later when he hadn't just downed a couple pints of ale.

"Fine, fine." She waved a hand.

"And third, I want the four-hundred bucks your ex owed me, plus a thousand-dollar deposit on the upcoming work. Up front."

In response, she tapped at her phone. "Okay. What's your Venmo?"

Not even a pause. Interesting. Everett wondered about the state of her finances and how that intersected with the state of Cannon's finances. "Not yet," he said. "Wait until I talk to the sheriff and send you a contract to sign."

"But you'll do that soon?"

"I'll work on it tomorrow."

That seemed to satisfy her. They exchanged phone numbers and then she was off, striding quickly across the floor as if she couldn't tolerate one more minute in Gulch.

Everett wrote another name on the yellow pad: Izzy Kincaid.

CHAPTER SIXTEEN

Despite his promise to Izzy Kincaid, Everett did not begin her business on Tuesday morning. It was simply too beautiful outside for that kind of thing. Instead he had coffee and gossip at Rising Times—the gossip was about one of the wine-tasting rooms abruptly closing, not about the murder—and then got into his truck and drove east. Janet seemed to enjoy the outing, taking the curves faithfully and chugging along happily even on the steepest hills.

The nearer he got to Calaveras Big Trees State Park, which was about two thousand feet higher than Gulch, the more fall color the trees displayed. It was definitely chillier at the park, and of course the forest there was much more dense. Although some areas around Gulch had a lot of trees, such as the former Miracle Creek Campground, their specimens weren't as impressive. Here the giant sequoias reached impossibly high, with trunks as wide as a small house. There were lots of other trees too, as well as smaller plants in the understory, and undoubtedly Everett could have identified some of them if he'd picked up a brochure at the information center. Instead he simply ambled along the trails, inhaling the forest scents and pausing to watch birds and squirrels. He was thankful for the hiking boots he'd bought the other day.

Standing alone in one grove, he became aware of being more content than he'd been since... well, in a long time. The natural beauty, the peace, the solitude, the healthy exercise: all of these were balms for the soul. Izzy Kincaid was blind not to see that.

Could Everett imagine living in this area permanently?

He mulled that over as he continued his walk, but by the time he returned to his truck he still hadn't found an answer.

Everett drove home after a quick burger in a town called Arnold, but instead of climbing out of Janet right away, he sat inside while parked in the driveway. Grumbling at himself to stop procrastinating, he pulled out his phone and brought up the contact information that Sergeant McBeth had oh-so-helpfully shared with him.

Need to talk to you about Cannon.

The answering text came almost immediately.

Ready to confess? I should probably Mirandize you first.

Hilarious. Man, Everett could picture the smirk precisely. *When can we talk?*

Now's fine. Come over to my house.

Everett stared at the phone as if the words might change into something less weird. They didn't. Finally, he simply wrote *OK*.

Because McBeth's place was less than a mile away, and because Everett was feeling virtuous about exercising today, he walked. He passed a few people who looked familiar and exchanged greetings with them. He couldn't tell whether they knew he was The Man Who Found the Dead Guy.

When he got to McBeth's house, the sergeant was standing on his front porch waiting for him, a coffee cup in one big hand. He was definitely out of uniform, wearing gym shoes, khaki shorts, and a gray T-shirt emblazoned with a Sacramento State University logo. "Want a cup of joe?" he called before Everett could say anything.

"Do people in real life call coffee joe?"

"I do. Want some?"

This was getting even weirder. "Um, no thanks."

"Sorry about the... this." McBeth gestured vaguely with his free hand at the surroundings. "My day off. It's just as convenient as the station anyway."

Everett winced. "Oh, shit. I'm sorry. I didn't mean to bug you when you're off work." In fact, it hadn't even occurred to him that McBeth would have days off, which was dumb.

"No big deal. My daughter's still home sick, so I'm playing nurse and puttering around the house. By the way, tell your sister that Sophie has already finished two of those books. I think her reviews are going to be positive." He laughed.

Well, damn. Everett had been thinking of this man as Sergeant McBeth, but he was actually a fully fledged human being with needs and interests outside of his job. And with really good legs.

"I'll tell her." Everett walked up the steps and onto the porch. "You're sure it's okay?"

"It's fine. Probably better than meeting somewhere with lots of ears anyway. Which is pretty much everywhere in town. I'd invite you inside, but I don't know how many germs Sophie has spread around. Kids are like plague factories. Anyway, it's a nice day. Good to be outdoors."

"It is. I went to Big Trees this morning." A thought hit him. "That's not outside my safe zone, is it?"

McBeth's eyebrows rose. "Safe zone?"

"You told me to stick around until you wrap up the investigation."

McBeth smiled. "I didn't mean you literally couldn't step foot outside the city limits. I'm just requesting that you don't move away or spend too much time far afield. I still don't consider you a suspect, but you are a witness."

Fair enough. Everett considered how to continue. Word choice was critical; he'd learned that as an attorney. However, picking the right ones wasn't always easy outside of a legal memorandum. "Look, Sergeant McBeth, I—"

"Cole. Call me Cole, and I'm gonna call you Everett, if you don't mind. We're neighbors."

This wasn't at all how Everett had pictured the meeting going. "You people take community policing really seriously."

"We do." Cole's usual amused expression was replaced with earnestness. "This is my home, my family's home, and I love it. I care about

Gulch and the people who live here. Even the ones who are sorta jerks." The smile returned.

Everett wasn't sure whether Cole was referring to him or Cannon and decided he'd rather not know. "This isn't how cops are back home."

Cole made a sweeping gesture with his hand and spoke in an exaggerated drawl. "In case you haven't noticed, this ain't Chicago." Then he pointed to one of the honest-to-god rocking chairs on the porch before sitting in the other, his long legs stretched out before him.

Everett almost asked whether he was going to start playing a banjo next but realized that would make him sound an awful lot like Izzy Kincaid. Who was supposed to be the topic of conversation. So he lowered himself gingerly into the other chair, which proved annoyingly comfortable, with the softest little creak whenever he moved.

He found it pleasant to gently rock on a warm autumn afternoon, a few fluffy clouds sailing tranquilly through the sky while a jay and a squirrel waged a tiny battle in the neighbor's oak tree. No sirens or strident voices, no gunning engines, no reek of garbage or exhaust. And a handsome man with impressive calf muscles sitting next to him.

"You wanted to talk to me?" Cole eventually prompted.

Oh, yeah. That. Everett took a deep breath. "I think you ought to investigate Izzy Kincaid as a likely suspect."

"Oh? Why is that?"

A little disappointed that he hadn't even earned a raised eyebrow, Everett explained. "Because statistically, the most likely person to murder someone is their spouse." He paused. "Um, that's true for female victims, at any rate. I'm not sure about men." The Crim Law professor who'd discussed this hadn't mentioned male victims at all. Or, for that matter, people in same-sex relationships.

"I appreciate the advice, Everett. But I am aware of the statistics. And I can't lock someone up just because she was married to a dead guy. When we do a murder investigation, we have to be really careful not to jump to conclusions. Sloppy police work can lose a case."

That reminded Everett about his earlier ruminations on inductive reasoning. An investigator couldn't just gather a piece of evidence and be done with it—they had to build a case, had to also look for anything that could disprove the theory.

When it came to Izzy Kincaid, however, there was more evidence. "Okay, but she couldn't stand him. They were in the midst of a divorce. She was pissed because he expected her to move here, and I also think she wasn't happy about how he was handling money. Oh, and he was mean to Belle. That's her dog."

Cole studied him closely, head a bit cocked. "And how, may I ask, do you know these things?"

"She told me." Everett sat back, crossed his arms, and tried to replicate Cole's smug face.

There was the eyebrow lift. "I hadn't realized that you and Ms. Kincaid were acquainted."

"We weren't—not until last night. I was sitting at the Gulch Inn's saloon when she walked up, introduced herself, and offered me a job."

Cole went very still for a moment before setting his mug on the porch floor and leaning forward. "Izzy Kincaid offered you a job. Doing what, pray tell?"

"Finishing the work I started in Cannon's house."

"But why—"

"Why me? She said it's because she doesn't want the hassle of finding another handyman around here. She, uh, doesn't have very flattering things to say about Gulch. She wants the house fixed up pronto so she can sell it, which I'm not sure she can legally do right now, but I'm not her lawyer so that's not my problem."

Instead of being grateful for these nuggets of information, Cole looked as though he had a headache. When he spoke, it was slowly, as if he were reluctant to hear the answer. "Did you tell her yes?"

"I told her I had to speak with you first," Everett said primly. This was him demonstrating that he was law-abiding and rule-observant. Which he mostly was, nowadays. Had been for a long time, in fact. It was a little boring, albeit considerably safer.

"Are you really that hard up for money? I can point you in the direction of some folks who are hiring right now."

"I'm not desperate yet, thanks, and I'm not looking for a regular gig. I had enough of that to last me awhile."

"Right. You're... finding yourself. Or something." Cole narrowed his eyes. "She's really pretty. Were you hoping maybe to, uh...."

Everett snorted. "Get in her designer pants? No. I was married to a man, remember?"

Cole responded with a shrug. "So? A person can be married to a man but also attracted to women. Or vice versa. Or be attracted to nonbinary folks, or—"

A muffled burst of female laughter interrupted him.

Confused, Everett looked around, but Cole only heaved a sigh before speaking loudly. "Sophie Beatrice McBeth, are you eavesdropping?"

Another laugh, and now Everett could tell that it came from nearby, on the other side of an open window covered by curtains.

"I'm not," came a disembodied voice that, presumably, belonged to Cole's daughter. "I came in here to get something."

"Get what?"

"Kleenex. I'm out." The sneeze that followed would not have earned an Oscar.

"Soph, you're supposed to be resting. And we're discussing police matters."

"I heard what you were discussing, Dad." More laughter, this time followed by the sound of running footsteps.

"She's going back to school tomorrow," Cole muttered to himself. Then he looked at Everett. "Sorry about that. She's a really great kid, but she's a teenager now, and...."

Everett, amused by the whole thing, shook his head. "It's fine. This is her house too, after all."

Seemingly relieved at Everett's understanding, Cole leaned back in his chair and picked up the coffee mug again. It was probably cold by now, but he took a sip anyway. Then he scratched his cheek, which was slightly more stubbly than usual. "You were explaining why, exactly, you think working for the ex-wife of the man you discovered deceased feels like a good idea to you."

"I mean, the money would be nice. She'll have to pay what he owed me too. But also, the work needs doing, and I hate leaving things unfinished." That was true, and it was one reason why leaving the law firm—and Sam—had been painful. He would have quit his job years ago, actually, if not for the pay and a sense that he would be abandoning a duty. And despite all his flaws, he was reliable.

Okay, yes, he also wanted the chance to snoop around some. But Sergeant McBeth didn't need to know that. Everett used his most precise lawyer voice. "Is there anything stopping me from taking this job? From a legal standpoint, I mean. Are you concerned I'll get fingerprints everywhere?"

"You already have fingerprints everywhere. In this particular case, the only prints that would help us would be on the murder weapon, and even then they're only of use if the killer has prints on file—which can take several weeks to find out. Plus in this particular case, as you might recall, the weapon ended up shattered into tiny pieces and soaking in blood and wine, which considerably reduces the likelihood of getting a usable print anyway. So, Everett, you can leave all the prints and trace evidence you want at that house—which we've already swept, by the way—without affecting the case." Apparently pleased with his lecture, Cole set down his mug and crossed his arms.

Everett waited a few beats. "So nothing is stopping me from taking the job."

"Common sense is stopping you!" Cole exclaimed, throwing up his hands.

"Nobody ever accused me of having too much common sense."

Yeah, Cole probably did have a headache coming on, judging from the way he rubbed his scalp. "Talking to you is like talking to Sophie."

"Except she has to listen to you and I don't. Unless I'm breaking the law, which I'm not." Everett stood and brushed imaginary crumbs from his jeans. "Thank you for the neighborly chat. I hope you decide to give Izzy a close look."

"I hope you decide not to do anything stupid."

Sophie's laughter followed Everett down the walkway.

On Wednesday Everett spent the morning grocery shopping and then meal-prepping for the Rollins-Rosses. He did this at their place, about a mile from his, on a block of faux Tudor houses all built in the early nineties. "It was supposed to be a whole subdivision," Gary explained as they led Everett into the kitchen, "but the developer gave up."

Tom wrapped an arm around his husband's middle. "He promised to treat me like a prince, but this is the closest I'm getting to a castle."

Everett looked around. The furniture was a pleasing mixture of modern and antique pieces, the latter of which might have come from Carol Allen. Everything looked welcoming. "It's really nice, though. And it looks as if it's in great condition."

"That's because my darling hubby didn't balk at spending a fortune updating it. It had track lighting. Sponge-painted walls. Zebra-print curtains." Tom shuddered.

Thinking of the house he and Charlotte had lived in during the nineties, Everett figured these guys were lucky they had a roof that didn't leak and a furnace that didn't decide to die at the most inconvenient times. Then he remembered that Tom's parents had kicked him out when he was still a teen. Everett was glad that Tom now got to live in a nice house with a loving husband.

Not surprisingly, the kitchen was extremely well equipped, although Gary said they rarely used any of the fancy gadgets and cookware. "A Zojirushi," sighed Everett, petting the bread machine. "And All-Clad skillets."

Chuckling, Gary gestured expansively. "Have at it, my good man."

The Olive Branch opened at eleven, which meant that Gary left the house around ten. Tom remained perched on a barstool at the kitchen counter, schmoozing. He was good company while Everett chopped, diced, and sautéed, and like Xochi, he was a good source of local gossip. He also talked about some of his favorite books, movies, and TV shows.

"I can't believe you haven't watched *Steven Universe!*" Tom said as Everett spatchcocked a chicken.

"But it's a cartoon."

"It's an animated series, yes, Mr. Snobbyface. The characters are queer, nonbinary, and gender fluid, not to mention multicultural. There's an alien lesbian wedding! And it has lovely messages about emotions and relationships and respecting people's identities. You're adding it to your watchlist."

"Fine," said Everett, giving in to the inevitable. It might be better for him than last night's binge watch of *The Great British Baking Show*, which had nearly caused him to attempt macarons at eleven p.m.

Mission accomplished, Tom got up, put his teacup in the dishwasher, and glanced around. "It smells amazing and you're tons of fun, but I can't leave my honey stranded all day. Just call if you need anything, and let yourself out when you're done. Don't be shy about taking some of your masterpieces home with you. Wouldn't want you to starve at our expense."

Not long after Tom left, Everett reached a point where all the food was roasting, simmering, or otherwise in progress. He'd eaten bits of this and that as he cooked, and now he helped himself to a cappuccino from a machine that probably cost a thousand bucks retail and cataloged the rest of the kitchen's wonders. Now that he knew exactly what he had to work with, future meal-planning could take advantage of the slow cooker, the juicer, the panini press, and whatever that gadget was that looked like a rocket ship. He'd even use that upscale bread machine.

He realized that he was whistling contentedly, something he'd never done while toiling over contracts and briefs. And speaking of contracts, he needed to deal with Izzy. He'd brought his laptop with him, so he sat down and wrote up a contract for her. Nothing too complicated, but it plainly set out their respective responsibilities. Using his phone as a hotspot, he sent the contract to her, along with a bill for the outstanding four hundred bucks plus the thousand-dollar deposit.

Less than five minutes later, he had a signed contract back. There was no way that she'd read it that fast, but most people barely skimmed before signing things. A payment for fourteen hundred came through on Venmo just afterward, so he had no cause to complain. He dashed off a text to Izzy: *I'll start tomorrow morning.*

She replied with a thumb's up.

It was midafternoon by the time Everett tucked the last food storage container into the fridge and put away the last cleaned pot. He'd already labeled all the containers, written out a series of reheating instructions, and left the note on the table for Tom and Gary, so after a final wipe-down of the counter, he looked around with satisfaction and left.

His feet were a little sore from all the standing, but he felt uncharacteristically filled with energy and purpose. He was pleased to know that, thanks to him, his new friends would have tasty meals without the hassle of cooking or major washing up. That was an accomplishment for sure.

But what else to do with his day? It was a little late for another forest hike, and anyway, he wanted to give his legs a rest. He remembered the yellow legal pad with the list of suspects, currently on his couch at home. Today would be a good day to meet Junior.

Of course, that meant he had to figure out where Junior lived, and he couldn't think of how to ask Carol Allen without making her suspicious. But he had other sources. He drove home, parked, and walked swiftly down to Main Street, where he entered Rising Times thirty minutes before closing time. The pastry case was mostly wiped out, but the heady aromas lingered, and Xochi greeted him with a smile as she swept the floor. "I hear you're Gary and Tom's personal chef now. Sweet!"

"They own every kitchen gadget ever invented."

"I bet they do. Last year they talked me into an air fryer. I figured, what do I need with a thing like that? But Tom was persuasive and they gave me a discount, and let me tell you, I use that thing almost every day."

Everett didn't currently own an air fryer. Maybe he should remedy that, now that Izzy had paid him. "Could I get an Americano? And some info?"

She leaned the broom against the wall. "I got plenty of both."

He waited while she washed her hands, pulled the drink, and handed it over. She also gave him a miniature creampuff with ube frosting. "On the house. It won't be any good tomorrow."

No way was he going to refuse a free pastry. After taking a bite, groaning happily, and swallowing, he looked at Xochi. "Do you know Carol Allen's cousin Junior?"

"Oh yeah, sure. He doesn't come into town real often, but every now and then he spends a few hours at the Oasis."

"Could you tell me where he lives?"

Her eyes sparkled. "And why on earth would you be looking for Junior Lum?"

If he told her, pretty soon half of Gulch would know. So he mimed locking his closed lips. "Top secret. Sorry. But I promise I'll tell you later."

"Okaaaay." She set her elbows on the counter and rested her chin in her palms. "But you owe me a favor, okay?"

"Are you a Mafia don?"

"Sure." She waved a hand. "All this is just a front for my money laundering."

Leaving future compensation unspecified was unwise, but what the hell. So was talking to Junior in the first place, probably. "I will owe you a favor," he intoned seriously.

Xochi rubbed her hands together and cackled. "Okay. Head east on the highway a couple miles past town. When you see a ruined adobe building on your left, turn just past it. That's Glory Hole Road, but people kept stealing the sign and they gave up replacing it."

"I bet," said Everett after an amused snort.

"Follow that road for another mile, and when you see a gravel driveway with a gate across it, park there. That's Junior's property, but you're gonna have to walk to the house."

He tried not to wince and finished the cream puff instead. "What are the chances he shoots me for trespassing?"

She just shrugged and grinned.

Then Everett had another thought. "Is it very difficult to make macarons?"

CHAPTER EIGHTEEN

He couldn't stop himself from snickering when he turned onto Glory Hole Road, even if the sign was missing. He wondered about the story behind the adobe ruins. It looked to have been the size of a large, two-story house, but now the roof was gone and most of the walls had tumbled. He'd have to remember to ask Charlotte about it.

The area around the road looked like pastureland, but after he crested a steep hill, he saw an uneven terrain covered in small trees and heavy shrubbery. Something about it looked very Western to his eyes, as if someone might be robbing a stagecoach nearby or riding off into the sunset on horseback, Stetson cocked just so, a woman in a calico dress with petticoats left behind, sobbing.

And as promised, there was the wide gravel driveway blocked by a sturdy metal gate. Everett parked there, leaving enough space for someone to pass in the unlikely event there was other traffic. The gate was locked, but since there weren't any No Trespassing signs, after a brief hesitation he climbed over the gate. An awkward landing on the other side created a twinge in his right ankle.

Limping, he trekked up a rise, dust puffing around his feet and insects whirring beside him. If anyone had ever used this land for farming or pasture, it had been long ago; now everything was wild with some kind of fairly tall greenery. Birds chirped. Something small and furry darted just in front of him, nearly making him yelp before it disappeared into a bush. That left him wondering whether there were snakes here too, specifically rattlesnakes. He was fairly certain there were things one could do to avoid rattlesnake bites, but he had no idea what those things might be. Apart from returning to Chicago; not too many rattlers there.

The driveway curved around some enormous boulders and stout little trees, and then he spied a house. It was small, the white paint weathering to gray, the area immediately near it bright with white, yellow, and red flowers. The effect was rustic—except for the solar panels on the roof, which were an unexpected sight.

He couldn't see the front of the house from this angle, but it did look as if the windows were open, which he took as a positive sign that someone was home. "Hello?" he called as he tromped closer. "Hello?" Trying to make it clear that he wasn't attempting to sneak up on the place.

It sounded as if a door slammed. A moment later, a barking, howling pack of beasts rounded the corner of the house and galloped toward him, their combined sound loud enough to wake Gulch's eponymous dead man.

This time, Everett did yelp. He also spun around and started running at full speed... or at least that was his intention. But he got only a few steps before his iffy ankle gave out and he crashed onto the ground. Pain spiked in his knees and hands, but that was the least of his worries as the pack descended upon him, jaws wide, teeth gleaming, drool flying....

And began to lick him. All of them. Some piled on top, making him collapse entirely, while others came in from the sides—every one of them intent on swiping its tongue across his mouth and eyes.

"Brandy! Oscar! Lulubelle! Horatio! Get off him! Down! Sit!" The dogs paid no attention to whomever was shouting. Everett tried to curl into a fetal ball, but furry paws kept getting in the way. "Get back, mutts! Oh, for pity's sake, Lulubelle, get off his head!"

For the record, Lulubelle was approximately the size of a teenaged elephant.

Once the man arrived, the dogs barked some more but then moved away from Everett to dance around their owner. This gave Everett the opportunity to sit upright. As he started to brush dog spit and dust off his face, he realized that his hands were bloody—and stinging.

"Mr. Lum?" His voice might have been a tad shaky.

"Who on God's green earth are you?" Lum—if that was indeed him—patted absently at the dog now sitting peacefully beside him. The remaining dogs had scampered off, evidently in search of something else to terrorize. Lum was tall and broad but slightly stooped. His gray hair and beard were shaggy, but his jeans were in decent shape, as was his Nature Conservancy T-shirt. Thankfully, he wasn't carrying a gun, at least as far as Everett could tell.

Groaning, Everett made it to his feet, taking care not to put his full weight on the right ankle. "I'm Everett Vaughn." He almost put out his hand for a shake but remembered the blood. "I'm here to ask you some questions about Blake Cannon."

"You're not a cop."

"No, I'm a lawyer." Technically true.

"You're not going to sue me over the dogs, are you? This is my property!"

"No lawsuit. I doubt I've suffered any financial loss and anyway, you're right. I'm the one who climbed over the gate. But I do want to talk about Cannon."

Lum's expression hardened. "Are you his lawyer?"

"God, no. And, um, you were aware that he's dead?"

The scowl turned into a smile. "Yup." Then Lum sighed and took a step forward. "You better come sit down. You took a good fall there."

He didn't mention that his ravening hounds had been the cause of that fall. And Everett decided not to mention it since at least two of the hounds in question were currently sniffing at a butterfly, while another was scratching itself as its companion took a leak.

"Okay. Thanks."

Everett was limping badly as they picked their way through the foliage to the front of the house. The garden there—if you could call anything that wild a garden—was even more colorful. A crow squawked loudly from inside a large aviary on the porch. "Hush now, Mortimer. He's allowed to be here too," chided Lum.

"Mortimer?"

"He got attacked by someone's cat in town. He's doing pretty good now. I should be able to release him in another week or two. Don't let your cats wander unattended outdoors, Everett. It's not healthy for the cats—cars, coyotes, fights, disease—and they kill over a billion birds a year. A billion. You need to build 'em a catio." He pointed to a plywood-and-wire structure at the edge of the porch. Several cats gazed back from various perches.

"Catio?" Everett asked weakly.

"Sure. I bring 'em out when the weather's nice. Well, except for Miss Mushroom. She prefers to stay indoors."

"Um... okay."

They went inside the house—all four dogs nearly toppling Everett yet again as they rushed in—and he found himself in a 1950s-vintage kitchen. Whatever was bubbling in the large pot on the stove smelled delicious. Everything was clean and orderly, and the only odd things were the big plastic bins stacked against one wall.

"You need first aid?"

Everett looked at his hands and shook his head. "Could I just wash up?"

"Help yourself." Lum pointed at the sink.

The water and hand soap hurt, but they did remove the blood and embedded plant material. And, Everett hoped, the dog slobber. At his host's gesture, he sat on one of the turquoise vinyl chairs. One dog, a shaggy sandy-colored beast, immediately hopped up onto the chair next to him, while the German shepherd sprawled on its side near his feet and the other two disappeared under the table. Lum sat opposite Everett and stared.

"You, uh, rehabilitate crows?" That seemed like a gentle way to begin a conversation.

"I rehabilitate lots of critters. Don't have many right now. I get most of 'em in the spring, when birds fall out of nests or mothers get killed on the highway, leaving their poor babies behind."

"Is it hard work?"

Lum grunted noncommittally.

"Okay, well, I came here to ask you some things about Blake Cannon."

"That son of a gun was the most low-down sneak I ever did meet, and I ain't one bit sorry he's gone. I oughta thank whoever did it."

By now, Everett should have been used to hearing people say unflattering things about the deceased, but Lum's vehemence took him by surprise. "Why are you happy about his death?"

"'Cause maybe now things are gonna work out okay."

"What do you mean by that?"

Lum ran fingers through his beard. "He was buyin' Miracle Creek Campground from me. I just can't keep on top of it, and the taxes are about killing me. He told me he was gonna reopen the place. That would be real nice. And I could sure use some extra money to feed my critters. But then I found out he was gonna tear the whole thing down. Rip out all the trees and plants and put in a golf course and a spa and who knows what all. Taking away all that wildlife habitat. There could be endangered plants there! Plus wasting all that water and electricity."

The shaggy dog hopped off the chair, waddled around the table, and jumped into Lum's lap. He scratched its ears as it licked his chin.

"Mr. Lum, did you, um, cause his demise? Maybe by accident during an argument."

Lum looked horrified and clutched the dog to his chest. "I'm a vegetarian!"

"I didn't suggest you planned to eat him. I just think you had a pretty good reason for being angry at him."

"'Course I did. But life should be protected, even when you don't like it much. I got a nest of yellowjackets living in an old tree stump behind the house. The miserable little creatures have stung me three times this summer when I wasn't doing nothin' to bother them. They do that. They prob'ly think it's funny. My cousin Carol, she tried to talk me into killing them with poison. But that ain't fair—they got a right to live too. So I put up a fence around their nest so the dogs and I remember to stay away, and there you go."

Everett spent a moment trying to parse this little speech. Then he had a thought. "How'd you know that Cannon planned to destroy the campground? Did he tell you?"

"Naw. Carol did. She said she saw the drawings."

Huh. "Do you know who killed him? Or do you have any suspicions?"

Lum shook his head. "I don't much keep up on things in town. My critters are better company than most of those folks. I go in once a week to volunteer at the humane society and do my shopping, and that's about it."

"Do you know what's going to happen to the property now?"

"Naw," Lum said glumly. "He ain't paid for the whole thing, you know, so maybe I'll get it back. But even then I don't know what I'm gonna do with it. I still need the money. If I sell to someone else, they could be just as awful." Then he brightened. "Hey, you're a lawyer. You could help me."

Now Everett felt bad. "I can't. Sorry. It would be unethical for me to represent you under these circumstances." Not to mention unwise and illegal, since Everett wasn't versed on California property law, nor was he licensed here. In fact, his Illinois license had probably lapsed by now.

"Yeah, okay."

After a long pause, Everett stood. He wanted to get home and ice that damn ankle. "Thanks for talking to me today, Mr. Lum. I appreciate it."

Lum stood as well. "Lemme walk you to your car."

Everett didn't know whether this was out of chivalry over his injuries or to ensure that he didn't wander off. Accompanied by the dogs, who seemed delighted by the adventure, he and Lum crossed the property. Along the way, Lum pointed out various species of plants and gave a lecture on the importance of preserving native habitats. When Everett mentioned rattlesnakes, Lum waxed enthusiastically about several he'd recently spotted sunning themselves on rocks, and Everett was sorry he'd asked.

Lum opened the gate for him, saving Everett the task of climbing it with his sore hands and bruised knees. Once Everett was standing—

slightly awkwardly—on the other side, Lum asked, "You have any pets, Everett?"

"No."

"Well, you oughta. They're good for you. Just make sure you adopt, don't shop."

Then Lum and his pack turned and headed out of sight, leaving Everett to reflect on the fact that he'd neither proved or disproved Junior's involvement in the murder.

That night, Everett watched a couple of episodes of *Steven Universe*, mostly so he could report to Tom that he had. It gave him something to do while sprawled in the recliner with ice packs around his ankle—and the episodes were short, which suited his attention span tonight.

The soreness in his ankle, knees, and hands bothered him a little, but not as much as what was going on in his head. Although he hadn't realized it at the time, he now knew that he'd hoped to have a breakthrough while talking with Junior. He'd pictured it so perfectly: Everett cleverly cornering Junior with exactly the right questions, Junior helplessly capitulating and confessing, Cole congratulating Everett on his invaluable work.

Wait. Sergeant McBeth had not been part of Everett's little fantasy. Why would he be? Everett found the guy insufferable enough in real life.

Anyway, nothing had worked out according to plan. First there had been the attack of the hounds, which had wounded his pride more than his body. Then there was Junior himself, who, although suitably rustic, wasn't what Everett had expected. And finally there was the interrogation, which hadn't been one at all because Everett had stumbled over which questions to ask. In the end he'd learned almost nothing—except that Carol Allen had been aware of Cannon's plans to destroy the campground. And that she wasn't averse to poisoning troublesome creatures.

Of course, there was a big gulf between killing yellowjackets and killing a human being. But still.

And... wait. When, exactly, had she seen the resort blueprints and under what circumstances?

Everett closed his eyes and groaned. He wasn't cut out for this kind of thing. He should have stayed in his little office with his laptop and his tidy little contracts and his Zoom meetings about codicils and addenda. Or he should just stick to his hammer and wrenches.

But as he wallowed amid the threadbare upholstery roses, he remembered that he hadn't always been skilled at handyman jobs. His first attempt had been when he was nine and tried to repair the stopped-up toilet in their house—the only toilet in their house. That... hadn't gone well. It had taken him all afternoon to clean up the resulting mess, and for several days, he and Charlotte had to resort to using the bathroom at the Burger King two blocks away.

After that, back in those pre-YouTube dark ages, Everett had checked out a library book on plumbing repair. He'd taken a bus to the nearest hardware store, described the problem to the clerk, and listened carefully to the clerk's advice. And then Everett had fixed the damn toilet. Maybe it didn't look pretty, but it worked just fine.

All his other DIY abilities had been gained the same way: by study, asking the right questions of the right people, and diligent practice.

Law had been the same situation. It hadn't come easily to him; really, academics in general had been an uphill battle. Yet he stuck with it. Applied himself. Learned from his mistakes. And in the end, he'd done well enough to get hired by a law firm. Nothing flashy. No penthouse suites, no jetting off to meet with clients in Dubai and London. But enough to pay the bills.

If he could manage all that, maybe he could dig up a credible suspect—or at least unearth some valuable clues. Feeling a little better, he readjusted the ice packs and cued up another episode of *Steven Universe*.

CHAPTER NINETEEN

It was really weird to be in Cannon's house again. Chills had run down Everett's spine even before he'd keyed in the entry code, and once inside, he jumped at every little sound the building made—and it was a very creaky structure. He had the sense it had been sloppily built, and it probably didn't help that it was tucked into a hillside that itself might not be entirely stable. As a native of Chicagoland, he was of the conviction that hills were all very well for hiking and admiring views, but homes should be situated on nice, flat land.

In any case, the interior looked different from when he'd been here last. The blueprints and other papers were no longer in the kitchen, or anywhere else that he could see. He didn't know whether they'd been seized as evidence, moved elsewhere by Izzy, or discarded. Also, the place was a mess, with dirty shoe-prints on the floors, bits of plastic and scraps of paper on the counters and tables, and smudges on the sink and appliances. He wondered for a moment what the basement looked like, but then his stomach lurched and he pushed the thought away. It didn't help that the kitchen had a faint odor of rotting food or old garbage.

He considered texting Izzy in protest, demanding that she get the house professionally cleaned before he began. But it actually made more sense to clean after his repair jobs, and besides, in its current state he was more likely to stumble upon a clue.

His first task, he decided, would be the bedroom that needed painting. It was a good distance from the kitchen, and the latex smell would cover less-pleasant ones. Besides, he enjoyed painting. Not so much the climbing-a-ladder part, but the task as a whole satisfied him. While he worked, he envisioned himself in sixteenth-century Florence, wearing hose, doublet, and those puffy shorts, creating a masterpiece that would be admired for centuries to come. And yes, he knew that Michelangelo didn't use a paint roller to cover a wall in millennial gray, but pigment was going onto a surface, and that was close enough. He was thankful he didn't have to paint the ceiling; that must have been an uncomfortable project.

It was a small bedroom, and the painting was done by lunchtime. Feeling only slightly guilty, he detoured into the master bedroom, which looked pretty much untouched since last time. Except, interestingly, the wedding photo was gone. Izzy hadn't seemed likely to want it as a keepsake, so maybe she'd thrown it away. She might have thought it was too personal to display in a house for sale. Or... maybe looking at it made her feel guilty because she was the one who'd offed the man in the photo.

Something to consider. Maybe Everett should mention the missing photo to Cole.

There were quite a few additional tasks on his list, but since his ankle was throbbing, he sent Izzy a text.

Four hours of work today. Calling it quits. I'll be back tomorrow.

It had really been closer to four and a half, but he didn't mind rounding down as long as he was paid promptly.

She responded almost immediately.

Fine. Tomorrow @1 guy w/truck is coming for stuff in basement. Need u to help him carry.

His brain very helpfully treated him to a vivid image of what he'd previously seen in the basement, and again his gorge rose. He took a few calming breaths. She meant, of course, the wine cases. Surely Cannon himself was long gone, but what if the floor was still covered in.... Ugh.

For several minutes, Everett stood with phone in hand, seriously considering refusing. Then he decided that would be stupid if the scene had been cleaned. So, still without answering her, he straightened his shoulders, girded his loins, and headed down the stairs.

The garage didn't bother him. The police had left debris there too, and some new cardboard boxes were now stacked against the shelves he'd assembled, but otherwise there was nothing of interest. That left the basement itself.

Everett wasn't a superstitious type and didn't believe in ghosts. In fact, he'd been able to land a hell of a deal on a basement apartment when he was nineteen because the old house had a reputation for being haunted. He'd been happy just to have a roof over his head, and the place was in better condition than his childhood home had been. He wasn't thrilled with having mice and roaches as roommates, but he hadn't worried about visitors from beyond the grave.

Still, he now broke out in gooseflesh as he slowly descended the stairs—and not because of the chill in the air. A strong odor of wine persisted, and his imagination picked up an overlay of damp iron that could be emanating from the stone... or could be blood. *Shut up*, he told his imagination. *You're not wanted here.*

He reached the bottom of the stairs and found... nothing. No corpse. No broken glass. There was a dark coloration on the floor, but that could easily have been variations in the stone itself. Or a stain from the spilled wine. "It's definitely not blood," he assured himself aloud. And definitely not something he should worry about. "No big deal. De minimis non curat lex. Or, um, non curat Ev."

There was something weirdly soothing about saying things in Latin, he thought. English—*Ev does not concern himself with trifles*— just didn't have the same effect.

Stepping carefully around the thing-that-wasn't-a-bloodstain, Everett took a closer look at the cases of wine. There were about fifty of them, each containing twelve bottles, according to the legend printed on some. As he'd noticed during his first visit, a few of the cases were open and missing a couple of bottles. He lifted a box to see how much it weighed. Not too bad, although he'd be able to carry only one at a time due to his ankle. Even with someone else working with him, that meant a lot of trips up those stairs. Well, he'd get his work-out, at least. No need for a gym after all.

Quite a few of the boxes were entirely unmarked. Curious, he looked at the names on those that bore an imprint. A couple were from wineries he recognized from the tasting rooms on Main Street. But most said *William Valko* in a fancy cursive font. Although it sounded vaguely familiar, Everett was fairly certain it wasn't one of the places he'd passed downtown. And in fact, when he peered more closely at one box, he saw that the address was in Salida, California. Since he didn't recognize the place name, he assumed it wasn't nearby.

Because the basement got crappy cell reception, he didn't answer Izzy's text until he was back outside, breathing in fresh air and gazing out at a peaceful, tree-filled vista.

I can help carry at 1 tomorrow.

It wasn't specifically mentioned in the contract he'd sent her, but he'd included a few vague phrases about the work that could be interpreted to include schlepping boxes.

She replied with a thumbs-up, after which Everett hopped into Janet and headed back to town.

CHAPTER TWENTY

"Why are you limping, Everett?"

He froze only a few steps inside Gulch Pages & Pastries. Several pairs of eyes were trained on him. There was Charlotte, who'd been the one to speak, frowning at him from behind the cashier counter. There was an early-teen girl also at the counter, holding a book in each hand. There was Jessica, who'd paused in the middle of wiping down one of her little café tables. And there were three customers in the café section and one at the paperback spinner rack, all looking at him.

"Bear tried to eat me," he said, remembering what he'd said to Sam a couple of weeks ago.

Charlotte rolled her eyes. "Did it decide you were too bitter and spit you out?"

Everyone within earshot thought this was hilarious. Everett ignored them and walked toward his sister with as much dignity as he could muster. His limp was slight, but of course she'd noticed—immediately, while otherwise occupied, and from several yards away.

The teenager was squinting at him. "In California, there's been only one verified killing of a human by a black bear."

He would have guessed a higher number. "Okay, but how many maulings and other non-fatal attacks?"

She set her books on the counter, pulled a phone from her jeans pocket, and poked away for a few seconds. Then she looked at him triumphantly. "Only a few a year. And that's from the state Department of Fish and Wildlife, a reliable source."

"A few a year. Okay. But that means it's not impossible, right? And there are bears around here, I presume." He almost commented on what bears were proverbially known to do in the woods but decided it might not be well received.

"Not impossible, no. But highly improbable. Injuries are much more likely from sports, work accidents, car wrecks, and carelessness."

Charlotte, who looked amused by the interaction, apparently decided to intervene. "Sophie, meet my baby brother, Everett Vaughn. Everett, this is my new book reviewer, Sophie McBeth. Who just passed along the interesting bit of news that you're doing some work at Mr. Cannon's house again." Her tone was brimming with false cheer.

He wasn't sure which was more of a problem—that he'd been ratted out, or that the rat was Sergeant McBeth's kid. Who was now grinning widely at him.

Luckily, as he scrambled to craft a response, his manners didn't fail him completely. "It's nice to see you, Miss McBeth. I understand you were one of my sister's star pupils. I hope you're feeling better."

She held out her hand for a shake and did a credible job with the grip. "I have questions for you."

He had no idea what this would be about, but it was certainly better than dealing with Charlotte's wrath. "Okay. What do you want to know?" He hoped she wasn't expecting a detailed description of the murder scene. Let her father deliver that if he thought it was appropriate, which Everett doubted.

"Let's go sit down." She glanced at Charlotte, who nodded, and then marched over to the nearest café table and took a seat.

Since Charlotte was clearly not giving any clue about what was going on, Everett sat opposite Sophie. "I'm not going to tell you anything gory," he warned her.

"I don't care about any of that. I have questions about you."

"Why?"

She pasted on an innocent look that was patently false. "I have my reasons." The smug expression that settled onto her face was entirely familiar.

In fact, she resembled her father closely, with the same square jaw, sharp brown eyes, and tall, lanky build. Her hair was lighter than his, however, and curly while his was straight. She had on a slouchy mushroom-patterned sweater that Everett couldn't picture Cole wearing.

While Everett gazed at her, she stared back just as closely. "How old are you, Mr. Vaughn?" she finally asked.

"Forty-three, and you can call me Everett, seeing as how your dad and I are on a first-name basis."

"Do you have any felony convictions?"

He blinked. "Um, no. Some parking tickets and a couple of traffic infractions, none recent."

"Uh huh." Thumbs flying, she typed on her phone. "How would you classify your economic situation? Do you have a lot of debts?"

"I have zero debts. I have enough in my bank account to tide me over for another six months or so, if I live frugally. But as you're aware, I'm supplementing with odd jobs."

More typing. "Uh huh. And what are your plans for your future?"

"No idea. I'm having a midlife crisis. Do they teach you about those in school?"

She barely even looked at him. "Marital status?"

"Divorced."

"Have any of your exes been murdered or died under mysterious circumstances?"

"No!" he replied indignantly. Was this kid interrogating him on her father's behalf?

"Are you dating anyone?"

"No. And why the third degree?"

"Just... some stuff I need to know."

This was weird. Kids were weird, and he'd never understood them —not even when he was one. That was actually one of the reasons he'd wanted to be a parent: you never knew quite what to expect from a child, and they kept life from getting too boring and predictable. Despite this weird kid having been the one to land Everett in trouble to begin with, at the moment she was protecting him from Charlotte, albeit inadvertently.

So he answered her questions patiently. There were a lot of them. His education, general health, and political views. His favorite books, foods, bands, movies, and TV shows. The podcasts he listened to. His thoughts on organized sports. What he would wish for if he released a genie from a bottle. His ideal vacation spots.

"Are you writing my biography?" he finally asked her. "It'll be boring. Nobody will want to read it."

She spent a moment scrolling through the notes on her phone. "I guess this is good enough. For now. I don't see any huge red flags."

"Were you worried that there would be? For what?"

Sophie tucked away her phone and leaned forward. "I worry about my dad. He's really important to me. He's important to the whole town. And I'm the only one who watches out for him."

"Um... okay?"

"Okay." She nodded as if something were settled, then stood. "It's good to meet you, Everett." Without another word or any attempt to explain, she marched back to the counter, picked up the two books, and left.

Another customer had some questions for Charlotte, so Everett twisted in his seat to look at Jess instead. Today she wore a caftan—an abstract floral in fuchsia, orange, and yellow—along with a pair of coordinating yellow tights and lime-colored ankle boots with wedge heels. "What the hell were all those questions about?" he asked her.

But she simply shook her head as if she were disappointed in him.

Everett waited until Charlotte was finished with customers before he approached her. "I was going to tell you. I just didn't get a chance yet. I did, however, inform Sergeant McBeth what I was doing, and he assured me it was all kosher."

"Maybe. But it's still stupid. And the limp?"

"No big deal. I turned my ankle. And I iced it and elevated it and it's fine. I'm not a kid, Char."

She got a distinctly wicked smile. "No, you're a middle-aged man."

"I'm not mid—" He stopped himself because, dammit, she was right. It didn't matter that she was a decade older; she had her life together. Loving husband, two great kids, a pension plan, a new book-store. "Let's just drop the subject, okay? I came by to see how things are going."

"Not bad." She straightened a little stack of bookmarks. "And I'm sorry. I can't help worrying about you."

Although he was still a little annoyed with her, he also he felt a pleasant warmth in his shriveled soul. It was nice to have someone who worried. Just like Sophie did about Cole, in fact.

"The ship is sailing smoothly?"

"No tempest. Oh, hey! I should do a Shakespeare-themed window display soon."

That made Everett snort. "Would you feature the Scottish play as part of it? In honor of our good sergeant, of course."

"Hmm. I'm glad you came by. There's something wrong with your cat."

"I don't have a cat."

Perfectly timed, the orange cat appeared from behind a shelf and sauntered over, tail raised in greeting. Rubbing against Everett's shins, it purred loudly. Somehow he found himself picking the thing up, which it didn't seem to mind. In fact, it slumped comfortably in his arms and did an excellent impression of an idling motor.

"It doesn't look sick to me." Everett did a quick under-tail check, hoping he didn't wound the cat's dignity. "Um, he doesn't look sick to me."

"I didn't say he was sick. He does need to get his shots, though. Make an appointment with Dr. Kelly at Sierra Pride Vet Clinic. Not with Dr. Hardesty. I think she's only good with cows and horses, maybe because she's a big horse's ass herself."

"But the cat isn't—" He let out a deep breath. "Why did you say there's something wrong with him?"

"He meows at me every morning when I open the shop, even when his food dish is full. Then he paces in the windows but doesn't want to go outside, not even if I hold the door open. He's unhappy about something."

Everett was scratching the cat's ear. He hadn't decided to do that, not any more than he'd decided to pick him up, yet here they were. "Is

Dr. Kelly a cat psychiatrist?" He pictured a feline stretched out on a fainting couch, talking about how he never knew his father and had been abandoned by his mother at eight weeks, while a white-coated guy with a goatee took notes.

Charlotte gave him a familiar look: a mixture of exasperation and fondness that he secretly treasured. It meant that even though he was a pain, she loved him anyway. "Dr. Kelly can make sure your cat isn't sick. You can figure out why the poor little guy is melancholy."

Everett was going to point out that not only was this not his cat, but also that Everett himself was not a cat psychiatrist, nor did he have any experience with despondent felines. But even as he opened his mouth, a voice piped up behind him.

"Cats read energies."

He turned around to see Willow from Granocchio Cellars. Today her long hair was in a braid and she wore a hand-knit sweater that looked as if it had, in fact, been attacked by several cats. She cradled an oversize hardcover in one arm. He couldn't read the title, but based on its shape, he figured it was either a cookbook or something to do with art.

Willow dipped her chin at the cat in his arms. "If people around him are unsettled, he'd be feeling it. Or there could be a restless spirit nearby. Cats sense those too."

Charlotte looked offended. "Ghosts don't exist, and even if they did, they wouldn't be in my store."

"Not ghosts—spirits. Unhomed souls. When a person dies, they're given the chance to make up for their faults and errors by living again in a new body and doing better. Sometimes after we die, we have to wait a little bit to be reborn, and our souls sort of float around in the interim. The next time someone in Gulch has a baby, I bet your spirit will disappear and your cat will settle down."

Everett and Charlotte exchanged glances. Neither of them was the type to trash another's spiritual beliefs, but Willow's was... out there. And she clearly took it very seriously. "That sounds kind of exhausting," Everett said. "I mean, you're finished with this world but instead of moving on you have to start from scratch."

"No, it's a wonderful blessing! The opportunity to progress, to improve, to make ourselves and the world around us better. It's such a better plan than eternal suffering for sins. How does that fix things?"

Maybe she had a point. But man, he was struggling enough to get through this existence. The thought of having to do it all over again was daunting, like working nonstop with no weekends and no vacations.

Willow, however, might have taken his and Charlotte's silence for a desire to learn more. "Unlike human souls, cat souls don't get recycled. I think that's because every cat is already perfect at being a cat, so they don't need do-overs."

"I thought they had nine lives," said Everett.

"That's a silly superstition." Willow gave him a withering look. "So although their spirits don't wander, they're sensitive to those that do, and that's why sometimes they seem to behave oddly for no reason or stare so intently at what we think is nothing." She walked past him, patted the cat's head, and set her book on the counter. It was a cookbook called *Eating Simply from Nature's Gifts*. The cover had a beautiful photo of dandelions, mushrooms, ferns, and berries spread across a picnic blanket in a mountain meadow.

Charlotte, clearly happy to change the subject, said, "I've seen good reviews of this title."

"It's for my older daughter. Such a smart woman, but she eats too many processed foods. I'm hoping this will inspire her."

Charlotte rang up the sale and offered to gift wrap the book, but Willow declined. "I'll use some pretty fabric from one of my old blouses. Unfortunately, it got too badly stained to wear anymore—working with wine will do that, sometimes—but this way I can still get some use from it."

She gave the cat another pat and was almost to the door when Everett had a thought. "Hey, Willow? Could I stop by later? If you don't mind, I have more questions about winemaking."

"Of course!" She dimpled at him. "Any old time. I'm glad you're seeing the light." From the doorway she waved at him, Charlotte, and then Jess, who was back behind the pastry counter.

"What light are you seeing?" asked Charlotte as soon as Willow was gone.

"The radiance of the great grape." He huffed a laugh. "She caught me drinking a beer the other day at the saloon and gave me a lecture. Wine is, apparently, far superior."

"It is healthier."

"Not for Blake Cannon. Hey, you don't suppose he's the spirit who's making the cat unhappy?"

"No. He wasn't welcome here in life and he's not welcome in death. If he's waiting for a body, he can go do it at his office." She gave a decisive pat to the countertop and walked away, probably to go straighten something.

That left Everett with the cat, who showed no inclination to leave his arms. "If it is him, tell him to get lost. Or no, tell him first to send me a message identifying the culprit. Then he can get lost."

The cat looked up at him and blinked, as if his request had made perfect sense.

"Wait. Office. I forgot he had one in town. I wonder if Cole and his buddies have checked it out yet."

Everett wandered over to the café section and gave Jess his most winning smile.

"You need to give your cat a name," she said.

"He's not— Um, Jess my dear, do you know who besides Cannon had access to his office? Did he have staff?"

"It was just him. Nobody around here would have worked for him even if he could pay them. Except you."

"I was helping him fix his house, not helping him with his evil scheme to conquer the world."

"Uh-huh."

Obviously, Jessica had no interest in helping him out right now. Fine. He had other sources. He set the cat onto the floor and received a reproachful look before the cat stalked away.

Looking forward to putting his feet up, Everett limped out of the store.

CHAPTER TWENTY-ONE

Everett arrived at Rising Times the next morning just before eight. The inside of the little bakery was warm and redolent of chocolate and coffee, and Xochi seemed pleased to see him.

"Are you looking for some work?" she asked as she handed over his Americano.

"You need an extra baker or barista?"

She laughed. "No, not for me. It's my abuelo's friend. He wants to do some planting but a bunch of stuff needs to be cleared out first—weeds, bushes, little trees. Could you do that?"

He thought for a moment. "Would I need to know anything about horticulture? Because I don't."

"Nah. Just how to dig and chop, I think."

Some outdoor tasks would be nice, he thought. Fresh air and, presumably for this project, Charlotte and Jess's approval. "Sure, I could probably do that."

She scribbled on a napkin and handed it over. "There's his name and address. He doesn't do texting, but he's always home. You can just drop by to talk to him."

"Thanks." He tucked the napkin into a pocket and then asked the question uppermost in his mind. "Do you by any chance know if anyone besides Blake Cannon had access to his office?"

Instead of looking suspicious about this odd question, she grinned wickedly. "The owner of his building. Who was preparing to evict him for missing rent payments."

So Cannon had owed someone else money. No big shock there. "Who's the owner?"

"Sanjeev Patel. He's my landlord too—he owns a lot of downtown."

Oh, right. Everett vaguely remembered Charlotte and Jessica mentioning him. Although their space had originally been a general store, it had closed in the sixties or seventies and been replaced by a dance studio and, successively, a music shop, a secondhand store, and a series of other businesses, none of which had ever made much of a profit, according to Char. The spot had been empty for some time when she and Jess put in an offer, and the real estate agent told them that Patel had been making lowball offers for years.

"Wasn't there some kind of scandal with him?" Everett asked. He thought that Char and Jess had discussed something about it, but he'd been building bookshelves at the time and hadn't paid much attention.

Xochi rocked her hand. "Not really a scandal, just drama. Sanjeev's brother is married to Angie Patel—she's our mayor—and there's conflict there. Sanjeev ran against her in the last election and lost."

Somehow it was comforting to hear about other families' dysfunction, especially since Everett's was mostly in his past. His parents were long gone, Sam was still back in Chicago, and Everett got along well with Rob and Charlotte, despite occasional minor sibling squabbles.

"Were Sanjeev and Cannon friendly with each other until the rent became overdue?"

"Oh yeah, very. They'd stop in here together sometimes so Sanjeev could get a coffee."

Did Cannon have political ambitions? Or did he want support from someone who might someday be in a position to help him achieve his agenda? Interesting questions to ponder. "Do you know where I might find Sanjeev?"

"Oh sure, that's easy. He's right over there." She pointed to a second-floor window directly across the street.

Sanjeev Patel sat behind a sleek desk, his hands steepled. He was roughly Everett's age but much, much better-looking. In fact, he was the Platonic archetype of a silver fox, with thick straight hair still showing much of the original black among the white, dark skin and darker eyes, and a fit physique that was well showcased by his finely knit cowl-neck sweater.

His office décor was largely minimalist, but a trio of framed, well-weathered gold pans gave a nod to the city's history. Everett liked the effect and thought that he might try to emulate it, should he ever be in the position to do up a local home. Maybe he could get someone to hire him as an interior decorator. He wasn't qualified, but he also wasn't technically qualified for most of the other jobs he'd been doing lately.

Now, however, he was supposed to be focusing on solving a murder, not admiring the office or its very attractive occupant.

"So you're the brother," Sanjeev said.

Everett cocked his head. "The brother?"

"It's a small town, my friend. We know who's who and who comes and goes. There aren't many secrets."

Sanjeev's demeanor was friendly enough, but Everett couldn't tell whether this was a veiled threat of some kind or simply a statement of fact. If it was a threat, Everett wasn't sure why it would be expressed— or what deep, dark secrets Sanjeev thought he possessed. Unless Sanjeev thought he was the murderer.

"I didn't kill Blake Cannon," Everett said.

"Thank you for the reassurance." Sanjeev's lips twitched as if he couldn't quite suppress a smile.

Everett wanted to smile back. Everything about this man was just so... pleasant. His good looks and tasteful office. His long fingers and manicured nails. The subtle scent of his cologne, or air freshener or whatever was making the room smell a little like spices and flowers.

But again, Everett was supposed to be on a mission. He pulled his thoughts back together. Maybe he should start with a direct question.

"Do you know who did kill him?"

Sanjeev shook his head slightly. "I'm afraid not. That particular secret hasn't yet been divulged."

It had been worth a try. At least the guy didn't seem offended or upset by the query. "Were you and Cannon friends?"

"Um...." Sanjeev looked slightly pained. "I wouldn't put it that way. Acquaintances. At first, I was a big supporter of his plans. You know, I grew up in Gulch and it's a great little place. But it's not perfect. Our schools struggle, we had a performing arts troupe that folded during Covid and hasn't revived, sometimes retail spaces sit vacant for too long. I thought an upscale resort would be a good addition to the county tax base and would provide some jobs. And frankly, a little modernization wouldn't hurt. You can't stay mired in the nineteenth century forever."

That all sounded perfectly reasonable. "You said at first. What changed?"

Sanjeev looked chagrined. "I got to know him better. And I found out more details about what he had in mind. He planned to hire employees from elsewhere—he claimed locals wouldn't be polished enough. He held contempt for almost everyone here. And he was going to do what he could to make sure his guests did all their spending on-site instead of here in town."

"And he owed you money."

"That too." Sanjeev gave a small smile. "I see I have no secrets either. He owed a lot of people money, I think. But as nice as it is to chat with you, I can't help wondering why you're asking me these things."

If Everett didn't know better, he would have thought that Sanjeev was being a little flirty right now. But wait—did he know better? Maybe those sparkling eyes and those upturned lips were trying to suggest something. Or maybe Sanjeev knew that Everett was gay— small town, no secrets, and Everett had never made a mystery of it— and was hoping to distract him.

Focus, Vaughn.

He went for honesty. "As you probably know, I found the body, and it wasn't pretty. I'm possibly a suspect too. So I want to know who did it."

"So does Cole McBeth, and he's a capable man."

"I'm sure he is. But could it hurt to have another set of eyes on the case? Sometimes an outsider can bring a fresh perspective." Huh, he hadn't thought of that angle until just now. He wished he'd mentioned it to Charlotte. And possibly Cole as well.

Sanjeev stared into space for a moment as if considering. "All right, I guess I can see that. And you came to me because...?" A thought seemed to occur to him. "Do you think I did it?"

"Not really, although if you did and you're ready to confess, I'd be happy to hear it." Everett imagined Sanjeev standing and giving a monologue about his evil intentions, like a villain in a cheesy movie.

Sanjeev chuckled. "I'm afraid I'll have to disappoint you on that count."

"Then... could you maybe just let me take a peek inside his office instead?" Everett tried his most winning expression, the one he formerly trotted out when attempting to get someone to concede to a contract codicil or agree to a settlement.

And to his mild surprise, Sanjeev nodded. "All right. There's something there you should probably see anyway."

"What's—"

"Come see for yourself. Better than me explaining it."

Everett followed him out of the office and down the flight of steep wooden stairs, then through the glass-paneled front door and out onto the sidewalk. It was only a couple of blocks to Black Bart Road, and along the way, Sanjeev gave a little background on some of the businesses they passed. Many of them, it seemed, were renting space from him. "Have you been in there yet?" he asked, waving toward a place called Heavens Scent. The display window showed crystals, incense, tarot cards, and wind chimes.

"Doesn't look like my thing."

"Yeah, you don't seem like the type to be in the market for moon charts or ritual kits. But the folks who run it also sell soap that they make, and it's amazing. I won't use anything else."

Everett wondered whether the soap was what made him—or possibly his office—smell so nice, but he didn't ask. Now they were in front of a record shop called Spin Me. "Vinyl has a warmer quality than digital, don't you think?" Sanjeev asked. "And they usually have great deals. They buy used records too."

The tour continued as they walked along. It was a little hokey maybe, and Everett hadn't actually asked for a guide to the retail delights of downtown Gulch, but Sanjeev seemed sincerely enthusiastic. Whatever his true feelings had been toward Cannon, he appeared a genuine fan of his own hometown.

They turned onto Black Bart Road and were immediately in front of a shop that advertised hemp and CBD products. The old two-room jail was next door. On one of his early tours of the town, Everett had seen tourists taking photos in front of the barred cells, one of which contained a life-size figure of a man slumped on a cot. He was probably supposed to be a drunk miner, but his paint had faded and his hair and clothing were covered in dust and spiderwebs.

Past the jail was a gravel parking lot, currently occupied by a pickup truck older and more beat-up than Janet, a couple of SUVs, and a sedan. On the other side of the lot stood a small commercial building that looked more midcentury than gold rush. Half of it housed Ornamentary, which had a window full of Christmas and was currently closed. The other door, flanked by a pair of large flowerpots containing very sad-looking marigolds, had a sign reading Cannon Development.

Sanjeev unlocked the door and ushered Everett inside.

The space was entirely unremarkable: rough commercial carpet on the floor, bland wine-themed art on the walls, and sturdy but plain furniture, including a conference table and chairs, along with a couple of desks and some cabinets.

"He rented the furniture," said Sanjeev as he switched on the overhead fluorescents. "From a place in Stockton. I've been trying to get them to come collect it."

"The office is not all that impressive."

"He intended it to be temporary. Long-term, he was going to have space on the resort grounds."

Of course.

Sanjeev looked nervous as he clutched the back of one of the conference chairs. "Look, a lot of people are angry with me—but like I said, I didn't understand at first what he had in mind or what kind of person he was. I thought some new ideas and new money would be good for Gulch."

Everett felt sorry for the guy, who seemed sincere. "When did you find out the truth?"

"I started having my doubts a couple months ago, when he fell behind on rent. He had a lot of excuses, naturally. And hey, I get it—sometimes you have to juggle funds when you're dealing with real estate. But the unflattering comments he let drop about local residents…. Anyway, about two weeks ago I got a peek at the blueprints." He winced. "I don't think he intended me to see them."

That was interesting. Everett decided to employ a strategy he sometimes used to encourage the opposing side to keep blabbing about something they probably shouldn't. He took a step back and looked away, ensuring there was nothing threatening about his presence. *Hey, don't mind me. I'm barely even here.*

"The folks who run the holiday shop next door were having some issues with blown circuits. They run a lot of lighting in there. I brought in an electrician to take a look at the circuit box for the building, which is through there." He pointed to an unassuming door at the rear. "While he was there, I, uh, might have nosed around a little bit, just looking at things that were left in plain view! The resort blueprints were spread out on a desk. They're gone now. Cops took them."

Sanjeev pulled out the chair and sat heavily in it, still managing to look elegant. "Cops. I might have ended up disliking Blake, but I didn't want him dead. And I certainly didn't want a murder investigation in my town. On my property!" He spread his arms to indicate the room as a whole.

But Everett wanted to take the discussion back a step or two. "So you saw the prints and realized the extent of the planned resort."

"He'd bought—or planned to buy; I'm not sure which—a huge chunk of land. Much more than I'd imagined. Some of the smaller parcels near the highway currently have houses or small ranches on them, which is fine. But then I saw that he planned to obliterate Miracle Creek Campground and the forest there. I was so upset that I called Carol Allen—the campground belonged to her family—but it turned out she hadn't known about it either."

Well, that was interesting. At least now Everett knew how she'd learned about Cannon's intentions. "Why were you so upset over the campground?"

"We need our forest lands!" Sanjeev slumped a little, looking sheepish. "Also, I knew my brother would be livid. We used to have our big family gatherings there when we were kids. Aunts, uncles, cousins… everyone would come to Gulch and rent cabins for a few days. Everett, you and Charlotte get along well, don't you?"

Everett frowned at what seemed like a non sequitur. "Most of the time, sure. I mean, she can be bossy and I can be a pain in the ass, but that's sort of our dynamic."

Sanjeev nodded. "Jay and I used to be really close, but in the past few years…. Well, you don't want to hear about my family drama."

Actually, Everett kind of did, mostly because stories like that reminded him that other people had dysfunction too. But he didn't want the conversation to veer too far from Cannon. In any case, Everett got the gist of it. Sanjeev had grown disillusioned with Cannon and had also feared that their business relationship would further the schism between him and his brother. All reasonable enough. Also a potential motive to get rid of Cannon.

"When did all of this happen?"

"Hang on and I'll check my calendar." He consulted his phone. "That's right, it was Thursday. The folks at Ornamentary were especially concerned about the lights with the Grape Gala starting the next day."

So… two days before Everett discovered Cannon's body. Huh.

While Everett was mulling this over, Sanjeev stood and walked to one of the desks. "That's not the only thing I saw that day. The cops didn't take this one." He motioned for Everett to join him.

They ended up standing very close, which was way more distracting than Everett wanted. It had been a year since he and Sam split, and during those months he'd hooked up only… God, only three times? No wonder he was practically drooling like a cartoon character over Sanjeev. He'd never used Grindr or any of the other apps, and he had no idea whether he'd find a match here in the boonies, but it might be worth a shot. If for no other reason than to help him concentrate. And wasn't Sam already dating someone sort of steadily? A boat instructor for goodness' sake.

"See?" said Sanjeev because, oh yeah, Everett was supposed to be looking at the desk.

There was a scattering of papers, most of which looked like receipts, as well as some mystery numbers scribbled on Post-Its. But what Sanjeev was pointing at was a single sheet of paper with a photo printed on it: a large two-story brick building with big display windows. Wine bottles had been poorly photoshopped into those windows, and over the door hung an even more poorly photoshopped sign for Il Vigneto Winery and Tasting.

"Do you recognize the building?" Sanjeev asked.

"No, I— Hey! That's the bookshop!"

"I saw Blake later that afternoon. I dropped by here to warn him that I was going to start eviction proceedings if he didn't pay up. Honestly, at that point I was hoping he'd simply go away. We ended up having a rather, um, spirited conversation. In the heat of things, I demanded that he explain this image." As if hesitant to go further, Sanjeev let his palm hover over the page, covering the image but not quite touching it.

"And?" Everett prompted.

"He said, 'When that harridan's'—sorry, Everett, his words, not mine—'bookstore fails, I'm going to take over the building.' He got a really nasty smile and said, 'Wouldn't it be a shame if it turned out she had a lot of expensive code violations?'"

Indignant on his sister's behalf, Everett scowled. "Was he going to create those code violations?"

"I wouldn't be surprised," said Sanjeev, "although he didn't admit as much."

"What did you do?"

"I like your sister and Jessica. I want them to succeed. I called Blake a variety of rather unflattering things. He threw a handful of wine labels at me and called me small-town trash. I told him I'd see him in court and I stomped out. That was the last time we spoke."

Everett wanted to crumple the stupid picture or, better yet, set it on fire. There was no point in that, however. And who knew, maybe the photo would end up being evidence. Apparently Cole and his people hadn't thought so, but they didn't know everything.

"Did you tell Charlotte what he wanted to do?"

Sanjeev nodded. "I stopped by the bookshop shortly afterward to warn them."

And she'd never mentioned it to Everett. Apparently he wasn't the only one to hide certain information from a sibling.

He spent a few minutes pacing the room and processing this information. Sanjeev walked around too, more slowly, possibly surveying the carpet and walls and calculating how soon he could re-lease the place, and to whom.

Midway through one of his circuits, Everett paused. "He threw wine labels at you?" As an attorney, he'd engaged in paper battles, but they didn't involve actual physical contact.

"I know. Not an effective weapon. But it was part of the discuss— Well, part of the argument. He needed a production facility for his wine, you see. He'd managed to get a contract on some grapes for next harvest, but he wasn't going to be able to do anything with them." He shook his head. "I don't know who he thought he was going to hire, even if he did acquire a facility. Skilled vintners aren't easy to find. Of course he didn't need to make the wine in that particular building, but I take it he was harboring a grudge against Charlotte."

The grudge wasn't exactly news; Cannon had threatened her after the altercation in the bookshop. And Everett had the impression that if they hadn't butted heads over that, something else would have set them off soon enough. His sister wasn't the type to suffer fools gladly. But there was something important here in Sanjeev's story—he was sure of it.

Still pondering, Everett decided it was his turn to take a seat. He chose the closest chair, the one at the desk with the photoshopped winery printout. The chair, he assumed, where Cannon himself had sat and plotted.

"Do you know anything about winemaking?" he finally asked Sanjeev.

"Some. I'm not in the business myself, but I've lived here my whole life. You pick things up."

That made sense. "Where I come from, nobody made wine. So bear with me, okay? Cannon was going to acquire grapes about a year from now, and he assumed that he'd have somewhere to turn them into wine by then, right?"

"Yes."

"But how long does that take—the grape-to-wine part? Don't wines need to age?" He had a general sense that it was true, although it was possible he was mixing up wine-making with the process for hard liquor like whiskey or tequila.

Sanjeev returned to the chair he'd formerly occupied and sat gracefully, elbows on the armrests and fingers interlaced. "It depends on the variety. A lot of whites just need fermentation time without additional aging, which means they're drinkable within a few months of pressing. But reds, especially complex ones, take longer. Sometimes several years."

"What kind was Cannon going to produce?"

After a moment of looking thoughtful, Sanjeev stood, walked to the desk, and leaned over Everett's shoulder. Before Everett could get too sidetracked by their very close proximity, Sanjeev opened the center drawer.

"This is where he kept them," he said as he pulled out a small stack of paper squares and set them on the desk.

They were, clearly, wine labels. Il Vigneto was written in fancy gold script with gold grapevines swirling around it. Beneath that was Milagro County, 2025—that was this year, Everett noted—and finally Sangiovese Reserve.

"Huh," said Sanjeev.

"Is that a red or white?"

"Red. One that's traditionally aged for a fairly extended time. Also, reserved wines are sometimes aged even longer, although that's not always the case. Reserved can mean several things, or it can be just a marketing term."

Great. Everett was trying to learn about an industry that apparently wasn't consistent with its terminology. That was annoying. Legal jargon might be garbled Latin, and it might be incomprehensible to most laypeople, but if he were to throw a subpoena duces tecum at any other lawyer, or a lex loci or sub modo, that lawyer would know exactly what he meant.

"Sanjeev, when would this wine be bottled—before or after aging?"

"It would almost certainly be aged in oak barrels for a few years before bottling. It might also be additionally aged in the bottle after that."

The gears in Everett's head were turning. "So... Cannon was going to get next year's grapes and, assuming he had a place to make them into wine, it would be at least a few years before he could bottle and sell it."

"Accurate." Sanjeev looked intrigued.

"I'm guessing that Cannon intended to get the resort built and running fairly soon?"

"Yes," said Sanjeev. "These things take time, of course, but my impression was that he wanted to begin construction very shortly. He said he's been pushing the permits through with the county."

If Cannon was juggling funding as precariously as Everett suspected, he wouldn't have wanted to take things slowly. Although Everett hadn't worked on real estate deals, he'd been involved with colleagues who did, and he'd heard of cases where delays had led to deals collapsing like, well, a house of cards.

"What wine did he plan to sell until his was ready?"

"I have no idea."

Neither did Everett, but he was certainly curious. Too bad he couldn't just ask Cannon. "I wish I knew where his grapes were going to come from," he mused.

"Oh, I can tell you that."

Everett twisted his head to look up at Sanjeev. "Oh?"

"It's not a common grape in this county. Only one family grows them."

"Who?"

"The McBeths."

CHAPTER TWENTY-TWO

"It's a conflict of interest!"

Everett waved his hands so wildly that he nearly knocked over his coffee mug. Luckily it only rattled a little, sloshing a bit of its contents onto the table. He shot Jessica a guilty look before mopping up the spill with a napkin.

It was very late afternoon on Friday, and Pages & Pastries would be closing in less than an hour. Technically the café was shut down already, but Jess hadn't yet cleaned the espresso machine when Everett wandered into the shop and sat down at a table with Charlotte. There were currently no customers, so Jess had brewed an Americano for him and an herbal tea for Charlotte before returning to her cleaning.

He'd been describing the morning's adventures with Sanjeev Patel, but neither woman had appeared upset over Cannon's plan to force them out of business.

"As if we'd let that happen," Charlotte had scoffed. "He didn't have nearly the pull in this town that he thought he did."

Having spoken to quite a few locals by this point, Everett believed it. His conversation had moved beyond that to focus instead on the really important matter: Sergeant McBeth was chief investigator in a case that might involve his own relatives. Hell, who was to say that the crime didn't involve him?

"Calm down," Charlotte said sternly, as if Everett were fourteen again. "Maybe you should switch to decaf."

"It's not the caffeine that has me riled up. It's him! His family was—"

"I know. Honey, everyone's connected to everyone else around here. Even I am, and I didn't move here until I was I was almost thirty. Families like the McBeths have been here for generations and they're tangled up all over the place. If Cole were to recuse himself from every case that could potentially involve a McBeth, he'd have no work left at all."

Frowning, Everett took a sip of coffee. At least it had cooled enough not to scald him. "You don't have to use your Reasonable Voice on me, Charlotte Anne. I'm not being off-the-wall on this."

"You're being off-the-wall on all of this. You shouldn't be investigating, period. And now you're casting aspersions on the person who is tasked with investigating."

"I'm not casting anything. I'm just saying—"

"Cole arrested one of his first cousins a couple of years ago."

Everett squinted at her. "For murder?"

"No. Dealing fentanyl. That cousin ended up with a stiff sentence, as I recall. Cole doesn't let family favoritism get in the way."

Hmm. "If you were a cop, would you arrest me if I were dealing drugs?" He pictured himself crouching in a shack among heaps of pill bottles and stacks of bagged white powder while Charlotte waited outside, clad in a blue uniform, her hand hovering over her holster.

"Drug dealer. Is that the new career path you're contemplating?"

From over at the espresso machine, Jess piped in. "Stick to the legal drugs, Everett! Wine and weed! And caffeine!"

It was clear that neither Charlotte nor Jessica was going to take his concerns seriously. He might have stomped out in a huff, but then the cat appeared out of nowhere and hopped onto the table next to his cup. It meowed until he rubbed its ears, at which point it started the deep rumbling. "Animals in a place that serves food," he muttered. "Now that's probably against code."

Jessica waved a dismissive hand. "He's your cat."

"He's not."

"And you still need to take him to the vet," said Charlotte. "And give the poor thing a name. I've done my part already."

Everett was suspicious. "Which is?"

"Added him to the payroll. Your cat has regular employment even if you don't."

"Doing what? Shedding?" Everett shook several strands of fur off his fingers. "I wasn't aware that was a career option."

"Rodent patrol. He's caught two mice this week. That we know of. And that reminds me—can you set some traps? I think the rodents are coming in from the wall we share with Miner's Stake. He's got so much junk crammed in there that he's probably hosting an entire rodent city."

"Maybe he should set the traps on his side, then."

Charlotte scoffed. "We almost never see him, and when we do, he refuses to have a civil conversation."

Fine. Everett would pick up traps during his next hardware store run. He felt slightly guilty about killing the little creatures, but he knew they could damage the shop contents, spread diseases, and freak out customers. "We'll partner up on this one." He gave the cat a rub under the chin as he considered. "And the cat's name is Warren. But to be clear, he's not mine."

"Why Warren?" Jessica asked.

"After Earl Warren, who was, like this cat I presume, a Californian. As well as a governor, attorney general, and US Supreme Court chief justice. Did some not-at-all-cool things but eventually regretted them and spearheaded a lot of progressive reforms. I don't know his stance on bookstore mice, however."

He might have expounded further on Chief Justice Warren's part in the due process revolution and then discussed how the Supreme Court decisions of that era, while somewhat eroded during the subsequent decades, placed restrictions on police behavior. Which was another good reason for him to be involved in the current investigation, since none of those Supreme Court cases limited what a private citizen could do. But he yawned instead of lecturing, and when he stretched, his back crackled like a string of firecrackers.

"Did you overdo it today?" Charlotte looked genuinely concerned rather than sarcastic.

"No. Maybe. I don't know." He groaned a little, yawned again, and then stood. "I helped move a bunch of stuff. Cases of wine. They were heavy."

Now his sister looked grim. "Cannon's basement?"

"Yeah."

"And you were okay going back there after...?"

He thought about it for a moment. "It was actually good for me, I think. To see the space under less gruesome circumstances. But it was hard work, so I'm going to go now and relax. Unless you need something done around here."

"I have a list, but it can wait." She stood, patted Warren—still on the table but now snoozing—and collected the dirty cups. "It's Friday night. Go live it up a little."

That made him snort. "Yeah, you too."

"Don't do anything I wouldn't do!" Jessica yelled.

Chuckling, Everett wandered out the door and onto the sidewalk. Maybe back in Wild West days, Deadman Gulch had been a happening place. He pictured saloon girls and saloon fights; prospectors losing most of their gold dust in crooked games of cards and drinking up the rest in rotgut; horse thieves creeping around, eyeing the animals tied up outside the buildings. But maybe that wasn't how horse thieves operated. He didn't really know. He'd never even ridden a horse, and he certainly hadn't researched the details of that particular form of larceny.

Unlike what he imagined about the gold rush era, most things were quiet here tonight. Voices carried from the beer garden at the Gulch Inn, but faintly. Leaves rustled in the evening breeze. A few tourists lingered outside the ice cream shop or walked to their cars, hands carrying wine totes and paper bags. Outside of Foothill Toys & Games, which had just closed, a toddler had a meltdown while the parents tried to cajole him into a stroller.

Everett was tired and sore, and some alcohol might have gone down nicely, but he was also unexpectedly melancholy. So much so that he pulled out his phone and very nearly texted Sam. If he did have a couple of beers—or glasses of wine—he'd likely give into that urge and regret it in the morning.

Then out of nowhere he remembered that, just this morning, Xochi had asked whether he'd be interested in some yard work for her grandfather's friend. Just stop by, she'd said. Well, it wasn't too late in the day for that, so he might as well take care of it. When he pulled out the napkin with the address, he saw that it was on Baskett Road, which ran from Main Street up past the cemetery and then, more steeply, to Baskett Cavern. He wouldn't walk all the way to the cavern today, but he could walk to the house and stroll back.

The house in question was even older than Everett's rental; it must have been one of the town's originals. It was small and painted pale yellow, with a welcoming front porch, lots of gingerbread trim, and an impressive assortment of yard ornaments hidden among overgrown saplings and shrubbery. When Everett rang the doorbell, a voice inside yelled, "Hold your horses! I'm coming!" A short time later the door swung open, revealing a tall, thin man in jeans and a sweatshirt. He probably wasn't as old as the house, but he was definitely not a youngster.

He peered at Everett through wire-rimmed glasses. "I'm not buying any, I'm not converting, and I gave at the office."

Everett took an immediate liking to him. "My name's Everett Vaughn. Xochi Reyes said you were looking for someone to do some yard work, and—"

"Oh, you're that boy."

It had been a very long time since anyone had referred to Everett as a boy. He grinned. "That's me, Mister... uh...."

"Ron Tosto. Call me Ron." He looked at Everett skeptically. "You're a little scrawny. This is gonna be hard work. Gotta put muscles into it. Not like sitting at a desk and typing things."

"I like physical work," Everett said honestly. "Cheaper than joining a gym."

Ron made a scoffing sound. "Gyms. We didn't have those when I was young. We got our exercise honestly." Then he sighed. "But I'm not up to it anymore. Spirit is willing, flesh is weak. And Doris—that's my wife—says she's tired of living with a jungle in the front yard. She wants to put in some orderly plantings, she says. I told her nature's not orderly and anyway the deer are going to eat it all, but she hasn't listened to me for sixty-eight years and has no intention of starting now."

"So what would you—"

"She's off with the grands and the greats in Hawaii for two weeks. What's an old lady doing gallivanting around a tropical island, that's what I want to know. I called her last night and she said she's eyeing all the young men on the beaches and mourning what she never had."

Oh yes, Everett definitely liked him. "So while she's gone you can ogle young women?"

"My eyesight's not up to it, and it's not worth springing for new glasses. Anyway, I thought that when she got back, I could surprise her with a jungle clearance. Might even let her believe that I'm the one who did it. Remind her that I have charms even if I'm not a handsome hunk with a surfboard." The best thing was that Ron said all of this completely straight-faced.

"Ron, I'd be delighted to help Doris appreciate you more fully."

After a pause, Ron nodded. "We can give you a try. Five hundred bucks and you can use my yard tools, if you want. I got lots." He gestured to a shed at the edge of the property.

Everett had no idea whether five hundred was a reasonable rate, but it was enough to keep him fed and Janet gassed up for a while. Besides, the weather was pleasant for outdoor tasks, and he'd enjoy helping Ron out. The front yard, while unkempt, wasn't particularly large. "I can clear things, but I don't know anything about planting."

Ron waved his hand. "That's Doris's problem, not ours. She'd complain about whatever I chose anyway."

"Fair enough. You should know that I'm kind of doing odd jobs as a temp gig. I'm not licensed or bonded."

That brought a snort. "You sound like a lawyer."

"That's because I was one until recently. But I've reformed my ways and decided to become an honest man."

"Clearly they're letting just anyone into this town." Ron clucked his tongue. "You're gonna bring down the property values. But in the spirit of necessity, I'm willing to overlook your unfortunate past."

"I appreciate it. And I pledge to not litigate on your property."

This time, Ron almost cracked a smile. "When can you start?"

Everett mentally reviewed his schedule. He still had a couple of days' work left at Cannon's house, and on Wednesday he had food prep for Tom and Gary. He also had a few odds and ends to do at the book-shop. And the cat needed a vet visit. Somehow, despite being officially unemployed and at loose ends, he'd managed to acquire a fairly hefty to-do list. He found himself liking that.

"I can work all day Tuesday, and then pick things up again Thurs-day. I think that ought to do it, but if not, I can do Friday too. Plenty of leeway before Mrs. Tosto returns, tanned and relaxed."

After a moment of consideration, Ron nodded. "That'll do. I'll go fetch your payment." He started to turn away from the door.

"Not yet. Payment upon satisfactory completion of the work." Because Everett was fairly certain that Ron was less likely to cheat him than Cannon or Izzy, and it wasn't as if he was hard up for the money right now.

"Do you want to put the terms in writing, counselor?" Another almost-smile.

"I'm fine without." Acting on intuition, he added, "If you don't mind me asking, what do you do for a living?"

"I am gainfully retired." Finally, a real smile broke through, although fleetingly. "But around these parts, I was once known as the Honorable Ronald F. Tosto of the Milagro Superior Court. Like you, however, I've reformed."

"It's a pleasure to make the acquaintance of a fellow former reprobate."

Ron shook his hand. "I'll see you on Tuesday. No need to announce yourself. The shed's unlocked."

Everett found himself grinning as he walked the short distance up the road toward the cemetery. He didn't explore much once he got there since it was growing dark, but he did stand for a moment to take in the fading view over Winter Camp Road. There were the trees of

Miracle Creek Campground, which he sincerely hoped never got razed by a developer.

At that point a memory hit him, followed by a realization. Both should have rattled loose in his brain days ago, but apparently he'd been too muddled with other things. Like that boat instructor. Anyway, he'd been hit now. The memory was of the last time he'd visited the cemetery, which was also the last time he'd seen Blake Cannon. Everett had been walking downhill toward town, while Cannon and the other man were going up. Everett paused and shared his new insight with the cemetery. "Cannon was taking him up for an aerial view of the resort site. I bet that guy was a potential investor."

And... huh. Wasn't that the day before Everett found the body?

Muttering about his own stupidity, Everett hurried down the road toward town.

CHAPTER TWENTY-THREE

"Is your dad home? I need to talk to him, please."

"Why?" Sophie McBeth stood in the open doorway of her house, wearing an oversize Gulch Pages & Pastries T-shirt and with a pencil clutched in one hand. Everett wasn't even aware that such T-shirts existed. He'd have to ask Charlotte about it later. Now he had more urgent matters to deal with.

"It's police business."

Inexplicably, she looked disappointed. "Tell me," she said airily. "I'll give him the message."

"This really needs direct communication."

She stared at him before announcing, "He's making dinner." And sure enough, Everett registered the sounds of running water and clattering pans coming from down the hallway behind her. And the scents of garlic and butter, which made Everett's stomach rumble. Apparently he was hungry.

"I'm sorry to interrupt. It's important."

After a moment of thought, she turned and bellowed, "Da-ad! Ms. Tabor's brother is here!" She managed to bellow with a sing-song inflection, an action which Everett wouldn't have thought possible.

Very shortly, Cole hurried toward them, wiping his hands on a towel. He wore a tank top and shorts, and despite Everett's best efforts, he found himself admiring those very toned arms and legs. Where did Cole work out?

"What's wrong? Everyone okay?" Cole demanded.

"Everyone's fine. I came by because there was something I'd forgotten to tell you about Cannon. Something possibly pertinent to the, uh...." He glanced at Sophie and stopped.

"The murder," Sophie said with an eye roll. "You can say it. I'm not a child."

Cole looked slightly exasperated, although Everett wasn't sure whether it had been he himself or Sophie who had triggered the expression. Maybe it was a group result. "Is it graphic or gory?"

"Um, no."

"Then you might as well come in and join us for dinner."

"You don't have to—"

"Food's ready. I don't want to wait and neither does Sophie, and we're not rude enough to eat in front of you without giving you a plate. So come in."

Unsure what he thought of this development, Everett followed Cole down a hallway lined with Sophie's school photos and into a brightly lit kitchen. The oak cabinets, white tile backsplash and countertops, and vinyl floor were like time travelers from the 1980s. The white range dated from that era too, but the stainless steel fridge was newer and liberally covered in magnets.

"Sit." Cole pointed at one of the six chairs around the table, and Everett obeyed as Sophie fetched him a set of cutlery.

"Anything I can do to help?" asked Everett.

"Nope. Almost done."

Sophie sat opposite him, leaned forward, and stage-whispered, "Don't expect it to be very good. Dad's cooking is mediocre at best."

"Hey!" Cole protested, wooden spoon in hand. "If you don't like it, you're welcome to take on the chore yourself."

"I am far too busy with school. Have to keep those grades up, right?"

They spent a few minutes squabbling over household responsibilities and priorities, and Everett didn't bother to hide his grin. It was clear that the two of them were close, that they loved each other, and that they were both strong-willed and tended to butt heads. He'd never had a relationship like that with either of his parents, but what he and Charlotte had together had been very like it. Still was, really.

Peace settled when the food was ready. Sophie helped Cole carry it to the table: an enormous bowl of salad, an equally enormous bowl of spaghetti with meat sauce, and a platter of slightly over-crisped garlic bread. "Whattaya want to drink?" Cole asked from behind the open door of the fridge. "We have water, milk, and... huh. Guess that's it."

"Water's fine, thanks."

"Sorry, I rarely have alcohol in the house. Don't drink it much." Cole filled three glasses from a pitcher, set them on the table, and took the chair next to Sophie. That left them staring at Everett—both with the same sharp gaze—which he found a little disconcerting.

"That's kind of ironic since your family owns vineyards."

"Have you been doing a background search on me, Everett?" Now Cole's eyes held a challenge that Everett didn't understand.

"In this town, it's impossible not to learn everything about everyone. Must make your job a lot easier."

"You don't know much about me at all. And by the way, I don't drink because I never know if I might get called in to duty. My relatives' businesses are irrelevant."

Before Everett could retort, Sophie groaned and said, "Oh my God," then reached for the spaghetti. All three of them filled their plates—although Cole had to remind her to take some salad—and dug in.

"This is good," Everett said after a few bites of the pasta. He wasn't lying. It wasn't spectacular, but few meals truly were.

"Just sauce from a jar plus some ground beef. Sophie's not exaggerating—I'm not much of a chef."

Everett shrugged. "You're busy. Single parent, demanding job. And you weren't expecting company tonight."

"We haven't had company in aaaages, have we Dad? It's tragic. You're so incredibly single, and—"

"Sophie."

Although Cole's tone was sharp and she did stop, Sophie didn't look the least bit chastened. She crunched through a big bite of garlic bread.

After considering for a moment whether he should say anything, Everett threw caution to the wind. "If you wanted, I could give you a couple tips to make a dinner like this more… gourmet. Not that you need to! This is perfectly fine. But if you wanted to, there are some easy steps you could take to upgrade." He hoped he wasn't coming off as a judgmental ass, because for once he wasn't trying to be one.

Cole paused, salad fork midway to his mouth, and gave Everett that searching look. "You're a chef now too? A man of many skills, it seems."

"I worked in restaurants. And I taught myself things. I like food, and I didn't always have the money to eat out. Besides, cooking relaxes me." That was maybe a bit more self-disclosure than he'd intended.

"What kinds of tips?" Sophie interjected.

"Change up the base now and then. There are some really nice veggie noodles at the Olive Branch. Different pasta shapes with things like spinach and carrots added to the dough. They cost a little more, but they're still plenty affordable, and the veggies add color and flavor. And vitamins, so maybe you could minimize the salad."

Sophie laughed and elbowed her father. "I could go for that. What else?"

"Well… making sauce from scratch is easy. You can make a big batch, portion it, and freeze it. Then it's just as convenient as jarred but tastier, and you can control exactly what goes into it. And if you felt like it, when you served the meal you could add some grated cheese."

"We have parmesan in the fridge," said Cole.

"But is it the kind in the can?" He waited for a nod. "Yeah, I thought so. That's fine and very simple. But again, if you want to bump things up a notch, try some freshly grated. Or sub asiago, pecorino romano, ricotta… whatever floats your boat. Tom and Gary sell a little hand grater that's cheap and kind of fun to use."

A smile played at the edges of Cole's mouth. "Are they paying you a commission?"

"Not yet. I'll have to raise the issue with them."

There was something new in Cole's expression. Something... intriguing and more than a little confusing. But then Sophie pushed the platter of garlic bread toward Everett. "Have another piece. And I like your ideas. Can you give me a sauce recipe?"

"Sure, I can write something down."

She beamed and gave her father another elbow nudge. "See, Dad?" Whatever that meant.

Cole's expression turned harder for reasons that Everett couldn't fathom, and then that cocksure smugness slid into place. "You did say you had something important to tell me. I hope it wasn't an emergency."

Oh yeah—Everett had come here for a reason, and it wasn't to impart basic culinary knowledge. He set down his fork and wiped his mouth with a paper napkin. "I remembered something today. It wasn't a big deal at the time, so it slipped my mind, but maybe it's important. You should check it out."

"Check what out?"

"The afternoon before I found Cannon, uh, deceased, I happened to run into him. He was walking up to the cemetery."

"Maybe he had a premonition!" Sophie interjected excitedly.

Cole gave her a stern look, then turned back to Everett. "And?"

"Somebody was with him. Fiftyish white man in expensive casual wear. Not a local, I don't think. I bet he was an investor and Cannon was taking him up to get a good view of the property. There's a nice one from the cemetery."

"I'm aware of the topography of my hometown, thanks."

Everett huffed. "That man could very well have been the last one to see Cannon alive. He could be the murderer. What if they argued over something and the guy just...." He mimed swinging a bottle, almost knocking over his water glass in the process.

"Why didn't you mention this to me when I questioned you, on the day you found the body?"

"I'd forgotten about it. Sorry. I wasn't really thinking clearly at the time. Discovering a corpse wasn't exactly on my agenda that day." No need to mention that Sam and the boating instructor had also been doing dumb things to his brain.

"Who was the man?" Cole looked intrigued, probably despite himself.

"Not a clue. Isn't it your job to find out?"

Cole harrumphed and stabbed at a slice of cucumber. "You haven't given me much to go on. And it's probably nothing anyway."

"But you don't know that. Not unless you already know who did it. Like... maybe a McBeth."

"What?" Cole stared at him in apparent astonishment.

"Cannon had a contract to buy grapes from your family."

"Who told you that?"

How to explain this without divulging that he'd been nosing around where he probably shouldn't? Maybe he could sort of gloss over that part. "Sanjeev Patel showed me wine labels that Cannon had printed up. They had the Il Vigneto logo and they said Milagro County, 2025—this year—and Sangiovese Reserve. Sanjeev said that the only people growing those grapes here are McBeths."

It looked as if McBeth was trying to control his temper. "Mr. Cannon attempted to persuade my cousins to sell next year's harvest to him. They said no because they already had contracts in place—a point that I'm sure you of all people can appreciate. Also, instead of paying in actual money, Mr. Cannon wanted to give them a small share in his resort and also, and I quote, 'exposure.' My cousins told him to take a hike. That was the end of their interactions with the victim. They disclosed all of this to me once the murder became publicly known. They have rock-solid alibis and no particular motive."

"Oh." Everett deflated a little. It wasn't as if he'd truly thought the McBeths were to blame, but their involvement had seemed important. "Charlotte told me you arrested your cousin a while back."

"That was a different one. He's still doing time at Pleasant Valley. Which is a shame because he wasn't a bad kid. He's about my age and we used to hang out when we were teens. But he picked up an addiction to painkillers after a car accident, and that led him down a rough path."

"So you arrested him."

Cole sighed loudly and pushed his plate away. "I didn't enjoy it, if that's what you're implying. I would much rather have gotten him into treatment, but there aren't many options for that around here—it's a real problem—and he wasn't open to the idea anyway. He was dealing dangerous drugs. The kind that kill people. And it's my job to protect my neighbors."

"That's fair enough. And addictions are never easy on anyone." Everett looked down at the table. "My father had... well, some issues. Big ones. He died young from them." Younger than Everett was now, in fact.

"I am sorry to hear that." Cole looked sincere in his sympathy.

"Thanks. And I'm sorry to eat and run, but I shouldn't have intruded on you in the first place." Everett stood, feeling suddenly awkward. "I'm grateful for the meal and your hospitality, and Sophie, I'll leave a recipe with Charlotte so you can pick it up the next time you're in the shop."

Cole looked at him gravely. "I appreciate you sharing information. And your cooking tips. Maybe there's not much hope left for me as a chef, but now you've got Soph interested."

They stared at each other as if neither could decide what to say or do next. Sophie saved them both by scooting back her chair and rising to her feet. "I'll show him out, Dad."

She led Everett to the front door and held it open for him. "I really do like your pasta ideas. Will you write down the cheeses too? I forget what ones you said."

"Sure."

"Hey, Mr. Vaughn?"

He smiled at her. "Everett, remember?"

"Okay, Everett." She said his name as if she were tasting something new. When she spoke again, she nearly whispered. "Hey, um, those labels you mentioned?"

"Sorry to upset you with talk of homicide over the dinner table."

Sophie was a champion eye-roller. "I don't care about that. It's just that I thought of something. Why would Mr. Cannon have labels already printed up when the wine won't be bottled for a few years? And when he didn't even have the right to buy the grapes?"

Everett supposed he shouldn't be surprised that Sophie McBeth knew things about winemaking. "I have no idea."

"It's weird. Also, how come the labels said this year?"

He frowned. "What does the designated year refer to, exactly?"

"Duh, the year the grapes are harvested."

Cannon definitely didn't have Milagro County Sangiovese grapes from this year. Huh. "You should ask your dad these questions."

"Nah. He'll just tell me I'm a kid and should mind my own beeswax."

"Well, I'm sorry I can't answer them, then."

"It's all right." She glanced over her shoulder toward the kitchen. It sounded as if Cole was washing up, and Everett felt a twinge of guilt for not staying to help. "You should totally invite yourself to dinner with us again."

"I didn't.... Your father.... I came by...."

Everett was still sputtering on the front porch as she laughed and closed the door.

CHAPTER TWENTY-FOUR

The city was quiet this morning. Too quiet. The detective narrowed his eyes as he strode down the sidewalk, his hand inches from his Colt, ready to draw if—

Nope. Everett wasn't a fan of firearms and couldn't pull one even in his imagination. He'd been okay when his illusory six-shooters remained safely in their holsters, back in his daydream cowboy days, but now that he was a daydream gumshoe, the phantom gun felt heavier. Maybe PI Vaughn didn't need a pistol. Maybe he was so smart and fast that he relied entirely on his sharp perception, lightning reflexes, and clever retorts.

Or maybe Everett needed to keep his head in real life.

Yawning, he entered Rising Times and deeply inhaled the delicious scents. No other customers were here this early on a Saturday, and Xochi greeted him cheerily from behind the counter. "You must have work to do today."

"Got it in one." He watched as, without being asked, she prepared a large Americano for him. He'd never before been a regular anywhere. It was nice. "Hey, thanks for the referral for Judge Tosto's yard work. I'm going to do that next week."

She set his cup on the counter. "Oh, good. I like him. He and my abuelo meet here every Thursday morning. They sit over in the corner for an hour and complain about the government. At the end, Judge Tosto waits for my abuelo to leave and, even though I'd totally comp them, he insists on paying for them both. And I'm not allowed to tell my abuelo." She slid open the back of the pastry case and grabbed a pair of tongs and a small paper bag. "Want some pan de muerto today? It's early for it, but I was in the mood."

"Sounds great." He watched as she slid a mini bread into the bag. "The little sugar skull on top is a nice touch."

"Not traditional, but it looks cute and the tourists like it. You think maybe Jess should carry some of these over at Pages & Pastries, maybe serve them as a special with some chocolate caliente?"

"Charlotte's considering a Día de los Muertos window display, so that would be perfect."

"Cool. I'll talk to Jess."

Everett handed over a ten. "Keep the change. Which is absolutely not enough to serve as a bribe, but I wonder if I could glean some information from you."

Her eyes sparkled. "You can glean for free."

"I found Blake Cannon's body the morning of September 27, but the murder probably happened the day before—a Friday. And it's possible that on that Friday afternoon, Cannon came into your shop with an out-of-towner who bought coffee. Do you have any memory of that? I know you get a lot of customers, but—"

"Oh, I totally remember that. Cannon hardly ever stepped foot in here, so it was a real occasion when he did. He didn't order anything. But his buddy did, and he was kind of a jerk because I didn't have coconut milk, just cow, oat, and soy."

That sounded on-brand for someone that Cannon would hang out with. "Do you know who the man is? Did you maybe catch his name?"

She shook her head. "Sorry. But while I was prepping his drink, I heard the guy complaining about his room at the Gulch Inn. Cannon said that's why we needed his stupid resort so much."

Also on-brand. And it tended to confirm Everett's suspicion that the man was a potential investor. "Interesting." While he mused, he tore off a piece of the bread and popped it into his mouth. "Oh, yum. Still a little warm even."

"Early bird gets the super-fresh baked goods. You know, right now Bret Faud's on shift over at the inn. I bet you could ask him about the guy."

"Why would he tell me anything? Isn't that kind of thing confidential?"

She smirked. "Dunno, but nothing in Gulch is confidential. Plus, Bret was one of Ms. Tabor's students—we were in the same class—and he was gaga over her. He thought he was gonna be the next Shakespeare or something."

Well, it was worth a try. "Thanks for the info gleaning." Everett lifted his cup and bag. "And the sustenance."

"Good luck!"

It was pleasant to meander across the traffic-free street, watching the sky brighten as he scalded his tongue on good coffee. Although temperatures were still warm during the day, the air had taken on a definite autumnal scent and storefronts showed seasonal décor. Ski boots, thick gloves, and snowshoes had joined the running shoes in the window display at Take a Hike, while Berg's Candy Kitchen had foil-wrapped chocolate pumpkins and marshmallow ghosts. Mother Lode Discoveries had several windows full of antique and vintage Halloween decorations and furniture upholstered in reds and golds.

The front of Deadman Gulch Inn looked almost the same as it had in the 1850s, with a long wood-floored porch on the ground floor; tall, thin windows with painted iron shutters; and a second-floor balcony, edged by a highly decorative wrought-iron railing, that ran the width of the building. Everett paused for a moment just to imagine all the historical figures who'd walked through the same door he was about to use, and he wondered what they had been thinking about at the time. Even merchant princes, stagecoach bandits, and well-heeled publishers must have spent at least a portion of their days wondering when they last saw a dentist or trying to decide where to eat lunch.

Everett transferred coffee cup and bag to his left hand and went inside.

The registration lobby was small and fairly cramped. To the left, a door led to the saloon, which of course was currently closed. There was a tourism brochure rack to the right, along with an enclosed stairway leading up and, nearby, a door marked Employees Only. Straight ahead was a table set up for coffee and tea service, a dark hallway that looked as if it led to some rooms, and the alcove with the registration desk.

A sleepy-looking young man behind the desk pushed the hair out of his face and said, "Welcome to the historic Deadman Gulch Inn. How can I help you?" He seemed slightly eager at the prospect of doing anything aside from half dozing. He was skinny and sandy-blond, and he wore a hoodie with the inn's logo.

"Are you Bret Faud?"

Now the kid seemed a little alarmed. "Uh... yeah?"

Everett closed the distance between them and leaned up against the counter. "I'm Everett Vaughn. I just moved to Gulch a few weeks ago, but my sister's been here for decades. Charlotte Tabor?"

Bret's expression lit up. "Ms. Tabor! Oh man, she's so cool. She was my favorite teacher."

"That's great," said Everett, pretending as if this was news to him. "I heard she's a tough grader."

"Oh yeah, she totally is. But she makes you want to work for that grade, you know? Because of her, I'm an author." Bret winced slightly. "I mean, I write stuff. I've only published it online so far. But someday I'm gonna write a novel, and it's gonna be a best-seller."

"I'm glad my sister inspired you." Everett meant that sincerely. Char may have grown tired of teaching, but he knew that she'd enjoyed her career and had made a difference in people's lives. Which was more than he could say about himself.

"For sure. I even changed my name because of her. I used to be Andy Moore, but that's boring, so I was gonna change to Bret Harte. 'Cause he was pretty famous for stuff he wrote around here. But that would be confusing—two Bret Hartes—so instead I'm Bret Faud. That means heart in Arabic. I looked it up."

It was too early in the morning to admire the innocence and enthusiasm of youth, but Everett did his best. "I wonder if I could ask you a favor?"

"Sure. You need a room? We have one vacant now and I can give you a discount. That room doesn't have a private shower, but there's a shared one down the hall. Historic building, you know?"

It occurred belatedly to Everett that he could have sweetened this kid up—literally—by bringing him something from Rising Times. Oh well. He'd just have to rely on his family connections and winning personality. "Thanks, but I'm renting a house just a few blocks from here. What I was hoping for was information. I need the name of a man who stayed here during the Grape Gala."

Bret pushed his hair away again. "Maybe. We were fully booked all weekend, so.... Can you give me some details?"

"White. Fifties. Rich. He was probably here by himself. That Friday afternoon, he was wearing, um, khakis, a polo shirt, a baseball cap. He wasn't happy about the accommodations."

"Oh, him!" Bret's expression brightened. "Yeah, he was, uh, dissatisfied. He said the room was too small, the floors were creaky, and the bath amenities were crap. He had one of the en suite rooms. He was so pissed that he checked out early."

Everett's ears pricked up. "Did he? When was that?"

"Uh, Friday morning. He'd checked in the night before, pretty late I think, and I heard later that he kept asking for an upgrade. But we don't have one. His room was as fancy as we get. So Friday morning he came down and asked again. I couldn't give him one, since, like, it doesn't exist, so he said he was leaving. We're not supposed to give a refund without at least two days' notice of cancelation, but my manager was here and didn't want to deal, so he gave him one anyway." Bret shrugged, his expression showing his general bewilderment at the vagaries of human nature. "It was okay, though. We had walk-in guests pretty soon after he left, and they were sure happy to get a room."

"What was the guy's name?"

Bret turned to the computer beside him and spent a few minutes typing. Because of the screen's angle, Everett couldn't see what he was doing, so he allowed his gaze to fall instead on the framed photos on the wall. They all showed the inn, the passing years recorded by differing outfits on people and differing vehicles on the street.

Munching on his sweet bread, Everett thought about what it would be like if old buildings had souls. What if everyone who entered a building left a little bit of their spirit behind, and once enough of these spirit-bits accumulated, the building itself would gain an essence? If so, Gulch Inn would be an interesting character. Would a demolished building's soul end up in a new structure built on the same site? He'd have to ask Willow about that.

"Here you go," said Bret, interrupting Everett's reverie and sliding a square of paper across the counter. *Paul Schmidt* was written in careful print. "I can't give you his contact details 'cause that would probably be a little too much, you know?"

Everett took the paper and slipped it into his jeans pocket. "I get it. Confidentiality."

"Yeah. Sorry. But, um, since you're Ms. Tabor's brother...." Bret leaned over the counter and spoke in a whisper. "You might want to look in the Bay Area."

"Thanks. And best of luck with the writing. When you publish that novel, I'm positive my sister will promote it at her store."

Bret pushed his hair aside and beamed like a lighthouse beacon.

CHAPTER TWENTY-FIVE

By two o'clock on Sunday afternoon, Everett's body had had enough. He'd spent the entire weekend at Cannon's house—which he supposed was now Izzy Kincaid's house—hammering, screwing, stripping, and a lot of other activities that sounded sexy but absolutely weren't. After he finished repairing the wonky kitchen drawer with the damaged track, he decided to call it a day.

Leaning back against the kitchen cabinets, he sent Izzy a text. *I've worked enough hours to use up your $1K.*

She responded almost immediately. *Is everything done?*

No. I'll send a list of what's left.

The little dots danced for a moment before she replied. *I can pay another $1K.*

He was temporarily tempted; it was nice to see his bank account growing instead of steadily shrinking. But he'd already committed to cleaning up Judge Tosto's yard, and anyway, Everett had pretty much had his fill of this house.

Sorry can't. Busy.

He was gathering his tools when the phone buzzed again. *How much r they paying u? I'll pay more.*

Apparently Izzy had a number of things in common with her ex. Lovely. Everett wasn't under the illusion that he was a morally superior human being, but he'd never been the type to break a promise or persuade someone else to do so. Maybe his childhood played a part in this. He knew what it was like when someone failed to follow through with their obligations—*thanks, Dad*—and also what it meant to have someone to rely on. That was Charlotte, of course, who was bossy well past the age when he merited it but who'd always made her younger brother a priority.

No thanks, Everett texted back. Then he put his phone on silent and tucked it into his pocket.

Main Street was lively this afternoon, the sidewalks bustling with pedestrians and the restaurants' outdoor seating packed. Everett peeked in the window of Pages & Pastries, and seeing a line at the cashier counter and all the café tables occupied, decided not to go in. He knew that Char or one of her employees would have made sure that Warren had food and fresh water, and the small list of chores that Charlotte had given him could wait.

That left Everett feeling a bit at loose ends. He felt too ancient and achy to go for a hike, and if he went back home, he suspected he'd spend the rest of the day snoring on the couch. So he strolled up and down Main Street a few times, pausing to look at window displays, and he waved at Gary, who was stationed at the door to the Olive Branch, offering free samples of fancy crackers.

Then Everett spied Cole McBeth half a block down, annoyingly resplendent in his uniform and smiling as he chatted with a group of tourists. Before Cole could glance over and see him, Everett ducked into the nearest business, which turned out to be Granocchio Cellars.

Despite the long, narrow space being full of people, Willow saw him and waved him over to the single unoccupied stool, down at the end of the tall tasting counter.

"I don't want to—"

"Sit. You can listen in." She gestured at the two people seated closest to him, a man and woman in their twenties. "I'm giving these kids a crash course on wine tasting. The important stuff—not the snooty BS."

Everett smiled at the couple, who were holding hands and looked horribly fresh-faced and optimistic. "Sure."

Willow placed a glass in front of each of them. "A bottle of wine is like a person," she said, holding aloft some pinot noir. "DNA matters, but that's just the beginning. The environment is what really shapes the personality. The terroir, of course, and also the specific weather patterns during growth, and all the zillion decisions made by the grower and producer. You can have two wines made with the same grape, and they can turn out totally different. And like snowflakes, no two wines are the same."

She spent the next twenty minutes expounding while they swirled, sniffed, and sipped. The young couple seemed enthralled, while Everett was impressed with Willow's enthusiasm. It didn't seem to bother her that there were other customers in the place; her husband Tim was helping them with more efficiency and less educating.

But her method turned out to be effective for sales too, because by the time she finished, the couple had signed up for the Granocchio wine club and bought a mixed case to take home. After ringing them up, Willow turned to Everett. "Have I converted you from beer yet?"

"Can't I be nondenominational in my alcohol?"

"You can, but it'd be a mistake. Want a full glass of that grenache? You seemed to like that one best."

"That'd be great, thanks." He waited for her to grab the bottle, and as she was pouring he remembered that he had questions for her. "Hey, do you mind if I ask you something? I know you're busy, so—"

"Ask away." She winked before pouring herself a glass too and taking a healthy swallow.

"It has to do with Blake Cannon."

She made a face as if her grenache were sour. "He didn't know the difference between decent wine and plonk, and he didn't want to learn."

"What's plonk?"

She sighed. "Cheap, mass-produced junk with no personality at all. Don't get me wrong—there are good inexpensive wines out there. But I'm talking about that stuff churned out by machines and glugged into three-hundred-thousand-gallon tanks. Like Wino Willy."

Everett, who was mid-sip, nearly choked. "Wino Willy?"

"You haven't heard of it? It's William Valko Wines, formally. Huge place down in the valley, in Salida. You can buy their swill for three bucks a pop, but you're better off drinking beer."

Everett recognized the name at once—he should, considering he'd hauled all those boxes emblazoned with it. "Cannon had a bunch of that in his basement."

"Doesn't surprise me a bit. But what did you want to ask?"

"Can you think of any reason why he would have had a bunch of wine labels printed with this year on them, for Milagro County sangiovese?"

Her eyes widened. "He did?"

"Saw them myself."

She muttered something under her breath. Everett doubted it was flattering. "It's because he was a liar and a fraud."

"You don't think he was producing some?" Maybe he had a facility that Sanjeev didn't know about. And maybe Cole was mistaken—or deliberately covering up the truth—about who his cousins had sold grapes to.

Willow downed the rest of her glass. "Only one vineyard in this county grows those grapes, and they sold their entire harvest to us and Kovacs."

"So why print those labels? It wasn't just one or two. I saw probably a hundred or so." It seemed like such an odd thing to spend money on. Maybe he was going to use them for promotional purposes, but Everett couldn't think how.

"Couldn't tell you. Want another glass?"

Everett looked at his empty one and then dismounted the barstool. "No thanks. I'm good for this afternoon. How much do I owe you?"

She waved a dismissive hand. "Not a penny. But maybe you could suggest to Charlotte that a window display with books about wine would be a great idea."

He grinned at her. "It would, and I'll be happy to." He went out into the bright late-afternoon sunshine and headed for home. Maybe a nap wasn't such a bad idea after all.

CHAPTER TWENTY-SIX

Fueled by wine and a couple days of physical labor, Everett's Sunday afternoon nap was long and deep. He woke up after sundown with wisps of dreams melting away like cotton candy in water. Something about grapes—no surprise there—and Sam had been in it, and also Izzy Kincaid's labradoodle.

Everett and Sam had discussed getting a pet during the pandemic lockdown. A lot of people were doing it, and Everett, who'd never had a pet, was at first open to the idea. But then they'd squabbled about what to get—dog or cat, youngster or adult—and how they'd divide the commitments of caring for a new family member. Sam had said that if Everett wasn't ready to accept the responsibility of a companion animal, how could he possibly be prepared for human children. Everett had accused Sam of using this as yet another excuse to not have kids. In the end, the issue was just another sign of the space that had grown between them.

Still recumbent on the rental-house couch, Everett sighed and very nearly reached for his phone. Then his common sense woke up, and he managed to stand and stretch and think about what do next—at least for tonight, if not for the rest of his life. He was going to have to deal with the latter decision eventually, but for now he could simply make up his mind about dinner.

Except he dithered about that too, pointlessly opening and closing cabinets and the fridge, until finally he couldn't stand himself a second longer and made a grilled cheese sandwich with canned tomato soup. Which hit the spot perfectly, in fact. Grilled cheese had been one of the first things he'd perfected back when he was a kid, along with mac and cheese, pancakes, and sloppy joes.

Instead of maturing through his midlife crisis, was he reverting to childhood?

Dinner eaten and dishes washed, he spent a couple of hours slumped in the armchair and scrolling on his phone, not really registering what was playing on the TV. He couldn't shake the post-nap grogginess. Or maybe it was a mini hangover, although he hadn't had enough wine to get truly drunk. He wondered whether some wines were more likely than others to cause hangovers. Maybe he'd ask Willow the next time he saw her.

Thinking about Willow reminded him of the information she'd shared today and the many cases of Wino Willy that had been stowed in Cannon's basement. Why would a guy who intended to run an upscale winery resort have hundreds of bottles of cheapo stuff?

As he mulled this over, he remembered something else: the man who'd been with Cannon right before he died. Paul Schmidt. An online search revealed that it was a pretty common name, which was frustrating until Everett added additional terms: *investment* and *San Francisco*.

And there he was, with a photo and everything—this time in a suit instead of golf clothes. Paul J. Schmidt, partner, Delta Sierra Capital. A moment's further research revealed that Delta Sierra was a private equity firm headquartered in San Francisco.

There was no indication that Schmidt had a history of murdering people... but the Internet didn't always reveal all.

Everett spent nearly an hour pacing the small house, considering whether to hand over this information to Cole McBeth. It might be valuable. On the other hand, maybe Cole already knew about Schmidt. Although he hadn't admitted this over their spaghetti dinner, he simply might have been keeping it close to the vest. And if he didn't know, well, he'd been previously dismissive of Everett's investigations.

A number of possible scenarios rolled through his head, but none of them resulted in the culprit's arrest. Everett had become invested enough in the situation to really want the bad guy behind bars. Not because Cannon's murder was an epic tragedy, but he hadn't deserved to die. Plus if Everett was honest with himself, he wanted to feel as if he'd accomplished something meaningful. Figuring out who'd done it would be meaningful.

He fetched his yellow legal pad from the kitchen table and wrote out a full list of suspects. It was, he thought, better informed than his previous list. He included Cole McBeth and his cousins, along with Carol Allen and Junior, Sanjeev Patel, Izzy Kincaid, and Paul Schmidt. He added the owners of the Gulch Inn, the Snooze-Inn, and the town's two bed and breakfasts. Then he started to write down the wineries, but stopped himself. His list was useless if he included half the town.

How would a real detective handle this?

Everett pictured himself in a suit and bowtie, with oiled hair and a waxed mustache, standing in a drawing room with dark wood paneling and rich upholstery. He held a cane—no, he held a pipe—and the room smelled of tobacco and sherry. An assortment of Gulch citizens in formalwear perched on uncomfortable furniture, watching him warily. Everett would give a speech in which he revealed each person's motives —gasps and exclamations would accompany each unearthed secret— and finally he would explain how he'd solved the case. He would pause meaningfully, then name the murderer. Who would stand and immediately confess.

Maybe this Everett should have a Belgian accent.

None of this, however, was going to happen in Deadman Gulch. There were a few Victorian-era homes that might have parlors, but they'd never hold his long list of suspects. Plus, how would he lure everyone in for the great reveal? Especially Paul Schmidt, who didn't even live here.

"If the mountain won't come to Muhammad," Everett said out loud.

It looked as if an excursion was in order.

He woke early on Monday and put on his nicest jeans, a white button-down, and a sport coat. It wasn't really a suit but—as the closest thing to business attire that he still owned—it would have to do. After gassing Janet up at the Chevron near the edge of town, he headed down into the Central Valley.

Traffic wasn't too bad at first, but it picked up an hour later when he merged onto I-5, and by the time he hit the East Bay, it crawled. God, he didn't miss the Chicago version of this at all. After he and Sam had married and bought their suburban townhouse, they'd awakened at five every morning just to beat rush hour into the city. Everett didn't mind being an early riser, but that was too much, especially during the bitter cold winter months when the sun hadn't yet risen to illuminate the dirty gray snow. Yet despite their efforts, there had still been plenty of other cars on the road.

Now as he drove, Everett passed the time listening to Spanish stations on the radio—even though he didn't speak the language—and looking at houses perched on the hillsides. He also realized that he'd forgotten to eat breakfast and was hungry. Janet's perpetual french-fry odor wasn't helping.

At long last he was crossing the Bay Bridge and trying not to think about earthquakes. Once he passed Treasure Island, his first glimpse of the city almost took his breath away. It was picture-postcard gorgeous.

He'd spent two weeks here during the early days of his Post-Divorce Wanderings, staying at a nice hotel near Union Square and doing all the touristy things. He'd even gone to a couple of bars. But that had never been his thing even when he was young, and years of marriage had shriveled whatever flirting skills he'd once had. Clutching his overpriced drink, he'd felt too old, too awkward, and too unhip, so he'd finished the booze and left. He'd enjoyed the rest of his time in the city but hadn't been sorry to leave.

Now he piloted Janet off the bridge and into the Financial District, trying to avoid pedestrians, bicyclists, parked cars, buses, and other drivers. She was a great vehicle to have in Deadman Gulch, but not so much in San Francisco. In fact, he would have preferred to not drive here at all, especially when he grew slightly disoriented and spent nearly half an hour circling the Embarcadero in search of a parking lot. He eventually found one, but maneuvering Janet was rough in the tight places and involved a lot of swearing.

He was relieved when he was finally on the sidewalk, back on his own two feet.

Schmidt's office was only a couple of blocks away, but Everett stopped for a cup of coffee and a bagel, trying to plan what should happen next. Unfortunately, nothing much came to mind; he was going to have to wing it. At least he was fed and caffeinated, although the coffee had not been as good as Jessica's or Xochi's.

"Dawdling won't help," he muttered under his breath, and gave himself a mental pep talk. He could do this. While most of his legal career had involved interactions with other lawyers and corporate flunkies, he'd dealt with higher-ups too. The type of men—and they were, almost without exception, men—who thought of the world as a food chain and of themselves as apex predators. And over the years, some of those men had ended up bowing before the power of Everett's legal skills. Okay, that was an exaggeration. But he wasn't afraid of them. He could handle Paul Schmidt.

If he could get in to see him, that was.

The first barrier was the attractive young man behind the reception desk in the building lobby. Everett marched up with the confidence of a person who fully expects to get his way. "Everett Vaughn here to see Paul Schmidt at Delta Sierra," he announced.

Maintaining a blandly pleasant expression, the man poked at his screen. "I'm afraid I don't see your name on the list," he finally said.

"It's regarding a private matter. Please call up now and tell Mr. Schmidt he'll want to talk to me before the police get involved." This was a risk since Everett didn't know whether the Milagro Sheriff's Department had already contacted Schmidt. But even if they had, Schmidt's curiosity might be piqued enough to let Everett up.

The receptionist's face didn't register any reaction to the state-ment, but he did type something. He really was very cute: black hair arranged carefully in place, slightly rosy cheeks, adorable cupid's-bow mouth. He was also half Everett's age and, Everett had to remind himself, not the point of this expedition. God, maybe he really needed to think about trying to date. Not that he had many prospects in Gulch.

"Mr. Schmidt will see you. He's on twelve. Turn right when you get off the elevator." The receptionist pushed a button to open the glass doors and waved Everett through.

Twelve was not a particularly high floor in this building, which probably meant that Delta Sierra was only a middling financial player. Everett didn't know whether that might gain him some advantage, but he'd keep it in mind.

The hallway was long and quiet, with photos of scenic San Francisco on the walls and commercial-grade beige carpet muffling his footsteps. He passed office suites for three finance-related companies, an insurance company, and something called World Ramen Enterprises. Delta Sierra was at the very end, behind frosted glass doors that opened at his touch.

The receptionist here was female and blonde, but she clearly came from the same mold as her compatriot downstairs. Attractive and carefully groomed, she showed a generic smile and no genuine emotion.

"Welcome, Mr. Vaughn. Please have a seat. Mr. Schmidt will be with you shortly."

There were a half-dozen chairs in the waiting area, together with a low table full of magazines that looked excruciatingly boring and a tinkling fountain that made him wish he'd stopped at a bathroom. Everything was in shades of white and soft gray, and the air carried both a wafting scent of fake lavender and jazz playing very faintly through a sound system. After Everett sat, he discovered that the chair was carefully designed to make sure you weren't too comfortable. Its back was at an angle almost guaranteed to give him an ache, and if he relaxed too much, he'd be at risk of sliding forward onto the floor.

He sat there for what felt like a long time, the receptionist studiously avoiding eye contact. Three times people entered the suite, greeted her, ignored him, and were buzzed through the door to the inner sanctum. Twice people left. Everett scrolled through nonsense on his phone, opened Instagram and almost checked Sam's feed, then quickly closed it again. He wished there was at least a window here, because there were probably some decent views. Not top-of-the-skyscraper panoramas, but something. His Chicago office had been on the fifteenth floor, and some of the senior partners had partial lake views. Everett's office had faced an exceptionally boring steel-and-glass building with opaque windows.

Just as Everett was about to reopen Instagram, a text message came through. His heart did an inexplicable little jog when he saw who'd sent it: Cole McBeth. The text was only two words long: *Call me.*

"Mr. Vaughn?"

Everett startled sharply and nearly dropped his phone, but the receptionist didn't show any surprise.

"He's ready to see you," she said.

Everett stood, tucked the phone away, and was buzzed through the door.

He found himself in another corridor, with a glass-walled conference room straight ahead and offices lining the hallway on either side. Most of the doors were closed, but he could faintly hear conversations coming from behind a few. Schmidt stood in his doorway at the far end left, looking impatient. He stood back so Everett could enter and then quickly shut the door.

Sure enough, this room had a sliver of bay view. The rest of the office had sleek, expensive-looking furnishings. Its walls held framed golf paraphernalia and signed photos of golfers. Schmidt was in some of them, grinning next to men who wore polo shirts and logoed caps. If Schmidt had any family, there was no sign of them anywhere. He pointed impatiently at a guest chair before collapsing into his own. "Who are you and what's this about?"

Right. Straight to the point. He didn't seem to recognize Everett from their brief encounter on the road near the cemetery. That tracked with Everett's expectation; people like Schmidt tended to ignore guys who looked like laborers.

"This is about Blake Cannon," Everett said, taking a seat. He watched carefully for any reaction on Schmidt's part and saw annoyance, perhaps tinged with disgust.

"You can tell him that I haven't changed my mind and I won't."

That wasn't what Everett had expected. "I can't tell him anything unless you want to hold a séance."

Now Schmidt frowned in confusion. "What the hell does that mean?"

"Cannon's dead."

"Dead?" If Schmidt was pretending surprise, he was an excellent actor. "What the fuck?"

"Murdered."

For a moment, Schmidt simply blinked at him. He certainly didn't look grief-stricken, and Everett almost felt sorry for Cannon. Yes, he'd been an ass, but no one—not a single person that Everett had spoken with—had shown any sadness about what had happened to him. Not even his wife. Everett might not be the most popular guy in the world, but if he dropped dead right now, at least a few people would genuinely grieve, and quite a few others would feel sort of bummed out.

"How did it happen?" Schmidt finally asked.

Everett sidestepped the question but stated what he was sure of. "Cops haven't yet made an arrest."

"Huh. And you're here because?"

Time to... prevaricate a tiny bit. "I'm an attorney representing one of Deadman Gulch's businesses. My client had some interactions with Mr. Cannon prior to his demise and is interested in learning more about his recent circumstances." A few words of that sentence were absolutely true; Everett was proud of that. In fact, when Charlotte and Jessica had begun the preparations for Pages & Pastries, he'd helped out with some of the paperwork, so it wasn't even a huge stretch to say that he represented them.

Although Schmidt was sour-faced, he didn't kick Everett out. "What do you want to know?"

"Just a few details about your relationship with the deceased."

"There was no relationship," Schmidt spat.

"But you met with him recently in Deadman Gulch."

Schmidt exhaled loudly through his nose and leaned back in his chair. "Cannon sweet-talked me into driving way the hell into the middle of nowhere so he could show me plans for a resort. You know about the resort?"

Everett nodded.

"Well, it was a shitty idea. Never gonna fly out there in Bumpkin Central."

Surprisingly, Everett was offended on behalf of the entire citizenry of Gulch. He kept his face neutral, however. "My understanding is that he intended to attract wealthy guests from the Bay Area and Southern California."

"So he said. But why the hell would anyone in their right mind go there when there's Napa, Sonoma, Santa Barbara? Anyway, even if the demand was there, Cannon couldn't have pulled the place off."

"Why not?"

Schmidt tapped a blunt finger on the desk while he thought, and a few moments passed before he answered. "He was a goddamn mess. He had nothing of value and was swapping things around to hide that. Robbing Peter to pay Paul. What little capital he did have wasn't really his—it was his wife's, and I got the feeling that she wasn't on board. And even if I had come in like a fairy godmother and financed the whole shebang, I'd never see any return. His entire proposal relied on winemaking, but he didn't have access to any grapes."

This was a lot of very useful information. "No grapes? You sure about that?"

"Oh, he claimed he did. But when I asked to see the contracts, he couldn't show me a goddamned thing. I'm not stupid, Vaughn. I've been in this business for a while. Don't show me a turd and tell me it's chocolate."

Everett thought for a moment. "Wouldn't you have known that the concept and finances were shaky without going to Gulch? Why did you bother?"

More finger tapping. "I had an inkling. But the bastard sweet-talked me. And because wine's not really my thing, I thought it was possible I was missing something. You know, once in a blue moon, a project that looks like a stinker on paper turns out to be more promising when you take a closer look." He scowled. "This project was not one of those unicorns."

Although Everett wanted to get up and pace, he remained in the chair, which wasn't any more comfortable than the ones in the reception area. "So... to clarify. Cannon gave you a song and dance, you agreed to come up to Gulch for a couple of nights to see the lay of the land. You weren't impressed—"

"Nobody would be. Why anyone lives in a shithole like that, I'll never understand, and I know that nobody with money is going there on vacation."

Gulch was not a shithole. It wasn't as sophisticated as some places, true, but it had charm. The locals were colorful, the history was interesting, and the scenery was beautiful. Dammit, Everett liked the place. Which maybe shouldn't have surprised him, considering that his sister had voluntarily made it her home for over two decades. But it *did* surprise him, and it was something he was going to have to ponder.

But Schmidt was still talking. "The property itself isn't bad. You could put a nice golf course there, if you got rid of all those trees. But in that location, you'd just hemorrhage money, and I'm in business to make money."

"Okay, you hated it. You hated Cannon's proposal, and honestly, it doesn't sound as if you were a big fan of Cannon either. You declined to fund him. You had a fight, and—"

"Whoa!" Schmidt put up a hand. "We didn't fight. I'd already wasted enough energy on him. I told him no. He asked me to reconsider. He promised me that he'd get his hands on good wine pronto. I told him I didn't care. I got in my car and got the hell out of there. I never heard from him again."

It was hard to hear from someone who was dead. "What time did you leave Deadman Gulch?"

"I dunno. Two-thirty, maybe three. I was back in the city in time for a decent dinner." Schmidt narrowed his eyes. "Why?"

"Cannon was killed that night or early the next morning."

"When I left him, he was alive."

If Cole investigated, he could probably dig around some more. Maybe Schmidt stopped to gas up his car on the way home, and there'd be receipts and camera footage from that. There would definitely be a record of when he crossed the Bay Bridge; now that the human tolltakers were gone, the state tracked license plates. Everett knew this from the couple of weeks he'd spent in San Francisco. It was also possible that there were witnesses to Schmidt's departure from Gulch as well as his arrival in the Bay Area. But Everett didn't have access to any of that information.

He sighed. "Did you at least drink some good wine while you were there?"

"I guess. I stopped in at a couple of the tasting rooms. Cannon served me a glass of sangiovese that he claimed was pretty good. Like I said, wine's not my thing. I prefer a nice whiskey. But he said it would give a good indication of what he planned to pour at the resort. It wasn't his, of course, and his prospects for producing anything in a reasonable time were zilch, although he claimed otherwise."

"Sangiovese?" Excitement sparked inside Everett, making his heart race. He knew this nugget of information was important. Somehow. "Whose label was it?"

"Dunno. He'd torn it off the bottle. So I'd be objective, he said. What an idiot."

Well, crap. Maybe it didn't even matter, but Everett sure wished he knew whose wine that was. He sat in the miserable chair, trying to formulate his next questions.

Schmidt stood. "Look, I'm a busy man. I don't know what you're after, but I can't help you."

Everett stood too. "One final question. Do you have any theories about who might have murdered Blake Cannon?"

"How the hell should I know?" Schmidt spread his hands. "Cannon was a loser. Probably pissed off a lot of people. Not to mention he was surrounded by uncivilized yahoos. Maybe one of them mistook him for a bear."

Everett had had enough. "The violent crime rate in Milagro County is considerably lower than in most urban areas, including San Francisco." He didn't actually know if this was true, but probably neither did Schmidt. "Many of the locals are well educated, the stores and restaurants don't price-gouge, and you can walk down the street without getting run over by a bus. The sidewalks are clean. Food is unpretentious and good. You can sleep at night. And you don't have to spend your days surrounded by pompous dicks in suits!"

Oops—he was yelling now. He hadn't intended to, and Schmidt looked furious.

"You unprofessional twit!" Schmidt sputtered. "I could have you disbarred."

"Good luck with that." Everett strutted out of the office. He was still laughing when he reached the sidewalk.

Prior to heading up to Schmidt's office, Everett had assumed that he'd stick around afterward for lunch. The Ferry Building was nearby, and although there was no farmer's market there today—he'd memorized the schedule during his recent stay—there were plenty of fancy food vendors with permanent spots inside. He'd been considering picking up some nice cheese, an assortment of mushrooms, a couple of sausages.... But now, with the buffeting noise and car exhaust, he found himself eager to get back home.

Home. Deadman Gulch was sort of feeling that way.

He'd already buckled himself inside Janet when he remembered the text from Cole. As instructed, Everett called him.

Cole picked up immediately. "Where are you?"

"Oh, hello, Sergeant McBeth. Yes, I'm having a lovely day and I feel well. How about you?"

Cole's sigh was clearly audible. "I don't have time for this. Where are you?"

For the third time today, Everett's heart sped. "What's wrong? Is Charlotte okay?" He pictured her buried under a collapsed bookshelf, which would be his fault for improperly building it. Or she might have choked on a chocolate chip cookie, which would be partially Jessica's fault for not chopping the chocolate finely enough. Unless Xochi baked that batch; then she would be responsible. Or Charlotte could have been heading down to the basement for some reason, and she could have tripped over Warren on the stairs, and then—

"She's fine. Where are you?" That came out as a credible growl.

Everett let out a breath. "I'm in San Francisco. And I'm not escaping my zone of containment—I'm just here for a couple of hours. In fact, I'm about to head back to Gulch. Why?"

"Do I want to know why you're in San Francisco?"

"Probably not. Cole, what—"

"Cannon's house has been burglarized."

CHAPTER TWENTY-SEVEN

"Well, I didn't do it." That was Everett's first response to the news.

"I don't know that to be true."

Although Everett was aware that Cole couldn't see him, he rolled his eyes anyway. "Do you want me to drive back really fast so you can slap handcuffs on me?"

There was a long silence and then Cole cleared his throat. "When were you at Cannon's house last?"

"All day Saturday and then yesterday until two. Then I texted Izzy, told her I wouldn't be doing any more work for her, and left."

"And I assume you have proof that you've been in San Francisco today?"

"Bridge toll," Everett replied promptly, remembering his ruminations about potential alibis for Schmidt. "And a receipt for breakfast. But how do you know the burglary happened today?" He realized he was undercutting his own alibi by asking this, but he was curious.

"Ms. Kincaid arrived at the house yesterday evening and spent the night there. Early this morning she went to a yoga session. When she returned, the place had been tossed."

"If I had wanted to steal stuff from there, I would have had a couple of days to do it. I wouldn't have made a mess."

"Unless you wanted to make it look like someone else had done it."

It was hard to tell over the phone, but Cole sounded a bit amused. He was probably wearing that smug grin. Well, at least that meant he probably didn't truly suspect Everett. Again.

"Still no functional security cameras, I take it?"

Cole snorted. "Nope."

"You know what?" said Everett. "You are welcome to search my house for whatever was stolen. And when I get back, you can search my truck. Although I guess I'd have plenty of opportunity before then to dump the loot if I had it with me. Which I don't," he added hastily.

"That's very generous of you—the consent to search, not the hypothetical dumping—but we don't know what was taken. In fact, once I've confirmed your alibi, I might ask you to see if you can tell what's missing. You're likely more familiar with the house's contents than Ms. Kincaid is."

This was interesting, and now Everett was especially eager to get back. But his old truck lacked Bluetooth, which meant he had to hold his phone to have this conversation. And he wasn't about to illegally use a phone while driving—especially through a busy urban area—when a cop was on the other end. So he didn't turn on the engine yet.

"I guess I could do that. I haven't opened drawers and closets and stuff. Didn't you guys do some of that when you were investigating the murder?"

"Some."

Thinking, Everett used his free hand to tap a tune on the steering wheel. "Maybe the burglar was someone who knew about the murder, assumed the house was vacant now, and figured it was a good time to come in and take stuff."

"Except the dog was there."

"Oh." Everett had forgotten about Bella. "She's not much of a guard dog, huh?"

"That dog was probably thrilled to show the burglar around the place. Look, just let me know when you're back in town, okay? In case I have more questions."

"I'm leaving now. Should be back by dinnertime."

"You gonna invite yourself over and then criticize my cooking again?"

"I didn't!" Everett's protest came out as a yelp. "Your cooking was fine. I just thought that if Sophie had a little inspiration, she might try making some meals too." Then he had an idea. Possibly a bad one, but oh well. "Come over to my place. I'll cook this time, and it'll be your turn to offer helpful hints. You can search the joint while you're at it."

He wasn't sure why he was making this offer, but it was too late to retract it. Something about Cole McBeth made him say stupid things.

"I have no helpful hints about cooking," Cole said. "Can I just criticize instead?"

"Be my guest. Literally." Everett silently told his heart that it had done enough already today, thank you very much. It didn't need to speed up just because an annoying cop was coming to dinner.

Cole chuckled. "I'll see you when you're back in town." And then he ended the call.

Maneuvering out of the city took all of Everett's concentration. But by the time he was over the bridge and past Oakland—when traffic lightened and the route simplified—his mind had a chance to wander.

The first thing he considered was what to make for dinner. Even though it wasn't the most important matter in his life right now, it was the most pressing. He wouldn't have time to prepare anything complicated. But he had a couple of good steaks in the fridge, and it wouldn't take long to roast the butternut squash he'd picked up during his last grocery trip. He could whip up some flatbreads too, add a nice salad....

A Lexus cut abruptly into Everett's lane, making him stomp on the brake and swear, but at least he avoided a collision. He patted the dashboard. "Not today, Janet dear, not today."

Should he serve wine with dinner? He had a couple of bottles from Granocchio at home, but he wasn't confident in what to serve with steak. Red wine, right? Yeah, probably red. But which red? McBeth clearly knew wine and would say something—or maybe just make that face—if Everett got it wrong. On the other hand, maybe that wasn't such a bad thing; it would make them sort of even after Everett's critique of the spaghetti. But Cole said he didn't drink often. Would this be an exception? Or—

"It's not a date," Everett reminded himself sternly. It was a search and interrogation... with food.

He needed to think about something else. Like the burglary.

Someone had gone into Cannon's house to steal things. Or... to search for something. They'd done that even with the knowledge that someone was staying there, which implied that they wanted something right now. Otherwise they could have waited until Izzy left town again. But presumably, they'd known that she wasn't home at the time. If they knew her, they might have seen her head to yoga class. But Everett had the impression that Izzy hadn't spent much time in Gulch, so how many locals would recognize her? And would this person also be aware that Bella wasn't a threat?

That was a lot of unknowns right there.

Of course the biggest question was whether the burglary was related to the murder. Maybe even committed by the same person. If that were the case, then the key was to figure out what they were trying to steal. Except if the murderer wanted something, why didn't they take it right after killing Cannon? Or why didn't they come back for it anytime since, when the house was usually unoccupied?

"Because maybe they didn't know the thing was there until just now," Everett said out loud. Maybe they realized that they'd left a crucial piece of evidence behind—something that might not have been found during the search right after the murder but that would eventually turn up.

Everett hit the steering wheel. "An affair!" Cannon, whose divorce hadn't yet gone through, was having a fling with a local. "Cannon and his lover go down to the basement to grab a bottle. They argue over something. The lover hits him with a bottle and then runs. And then just recently she—or he; let's not make assumptions—remembers that they left something behind and goes back to get it before it can tie them to the scene. Underwear? Jewelry? Love letters?"

He was definitely going to propose this theory to Cole. It might actually make up for serving the wrong variety of wine.

CHAPTER TWENTY-EIGHT

"Blake Cannon was not having an affair." Cole McBeth had a fork in one hand, a steak knife in the other, and exasperation in his eyes.

"How do you know that? His marriage was rocky at best, and men like that... you can't trust them about anything."

Cole gave Everett a long look. "Like your ex?"

"No! Sam is nothing like him and never cheated on me. Sam's pretty great, actually. We just didn't fit well anymore." Defending Sam was not how Everett had intended this conversation to go, but it would have been unfair to let Cole think badly of him.

"How long were you married?"

"Ten years. Is this part of your interrogation?"

"Nope. Just curious." Cole speared some pieces of squash and popped them into his mouth. It was his second helping.

"Well, there's nothing nefarious about Sam and nothing suspicious about our divorce. Sometimes it's just better if people go their separate ways."

Cole sighed and swallowed. "Yeah, I know what that's like."

Everett had been so wrapped up in everything else, he'd forgotten that Cole was also divorced. "It must be hard, being a single parent."

"Sometimes, sure. It's probably rough on Sophie sometimes too. She has to endure my cooking, for one thing. But we have a lot of family around here, and they've always stepped up when we needed them. And Sophie, well, she's pretty special. Best thing that ever happened to me."

Hopefully, Everett's little stab of envy didn't show on his face. Anyway, they were supposed to be talking about Cannon's personal life, not Cole's or Everett's. "Why are you so sure Cannon wasn't having an affair?"

"Zero evidence of it. It's also really hard to keep a secret like that in this town. Everywhere you walk or drive, people see you. The hills have eyes, Everett."

The joke was so unexpected that Everett nearly choked on a piece of steak and had to wash it down with some water. Eyes sparkling with humor, Cole waited for him to recover while taking a sip from his own glass. He'd declined wine even though he wasn't technically on duty. Which had saved Everett the risk of being grape-shamed, at least. In solidarity, Everett had stuck with water too.

"Okay, I'll concede that Gulch is one big gossip cauldron. But still, it's not absolutely outside the bounds of possibility that he and someone else managed to hide an affair from all of you."

"Did you see any evidence of it in his house?"

Everett wasn't sure what such evidence would look like. Panties strewn around? Cutesy gifts? After thinking for a moment, he shook his head. "He had a wedding picture up in the bedroom," he admitted.

"Uh-huh. Anyway, the burglar didn't appear to mess with anything in the bedroom. But all the drawers were open in the room Cannon was using as a home office, and the kitchen was a mess. In my estimation, the burglar was looking for something specific. Something small. Could be jewelry or cash, I suppose, maybe some paperwork, or tokens of a torrid love affair." Cole pointed a fork at him. "Do *you* have any notion of what the burglar was after?"

"Sorry. Like I said, I didn't poke around that way, either before or after the murder. I was there to fix stuff, and I do have some morals." Also, he hadn't had any reason to suspect the drawers might contain anything particularly interesting or pertinent to the murder.

Cole didn't look overly devastated at Everett's failure to contribute to his investigation. In fact, he cut off another bite of steak and ate it with a little moan of appreciation. "Man, this is good. What did you do to make it so delicious?"

"I know my meat."

Cole raised his eyebrows, and when Everett realized his own accidental double entendre, he blushed. Which in itself was embarrassing enough to make his face redden even more, because Everett never blushed. He was a lawyer, after all!

"I mean," Everett said in an attempt to redeem himself, "I'm from Chicago. Hog butcher to the world. Um, and I guess cow butcher too? Anyway, we like our meat." That hadn't helped one bit, but he couldn't shut up. "I didn't have money for decent meat when I was a kid, but when I started earning a good income, I learned how to choose good cuts and prepare them well."

Mouth quirked in a half smile, Cole nodded. "I like to barbecue. Most of the secret there is in the sauce, though, and I have my family recipe for that. The McBeths manage ranches as well as vineyards."

"So you're a cowboy?"

Cole snorted. "No. I'm a deputy sheriff, remember?"

Right. And he was here because he was investigating a crime. Two crimes. Everett needed to keep that in mind.

"Can you tell me if you're close to solving this?" Everett asked.

"I've got a couple working theories. But I can't just jump in half-cocked, you know. Gotta get all my ducks in a row before I even think of makin' an arrest, or else some fancy lawyer gets involved and the whole case gets thrown out of court."

"You have to watch out for those lawyers."

"You certainly do." Cole had an odd expression, one that Everett couldn't read.

The rest of the mealtime conversation was about some of the things Everett missed about Chicago—which were surprisingly few, once he thought about it—and some of Cole's experiences growing up in a small, rural town. He talked about Sophie too, and was clearly bursting with pride over her even if she was currently slipping into some of the quirks common to teens.

When dinner was over, Cole didn't seem in a hurry to leave and even helped with the dishes. Which might have been a pointed comment about Everett's rude behavior when Cole had fed him, but Everett was happy for the help. And honestly, for the company. He hadn't realized it, but he'd missed having someone to talk to during mundane chores.

Afterward Everett filled a couple of bowls with maple praline ice cream from Dairy Heaven, and they went out to the pair of old wooden chairs on the little front porch. It was almost too stereotypical of country life to be true: crickets chirping, breeze lightly blowing, stars shining.

"Oh, give me a break," said Everett.

"What?"

Everett pointed at the street with his spoon. "Deer. There are three deer just strolling past." The creatures were perfectly quiet, their eyes reflecting a distant streetlight.

"You have something against them?"

"No, they're fine, I guess. I mean, Bambi and all that. It's just too damn perfectly bucolic."

"I like bucolic." Cole ate a couple bites of ice cream. With the porch light off, it was hard to see his expression, but he seemed comfortable.

For a long time they both sat there, eating, not talking, but it didn't feel awkward. It was pleasant to listen to the night noises—was that an owl calling?—and just be for a while. Even with a cop who Everett barely knew and who might still suspect him of crimes.

Finally, Cole groaned a little and stood. "I should go. Gotta make sure Sophie's homework is done and that she scrounged something to eat."

Everett winced. "Sorry—I should have said she was welcome too."

"That's real nice of you. But I think we'd have bored her to death."

After getting to his feet, Everett took Cole's bowl. "Well, good luck with the burglar. And the murderer. Who are probably the same person."

"Thanks for the insight," Cole said drily. Then he added with more sincerity, "But really, thanks for dinner. It was really good."

Instead of going back inside right away, Everett remained on the porch, watching as Cole walked down the sidewalk and disappeared into the darkness.

CHAPTER TWENTY-NINE

Tuesday morning dawned crisp and bright, and although the temperatures were predicted to warm up later, the trees seemed to have suddenly decided that autumn had arrived. Everett's stroll to Main Street was gloriously lined in vivid shades of crimson, saffron, and orange. He thought that he might like to learn to identify local tree species. Except he was going to move on in five months, so what would be the point?

At Rising Times, Xochi handed him an Americano and a pumpkin cream-cheese muffin, which he felt was a good way to fuel his upcoming project. He was her only customer at the moment and she was in an especially chatty mood, so he got the low-down on Marian Fisker's fender-bender in the grocery store parking lot, and Xochi's grandfather's scratch-off lottery win of a hundred dollars. "Oh, and you will not believe who came in here yesterday morning."

He couldn't even hazard a guess. "Who?"

"Junior Lum! He hasn't been here in, like, two years. He had one of his dogs with him—Lulubelle. I'm really not supposed to allow anything but service animals in the shop, but she's super sweet and he didn't want to leave her outside alone, so I broke the law. You won't tell Sergeant McBeth, will you?" She dimpled at him.

"Why would I...." Flustered, he stopped. "Your secret is safe with me."

"Thanks. Junior was super worried about her 'cause she has a lump or something, so he stopped by here while he was waiting for the vet to open. I hope she's okay."

Oh yeah, the vet. Everett needed to make an appointment for Warren. He pulled out his phone and set a reminder for later in the day. Then he looked back at Xochi. "Do you ever take a day off? I think I've seen you here every day of the week."

"You're sick of me already?" She affected faux sorrow.

"Never! You are a delightful way to begin my mornings. I just thought you must get really tired of working."

Xochi shook her head. "Nope. I love this place. When I was a little girl, I dreamed of owning a bakery. Weird, right? And when I grew up, I was lucky enough to have family members who helped that dream come true. I know that as careers go, it's not earthshaking. I'm not gonna change the world. But people come in and I make their day a little sweeter, and I figure that's a pretty good accomplishment."

He smiled at her. "It is."

Everett thought about Xochi's words as he walked to Judge Tosto's house. Bringing a taste of happiness to people was indeed a stellar achievement. Something that attorneys rarely managed. Sure, the world needed lawyers, and good ones could make lives a lot easier. But it was rare for anyone to be joyous over what their lawyers accomplished. The best that could be hoped for, generally, was a feeling of relief. And corporate clients didn't even feel that, considering that corporations were not people—contrary to a certain U.S. Supreme Court ruling—and couldn't feel anything.

He had a minor epiphany. What he needed was a job that not only paid the bills and satisfied his soul but that also made others happy. Like cooking... although he didn't want to be a chef. Too stressful. Fixing things could fit the bill. Cannon hadn't been appreciative, but Gary and Tom had. When Everett repaired their leak, he'd felt like a hero. Charlotte had also let him know how grateful she was for his contributions to her shop.

It was an intriguing line of thought.

But now he'd arrived at the Tosto residence where, sure enough, a deer was grazing on the shrubbery. It gave Everett a reproachful look, like a diner in a fine establishment being interrupted by a grubby peasant. "You could save me some work and just eat the whole thing," Everett said.

The deer took a few more bites and then walked elegantly up the road, probably on the way to complain to the manager.

Getting to the shed on the side of the house involved some stomping through the overgrowth, and Everett wondered, belatedly, whether he should be worried about poison ivy. Poison oak? Poison sumac? He really needed to learn about toxic plants. But it was too late now, so he pushed through. The shed was unlocked, as promised, the interior an arachnid paradise that made him wonder about venomous invertebrates. He noted that there were plenty of tools, and that they appeared to be in good shape. He pulled out loppers, hedge shears, and pruners and got to work.

Ninety minutes later, sweaty and already a little sore, he surveyed his progress. The area immediately around the walkway to the porch was cleared, as was a trail to the shed. As instructed by Judge Tosto, he piled all the debris behind the house in what was going to be the mother of all compost piles. Suitably sized branches would go into a wood chipper. He'd have to look into renting one... but maybe not while he was still a homicide suspect.

Everett was stretching his back and deciding what to tackle next when Ron Tosto appeared and handed him a thermos of water. "Figures that you didn't come prepared to properly hydrate," Ron said while Everett guzzled. "Kids today have no sense at all."

"I'm in my forties."

"I have shoes older than you."

Everett wiped his forehead with the grubby back of his hand. "Did you like being a judge?"

"Some days I liked it a lot. Some days it made me miserable. The good days outnumbered the bad." He got a distant look in his eyes. "My daughter wanted to be a lawyer. There weren't too many women in it back then, but she did well for herself. In fact, she became a judge too, down in Fresno. Then her oldest son decided he wanted to be a train mechanic, and she near about had a meltdown. She's a fine person, smart as a whip, but she's also a damned snob."

"What happened?"

The corners of Ron's lips twitched. "I had the good sense to keep out of it, but Doris stepped in. She told our daughter that our grandson had chosen a good career that suited him. And, more importantly, that there's pride to be found in any job done contentedly and done well. Nowadays that boy lives in Nebraska, of all places, but he's happy as can be."

"I'm glad," Everett said honestly.

"Look. I know I'm ancient, but I don't feel that way. My life has flown by. All human lives do. I reckon there's no use spending those short years in misery if we don't have to. And no use letting other's expectations guide our decisions."

He clapped Everett's shoulder with surprising strength. "That's more than enough sagacious wisdom for one day. I think I need a nap to recover from it all. Just come inside the house when you need to refill that thermos." He made his way up the porch steps and into the house, slow but straight-backed.

<hr>

Everett was a brave explorer, hacking his way through unmapped terrain in search of lost treasure and— Wait. That fantasy smacked a little too much of colonialism. Okay, Everett was a brave explorer on another planet that happened to have the exact same gravity and atmospheric conditions as Earth and that contained no sentient species. He was hacking his way through unmapped terrain in search of a special plant that, brought back to Earth, would both cure cancer and give drivers the uncontrollable urge to use their turn signals properly.

He wrestled with a pernicious knot of alien plants that looked remarkably like thistles—and poked like them too. Maybe it was time to take a break and have some lunch or—

"Everett Vaughn!"

He spun around so fast that he almost fell. Jo Rossi, the reporter, stood on the road at the edge of the Tosto property, waving broadly. As if he could possibly miss seeing her.

"Yeah?" he shouted back.

"Can I have a few words with you?"

He gestured at the still-wild yard. "I'm working."

"Won't take more than a minute or two."

He doubted that, but with a resigned sigh, he made his way over to her.

She gave a wary look at the hoe clutched in his hand, but then she seemed to gather her courage. "Is Cole McBeth narrowing in on a suspect yet? When does he expect to make an arrest?"

He blinked at her. "How the hell should I know? Why don't you ask him?"

"I did, but he has no comment. And I thought he might have let something slip. Over dinner last night."

Jesus. There really were no secrets in Deadman Gulch. "Was this the latest headline in the Milagro Daily Dispatch? Deputy Sheriff Eats Food with Bookshop Owner's Brother? Very exciting."

"Eats food for the second time, from what I hear."

For a moment, Everett seriously considered hinting that he and Cole were having clandestine trysts. That would be kind of funny. It would certainly annoy Cole. Wouldn't it?

Everett pushed the thought away. "He needed some info for his investigation and it was dinnertime. He most definitely isn't letting me in on his secrets, so I have nothing to share."

"Nothing at all?" She lifted her eyebrows.

"You need something to write about? How about a piece on how much Rising Times brightens everyone's day? Or Bret Faud's literary efforts?"

"Neither of those are news."

He huffed. "How about something on Miracle Creek Campground? It's a really nice piece of property. Carol Allen has some great photos of the place in the olden days. It's also not news, but it's locally relevant, and you can tie it in to Blake Cannon if you want."

For a moment he thought she might agree, but then she frowned and crossed her arms. "I don't need you to pitch story ideas to me. I came to you for info on the Cannon case."

"Can't help you."

Eyes narrowed, she took a step closer. "You're hiding something. Is it something in your past?"

"Okay. A, my past is pretty damn boring. B, nothing about my past has any relevance to the Cannon case. And C, it's none of your business anyway. So if you'll excuse me, I have weeds to clear."

He started to turn away, but she grabbed his wrist with surprising strength. "Gulch is my home. I care about it. I don't like the idea of a killer just running around."

"Well, I'm not too thrilled about it either, but—"

"Jo Rossi, are you harassing my employee?" Ron stood on the porch looking stern, despite the fact that he was wearing a Spiderman T-shirt and Bermuda shorts. He held a coffee mug in one hand.

Jo let go of Everett and took a couple of steps back. "I just have a few questions for him."

"I don't think he wants to answer. And in any case, Mr. Vaughn is currently on the clock for me, and I'm not paying him to chitchat with the press. Scram, Jo."

Her scowl deepened, and her shoulders sagged in defeat. "Fine. We can discuss this later, Everett."

"There is literally nothing to discuss."

He leaned on the hoe handle and watched her drive away before he turned back to Ron. "Thanks. She's persistent."

"Journalists have to be, I suppose. And she's a pretty good one. But she doesn't often have a murder land in her lap, and I'm sure that's a big deal." He rubbed his cheek thoughtfully. "Fifteen years ago, when I was still on the bench, she played a major part in uncovering a local scam artist named Digger Beltz."

"Digger?"

"Colorful, yes? He ran an auto repair shop on Gold Run Road. Folks would come in—especially old folks—and he'd pretend to do work on their cars but actually didn't. Sometimes he'd deliberately break things and then overcharge to fix them. Jo found out about it somehow and raised a fuss in the paper until the sheriff—not the current one—did something about it. Turned out Digger was also committing auto insurance fraud and a number of other dastardly deeds. I sentenced him to over ten years. Dunno what happened after he was released. He never returned to Gulch. Also dunno how many more victims he would've bilked if not for Jo."

"Hmm." Something in that little story started the gears turning in Everett's brain, but he couldn't latch onto what that something was. It was irritating, like having a popcorn hull stuck in your teeth. "You must have felt pretty good about locking him away."

"I was never happy about sending someone to prison. I was glad Digger wouldn't be stealing from anyone else, but prison... means we're giving up on someone, and I hate to do that. Always wished there was another way." He shrugged. "And now I'm the one helping you shirk." He raised his mug in a sort of salute and went back inside.

Everett returned to his thistles. It was natural that his mind remained on Digger, especially because Everett himself was digging at the moment. He wondered what had led the man to cheat his neighbors. Maybe simple greed, maybe he did drugs or drank too much. Everett knew from his own father how addiction could possess a good person and lead them to do rotten things. In fact, Dad had committed minor acts of fraud too, such as the time he—

Wait. Fraud. That was the word that had jogged Everett's mind. His subconscious had been putting a puzzle together, it seemed, and had only now decided to let Everett's conscious self see the picture. Well, part of it, anyway.

Had Blake Cannon been committing fraud? Not just moving money around creatively and failing to pay what he owed, but something more specific, related to wine. Something that might anger certain locals, if they found out about it.

Everett remembered how Cannon used to walk around town with a Peet's cup, but the coffee itself almost certainly came from the cheap pods he kept in his kitchen. And why did he do that? In an attempt to impress people. To make them think he was drinking something more prestigious—in his estimation, at least—than it actually was.

"Holy crap," Everett said to a nearby squirrel. "I think I know what he was up to, and I think that's what got him killed."

CHAPTER THIRTY

What Everett should have done was go straight to Cole with his theory and urge him to take action.

Obviously.

But Everett knew what would happen if he did that. Cole would listen to him and then, unbearably handsome and unbearably smug, would remind him that Cole was the cop, not Everett. And also that Cole knew way more about wine than Everett. Heck, Cole's thirteen-year-old kid knew more about wine. And then Cole would continue whatever investigative leads he was following, probably all in the wrong direction.

Sitting at his kitchen table that evening, every muscle reminding him that he was no longer youthful, Everett considered his other options. His yellow pad lay in front of him, the top page somewhat the worse for wear and covered in scribbles even he couldn't decipher. Three things were circled.

The first was a name, Junior Lum, who at one point had been Everett's favorite suspect. He still couldn't be ruled out, especially after conveniently making a rare appearance in town the morning of the burglary. Cannon's plans for the former campground could have been sufficient motive. And Junior might have had access to Cannon's house due to the discussions over their land deal.

A second name was also circled: Paul Schmidt, the San Francisco investor. Like Junior, Schmidt potentially had both access and motive. He also had an alibi—or so he claimed. But Everett had no way to check that. And heck, maybe Schmidt had hired someone to do Cannon in.

The thing was, Everett couldn't come up with a reason for either man to commit the burglary. It was possible that the burglar and the murderer were not the same person. Maybe the two incidents had no connection at all, other than happening at Cannon's house. That didn't feel right, however.

Then there was the third circle, which instead of a name contained the words *wine person*. This was the most frustrating theory because, deep in his gut, he believed it to be the right one. But he was missing the piece that would allow him to put a specific name there. There were a lot of wine people in Milagro County—some of whom were McBeths.

"Argh!" Gently thunking his forehead on the table didn't help.

If he wasn't going to go to Cole with his theory, the most logical thing to do was to give up on his informal investigation. It wasn't his business. He should let the sheriffs do their job and he should concentrate instead on getting his own house in order. Like figuring out what he wanted to do with the rest of his life. Despite the extra cash he'd brought in lately, in five months he was going to be unemployed, broke, and homeless.

Maybe instead of spending a year playing nomad, he should have stayed in Chicago and spent the money on therapy. Now he couldn't afford it and didn't have insurance. Which meant he should probably stop pounding his head against the table before he got a concussion.

A therapist would likely tell him that his preoccupation with Cannon's case was Everett's way of avoiding his own issues. "You're absolutely correct," Everett told the imaginary shrink. "But is that so bad in the grand scheme of things? I could be doing something much more self-destructive. And at least I'm not harming anyone else."

He got up from the table, poured and drank a glass of water, and wandered. This house really needed some work. Nothing structural, at least as far as he could tell, but the appliances were old and not energy-efficient, the surfaces were dated and worn, and there were lots of little things that needed fixing. Dinged-up drawers. Baseboards that had been bashed with vacuum cleaners too many times. A toilet that occasionally flushed itself. Sagging gutters. Dry rot at the top of a couple of the porch pillars. Discolored window blinds with knotted cords. The creaky floor in—

No. He didn't own this house and certainly couldn't afford to spend money fixing it up.

Wandering near the master bathroom, he spied the clawfoot bathtub and saw that it needed refinishing. He wasn't going to do that. But he could take a bath, which he hadn't done in... years, probably. It might soothe his aches as well as getting rid of residual grime from the day's labors.

He turned on the faucet and waited for it to get hot enough, which took forever. If he owned this place he'd consider installing an on-demand water heater, especially since water conservation was a major issue in these parts. Hey, maybe he'd put in solar panels too. He refocused and realized he didn't have any bubble bath or anything else fancy to add, so he googled for substitutes and ended up squeezing in a healthy dose of shampoo. It foamed nicely.

Finally he got in the tub and leaned back, waiting for the magic of healing waters to solve all of his problems. Nothing of the kind happened. His brain kept circling around the Cannon murder like water going down the drain.

"Wish I could talk to Charlotte about this," he said morosely. She was smart and level-headed and gave good advice. But his nosing around the murder was clearly a sore spot for her, and he didn't want to aggravate that sore spot.

He used to be able to discuss dilemmas with Sam, who was a great listener.

Somehow his hand, although he hadn't willed it to, reached for the phone on the closed toilet lid. Then that traitorous appendage managed to call Sam, miraculously without dropping the phone into the tub. At least his stupid hand chose a conventional call instead of FaceTime.

Sam picked up immediately, voice tight with concern. "You all right?" Everett had rarely called even when they were married. He preferred to text.

"I'm fine. I was.... Are you with anyone? Am I interrupting anything? Is your boating instructor there?"

"He has a name. Josip. And I'm here alone. We've only been dating a few weeks—we're not ready to jump into anything."

Everett put the phone on speaker and set it down. "We did. We were a whirlwind."

"Are you okay, Ev? 'Cause you don't sound like it."

"I'm sober and of sound mind. I'm just feeling a little... at sea." He chuckled drily and splashed.

"Are you in a *boat*?" Sam sounded as if that would be the most unlikely thing in the world.

"Dry land. Still in Gulch. Currently in the bathtub because I spent the entire day taming a jungle and I feel like I've been run over by a CTA bus."

There was a short pause. "Only some of that made sense, but I'm glad to hear you're not literally off the deep end."

"Courtesy laugh. Hey, my brain is stuck on a problem—"

"Your brain is like a starving dog, worrying at things. Not one of those smart breeds like a border collie or a German shepherd, though. Something kind of yappy. You have a chihuahua brain, Ev."

"Thanks." It felt good to smile. "Can I talk you through my current issue, maybe get some neutral input from you?" Everett sighed. "You don't have to do this. You're no longer contractually required to listen to me."

"I'll consider it pro bono work. Hang on." There was a slight rustling, the sound of a can popping open, and then that particular groan-sigh Sam always made when sitting down at the end of a long day. "Okay. I got my Goose IPA. Hit me."

"You're a peach. Josip is lucky to have you. Okay, well, it started when I found a dead guy."

"You... what?"

Smiling, Everett launched into his story.

By the time he finished the account the bathwater had grown cold, so he'd extricated himself and put on his softest sweatpants and NSYNC T-shirt, brewed a cup of joint-relief tea—provided without comment by Ron Tosto this afternoon—and climbed into bed. He might be discussing a murder, but he felt cozy. At the other end of the conversation, in a high-rise alongside Lake Michigan, Sam had switched from IPA to home-brewed decaf. He asked a few questions along the way for clarification or background information, but mostly he listened.

When Everett finally reached the end of his tale, Sam was silent.

"Did I put you to sleep?" Everett asked after a few moments.

"Gathering thoughts. You couldn't just get a facelift, buy a sports car, and have a fling with someone far too young for you, huh?"

"Not my style. How old is Josip, by the way?"

Sam mumbled something that sounded a lot like twenty-three, but Everett didn't push the point because Sam was doing him a favor. Then Sam cleared his throat. "I'm not going to tell you to back away because I'm positive Charlotte already told you that. And because I'm equally positive you won't listen."

"Well-reasoned, counselor."

"Then give me a sec. Something.... I'm trying to remember. Hang on." A rapid clicking noise came over the phone line, followed by, "Aha! There he is."

Intrigued, Everett sat up straighter. "Who?"

"There was this Indonesian guy several years back. I saw a few minutes of a documentary about him. He moved to California and ended up committing hundreds of thousands of dollars in wine fraud. He was convicted, did some time in a federal pen, and got deported."

Fraud. Just as Everett had been thinking this afternoon. "Tell me more."

"Yes!" Sam always spoke quickly when he got excited about something. "He was selling all these extremely expensive wines, like ninety-year-old burgundy for, like, a hundred grand—who the hell pays a hundred grand for a bottle of wine?—but it turns out they were fake. He was filling bottles with cheap stuff and slapping on fake labels."

Everett gasped. "That's what I thought Cannon might be doing! Putting his labels on Wino Willie."

"Apparently it's a whole thing. French and Italian cops caught a fake wine ring last year. The crooks cleared two million euros before they were stopped."

Leave it to Cannon to copycat a crime. "I don't think he was trying to make millions. He was probably just trying to fool investors and future guests. His whole concept depended on producing wine, and that wasn't going to happen for several years. Or later, depending how long it took him to get access to grapes."

Back when Everett had been a lawyer, especially in his early years, he would sometimes start on a client's case with only the haziest idea of what was going on. Then he'd read through everything in the file and research his fingers to the bone. Eventually he'd reach a point where everything would just click, like snapping a final Lego piece into place, and he'd know exactly how to proceed. He'd generally do some additional research, just to make sure, but it had never been truly necessary.

That was what he felt right now. Click. As part of Cannon's half-assed and convoluted efforts to finance his pet project, he'd attempted a low-rent version of what that Indonesian guy had done. Only in Cannon's case, someone found out what was going on—most likely when they saw the wine cases in the basement—and they'd meted out their own form of justice. Poor Cannon ended up with a sentence a lot heavier than a few years behind bars.

"Ev? Are you there?"

"Sorry. Thinking."

"At least you're not running out into the night to track down the killer."

Everett made a face. "Not yet. I know why he was killed, and although my pool of suspects has shrunk, it's still pretty big. Lots of people around here are connected to the wine business." In fact, it wasn't necessarily a local. Even if Schmidt wasn't the culprit, it could have been another potential investor.

"How would he possibly have thought this would work?" Sam asked. "In the cases I told you about, people were collecting the wine but not drinking it. But your guy... wouldn't folks have figured out the fraud as soon as they took a sip?"

"Not necessarily." Everett thought for a moment. "The investor I spoke with didn't know much about wine. Maybe the others didn't either. I bet his target resort clientele were the type of people who value the names of upscale brands but are clueless about discerning true quality."

"Hmm. Those people couldn't tell the difference between cheap wine and expensive?" Sam usually drank beer or, when he was in a midcentury mood, a classic cocktail: a Tom Collins or Manhattan. In fact, the only wine Everett could remember seeing him drink was champagne, on the night they arrived in Paris for their honeymoon.

Everett smoothed the blanket over his lap. "I've been doing some tastings while I'm here and trying to learn a little. Sometimes I can pick out the flavor notes that I'm told are supposed to be there. I definitely prefer some wines to others. But if you handed me a glass of Wino Willie and told me it was something fancy, I'd believe you."

Not that it particularly mattered, but he wondered whether Cannon could tell wines apart. He was clearly the sort who believed that labels matter.

"What are you going to do, Ev?" Sam sounded worried.

"Nothing stupid. I'm going to poke around just a little more to see if I can figure out what the burglar was after. That should help point to their ID. Maybe I'll have a chat with Izzy Kincaid."

It took a while for Sam to respond. "Okay. Just be careful, Jessica Fletcher."

"Hey! I like to think of myself as more of a Holmes or Poirot. Or Philip Marlowe!" Maybe he should buy a fedora.

"Just don't be Inspector Clouseau."

Everett snort-laughed. "Thanks for your help, Sam. You're a good friend."

"This is the part where I stop myself from telling you how much I miss you. Good night, detective. Keep me posted, okay?"

"Will do. And tell Josip I said hi."

When the call ended, Everett didn't really know much more than before, but he felt emotionally steadier. As if he'd found some bedrock to stand on.

Energy levels refreshed, he decided that instead of turning in early, he'd do some planning for tomorrow's task. He sent a text to Gary and Tom: *Confirmed for tomorrow at 9? Any specific menu requests or avoidances?*

Gary answered swiftly. *Yes 9 please. We enjoyed everything you made last week so whatever you want to make is fine.*

Before Everett could respond, Tom chimed in. *We trust u darling.* A string of heart and smiley emojis followed.

Grinning, Everett got out of bed and padded into the kitchen. Time to research some recipes.

CHAPTER THIRTY-ONE

Despite last night's soak and a thorough application of CBD lotion, Everett's body still felt the effects of wrangling Ron Tosto's jungle. And he was going to have to clear the rest of the yard tomorrow. By the time he finished his Wednesday morning shower, he vowed that he would get serious about an exercise program.

"Running," he promised himself over toast and tea. Then it occurred to him that perhaps late October in the foothills wasn't the best time to take up that hobby. At this elevation, he'd been told, snow wasn't frequent, but rain was. Not to mention short days and poorly lit roads. Plus he hadn't quite surrendered to the whole concept of hills. And he'd never enjoyed jogging even in nice, flat Illinois.

"Okay, then. I'll haunt Craigslist for a used elliptical or stationary bike. And a set of weights." There was plenty of room for those things in the second bedroom, which currently housed only a few large plastic bins labeled *Xmas Stuff.* Heck, maybe he'd look into yoga classes after all.

It wasn't just that he wanted to feel good, although that was a major motive. He might also want to look good. Eventually. In case he decided to enter the dating market again.

Ugh, the mere idea made him want to crawl back into bed and not think about anything for a while.

Today, however, he had grocery shopping to do and meals to prep. He also wanted to stop by the bookshop and see whether everything was in good shape—and check on Warren. Even though it wasn't his cat, Everett was willing to concede that he shared some responsibility for him. And damn, he'd forgotten to make a vet appointment. Best to do it now.

"Sierra Pride. This is Beau. How can I help you?"

"Uh, hi. I'd like to make an appointment. For a cat."

"Of course. Will this be a new patient?" Beau had such a gorgeous tenor voice; he should be making a living as a radio announcer or voice actor. Maybe he already was. Maybe the vet clinic was only a side gig. Everett would have happily listened to him read a list of veterinary infectious diseases, including a description of all their horrifying symptoms.

"Sir? Are you still there?"

Everett pulled himself back to reality. "Sorry. Yes, he's a new patient."

"Great. Can you tell me why he needs to see the doctor?"

Bedtime stories. Beau should record bedtime stories. He'd be great at that. Tight budget or not, Everett would buy everything he narrated.

Focus, Vaughn.

"Um, a checkup. And vaccines? He should probably get his shots, I guess."

"He definitely should. And is he neutered? Aside from not fathering unwanted kittens—our shelters are always full of cats—a neutered male is less likely to get in fights, urine spray, or wander. Also they won't get testicular cancer. I know a lot of men are hesitant to have their pets castrated, but I assure you it won't detract one bit from your own masculinity."

Everett hated being lectured to, and he was also plenty secure in his masculinity. But he didn't mind any of that now because it was Beau of the magical voice saying it. Everett wondered what Beau looked like and how old he was. Not that it mattered. But he wondered anyway.

"He's already fixed. But yeah, he needs shots. Also, I hear he's been acting sort of weird, so maybe the vet can make sure he's not sick."

"Weird how?" Beau sounded just as sexy when he was concerned.

"I haven't seen it myself, actually. But my sister... she owns the new bookstore downtown, and Warren just sort of showed up, and now—"

"You're Charlotte Tabor's brother? Is this the orange cat I've seen in the window?"

Wow. Apparently Warren was locally famous. As was Charlotte, but Everett was used to that. "That's him."

"Cool. Let's see.... Dr. Hardesty has an opening tomorrow at ten."

Everett remembered Charlotte's warning. "Actually, I was hoping for Dr. Kelly."

Beau chuckled, and that was sexy too. "Gotcha. How about Monday at eight?"

"Sounds good."

"The cat's name is Warren, and you are...?"

Everett gave his name and phone number and would have been happy to chat longer, but Beau had an actual job to do. For that matter, so did Everett, who was already running a little late.

"I'll see you Monday." Everett figured that was a neutral enough thing to say, right? He didn't want to sound like a creep.

He sighed after he finished the call, the magical voice gone.

He sent a quick text to Charlotte, who'd reminded him about the vet the last couple of times he'd seen her: *Warren to doc Monday @8*.

Then, since his phone was in his hand anyway, he texted Cole.

Can we talk this afternoon or eve? I have some info re Cannon.

No need to be specific—better to let Cole wonder. Hopefully he'd be curious enough to respond.

Everett finished the last of his tea, barely lukewarm at this point, and spent a moment considering whether to stop at Rising Times. It would be cheaper and faster not to. And he didn't especially need one of Xochi's delicious calorie bombs. But yesterday he'd spied some mini apple tarts in the pastry case, and they'd looked really good. Besides fruit was healthy.

"Tomorrow," he told himself sternly. "To fortify you for the rest of the jungle."

He was tying his shoes when his phone buzzed. He didn't recognize the number and considered not answering, but the area code was local so he picked up.

"Everett? This is Carol Allen."

He entertained a momentary fantasy that she was calling to confess to the murder, but then he remembered that she was no longer on his short list. "Hi, Carol."

"The weekend after Thanksgiving we do a big antique and crafts fair at the community center. I'm on the planning committee. I know that's over a month away, but I do like to get things arranged early. Can we hire you to help with the setup and takedown? It's about a week's worth of work in all. Cleaning up, assembling booths, arranging tables, hanging decorations... that type of thing. We'll have a small crew. Twenty dollars an hour. I know it's not much."

"But it adds up. And it's basically next door to me." He thought for a moment. "Sure. Just send me the dates and times that you'll need me." A contract was probably too much to ask for.

"Perfect. And while I have you on the phone...."

By the time he hung up, he'd also agreed to help her friend haul some junk to the county's solid waste disposal site and to complete a bathroom tile project that her husband had begun and then abandoned. His calendar was beginning to look pretty full.

But man, he really needed to get going. He was about to text an apology to Gary and Tom for running late, but his doorbell rang. That happened so rarely that it took him a moment to realize what the sound was. Then he set the phone onto the kitchen counter and hurried to answer the door.

Willow stood there with a bottle of wine in hand. Her outfit today consisted of a maroon corduroy jumper dress with a black blouse and black stockings. Her hair was tied in a kerchief, also black, and her Birkenstocks were light brown, as were her thin gloves, an apparent nod to the morning's slight chill.

"Hi!" she said brightly. "I was looking for something in the stockroom and came across this Montepulciano. We don't do a lot of Monte, but this is pretty special and I thought you'd appreciate it."

"Wow, that's really nice of you, and—"

Before he could finish the sentence, she'd walked right past him and into the house, the bottle still firmly in her grip. "I haven't been in here for years. Bev and I went to school together, you know."

"How nice." Bev was his landlady. He'd never met her in person, but she and Charlotte were friendly. "Hey, I really hate to be rude, but—"

"She and I were lab partners in high school chemistry. I wasn't much interested in science back then—didn't seem relevant to me. Of course, when I became a vintner I understood the importance of it." Willow wandered over to the bookshelf beside the fireplace. It contained a few cookbooks, a thirty-year-old set of encyclopedias, and an assortment of paperbacks, most of them by Tom Clancy. Apparently Bev was a fan of spy novels.

"It's generous of you to bring over the wine, but I really have to go. Can I stop by this afternoon and you can tell me all about it?"

Willow gave a small smile and set the bottle on the mantel. From where he was standing he couldn't tell for sure, but that didn't look like a Granocchio label. In fact, he thought it had the stylized image of a blacksmith's forge that he'd seen on the Kovacs label. Which was weird since she said the wine came from her storeroom.

"Can I ask you a question?" she said. With her hands in her jumper pockets, she looked relaxed, as if she planned to stay all day.

"Uh, sure." He glanced at his watch. Shit, he should already be at Gary and Tom's, and he hadn't even left for the store yet. He was usually a lot more reliable than this. He'd give them a huge discount to make up for it.

Willow tilted her head slightly. "Where are Cannon's sangiovese labels?"

It was such a non sequitur that it made no sense at first, and Everett spent some time frowning in confusion. "The... what?"

"I couldn't find them anywhere. But then, that house is such a monstrosity that searching could drive you nuts."

"You couldn't find...."

Oh no.

Just as the penny dropped, she took her hand from her pocket.

The morning light glinted off the barrel of a gun.

CHAPTER THIRTY-TWO

Everett had taken a Mass Communications Law class when he was a senior, taught by a professor known for his eccentricity. The prof was good, and Everett learned a lot. Or at least he thought so, until he sat down to take the final exam—which would provide his entire grade for the semester—and saw that it contained only a single essay prompt: *"The truth shall set you free." Comment.* The blood in his veins had turned to ice water, his stomach felt filled with concrete, and his mind was nothing but a blank whiteboard in a blizzard.

That was precisely how he felt now, with Willow pointing a handgun at him and making a resigned grimace.

"You," he managed to croak.

"I'm genuinely sorry about this. You seem nice enough, for a lawyer. And your sister is wonderful." She shrugged. "Sometimes that's just how things work out. Where are the labels?"

Everett backed away until he hit the couch and almost fell. He was nowhere near the door or any other escape route.

"I'm such an idiot," he groaned.

"Don't be so hard on yourself. You tried, and you were close to figuring it out, I could tell. But detective stuff just isn't your gig."

Everett didn't particularly want a pep talk from a murderer, but it was better than getting shot. "Willow, I think there's been a misunderstanding. Please put the gun away and we can talk about it."

"Can't. I'm usually all about nonviolence. But it's like... I'm a vegan, right? But if I was stranded on an island with nothing to eat except bunny rabbits, I'd eventually eat those bunnies."

"I'm not a bunny rabbit," he said in his most reasonable voice. It was the one he'd used with clients who wanted to do something incredibly stupid.

Willow shrugged again. "It's all life. People, rabbits, grapevines... all any of them want is to live. But sometimes a vine stops producing well enough to make it worthwhile. Or worse, it becomes diseased. Then you have to rip it out." She said the last part with enough vim to make him wince.

Maybe she was referring to Cannon and not him. "I'm not diseased. And I'm productive enough, I guess. Pay my bills. I've been helping people out."

"It was just a metaphor. Now, where are those labels? I don't have all day."

"Why do you care? Cannon's dead—he's not going to use them."

"What if Izzy does? And anyway, they tie me to his murder. If Sergeant McBeth finds them, he'll know exactly what Cannon was up to. It's only a step from there to me."

This didn't make sense. There were holes in her thought process, he was positive of that, but he couldn't clear his head enough to find them. And even if he pointed them out, he wasn't at all certain she'd listen. He'd already discerned that Willow was strong in her convictions. The only thing he could think to do was keep her talking. He didn't truly expect her to change her mind, and he certainly didn't expect a miraculous savior to appear, but every extra minute that she talked was an extra minute of him staying alive.

Willow took a step closer. The gun was a little unsteady in her hand. It looked bulky and old, but since Everett knew nothing whatsoever about guns, he couldn't identify it. Not that the make really mattered.

"The labels?" she said.

"Why should I tell you? You're going to shoot me anyway."

"Of course," she replied. "But if you tell me, I'll make it a nice, clean headshot. You won't suffer. And honestly, you should view it as an opportunity. You'll be recycled into a new body and get a chance to improve."

Although the mention of a headshot made him slightly dizzy, he tried to keep his voice even. "I'd prefer to improve in this body, thanks."

"Well, that's not going to happen. And look, I didn't want to have to do this, but if you keep being stubborn, I have no choice. If you don't tell me where the labels are, your sister is next." She looked thoughtful. "Poison instead of a bullet, I think."

His throat threatened to close up. "What good would that do?" he managed to choke out.

"None. It would be a real waste. But it's leverage, right? And I promise that if you cooperate, Charlotte stays safe." She briefly raised her free hand as if taking an oath.

"If you shoot me, people will hear. The cops will come."

She didn't look concerned. "Maybe. But by the time they arrive, I'll be back at my shop, getting ready to open for the day. And the wine on your mantel will point their interest at Kovacs, not me. I'm asking such a simple thing from you."

"You're willing to become a serial killer over wine labels?"

Her expression hardened and she came a little closer. When she spoke it was in a low growl. "It's not about the labels. My wines are mine. I care for them, worry over them. They're my children. What Cannon was going to do, it was like kidnapping! And can you believe he thought I'd be okay with it? He was proud of his evil scheme. He invited me over—he claimed it was to get some advice—took me down to his cellar, and revealed all. He thought that if he offered a cut of his profits, I'd hand my children over to him."

"And you lost your temper and beaned him."

It was funny. Everett hadn't previously made the connection between Willow and the murder because she didn't seem the killing type. But now that she was aiming a gun at him and he saw that gleam in her eyes, he could picture the scene perfectly: Cannon, panicking a little after Schmidt turned him down, desperate to get his hands on wine to show investors. He invites Willow and pontificates about his proposed fraud, confident that he'd be a success and oblivious to her reaction. Willow silently seethes. He turns his back, maybe to walk closer to some of the wine cases. She lifts a bottle out of the nearest open case, and... bam.

And she would have walked away with a clear conscience, positive that Cannon deserved it and would head into a better life next time around. She must not have known that he'd already printed up the labels that would provide clear evidence of her motive.

"There must be some other way to resolve this," Everett said.

"There isn't. I meditated on it. I drank some shroom tea and let that journey inform me. This is the only way."

He shook his head. "Put down the gun. Turn yourself in. I'll make sure you get a fantastic lawyer. They'll convince a jury it was self-defense. Worst-case scenario, you cop a plea to involuntary manslaughter and do two years, then you're out free." He wasn't sure whether this was sound legal advice, but under the circumstances, his reputation as an attorney was not his main concern.

"No," she said. "I'd rather continue to make wine. C'mon, Everett. Last chance. Where are they?"

Keep her talking. "How did you get into the house the second time?"

"I saw Cannon key in the code the first time I was there." She lifted the gun a little higher and sighted down the barrel.

This was a dumb reason to die. Would Charlotte bury him in the Gulch cemetery? Although he had a will, he'd never made arrangements for what to do with his body. He had life insurance, and he'd remembered to switch the beneficiary to Charlotte after the divorce, so that was good. But he'd never really thought about a final resting place. The cemetery here was a good one. And a pretty place. Nice views—not that he'd be enjoying them, but visitors would. In the unlikely event that ghosts were real, he'd have interesting company. And Deadman Gulch had—he had to admit—kind of grown on him.

He hoped Warren would be okay. Charlotte would make sure he

was well cared for. And Ron Tosto—would he find someone to finish his yard before Doris came home? Would Carol Allen find someone to help out at the antique and crafts fair, and to finish her bathroom? What would Cole McBeth think about the whole disaster?

He tried one last thing. "I'll take you there and show you."

Willow scowled. "I'm not that stupid."

Everett took a few clearing breaths. The near-panic had fled and he felt oddly calm. While he hadn't accomplished as much in life as he'd hoped, at least he'd never done anything awful. He had family who cared about him. He'd fallen genuinely in love, and even though the love had faded, he'd come out of the experience with a good friend. He'd fixed quite a few things that were broken.

He kept his gaze steady. "They're at his office next to Ornamentary," he said.

"Why on earth would he put them there?"

Before she could puzzle that one out, Everett ran. His goal was to make it to the kitchen, where his phone waited on the counter. There was also a nice sharp knife right beside the sink, and if he—

There was a gunshot.

The next events happened so dizzyingly fast that they were more like a series of rapid snapshots than like real life. Everett yelled—but didn't really hear himself, with the gunshot still echoing in his ears. He tripped over his own feet and fell. Willow shouted something. There was another bang, this one possibly more muted, coming from the direction of the front door. Someone yelled, "Freeze!"

Everett, who'd been trying to get upright again, froze, face-down in old carpeting that really ought to be replaced.

There was a mini storm of shouting, of running footsteps. He had the sense that someone else was in the house.

It occurred to him eventually that he wasn't dead and nobody was actively threatening him. He got his knees under him and, cautiously, rose onto unsteady feet.

The gun was on the floor. Willow was in handcuffs, looking miserable. And Cole McBeth stood next to her, holding one of her arms and speaking urgently into a radio. He turned and caught Everett's eyes. "Are you all right?" He looked furious. He was gorgeous.

"Um… yes?"

"Is anyone else in the house?"

"Not that I know of."

Cole nodded briskly. "Just stay put. Help's on the way."

It seemed to Everett that help had already arrived, but for once he wasn't in the mood to argue. He stayed put.

"It was self-defense!" Willow cried. "He lured me here and told me he was going to frame me for Blake Cannon's murder. Then he—"

"Oh, zip it!" Cole snapped. "You have the right to remain silent. Please do."

He had just finished Mirandizing her when several uniformed deputies stormed in through the open door. Everett recognized one of them, a young woman, from when he'd found Cannon's body, but he didn't know any of their names. Still dazed, he watched as Cole ordered them around. Within minutes, Cole had led Willow away, leaving Everett stranded in the middle of his living room.

The young woman approached him. "Mr. Vaughn, right? Can you tell me what happened here?"

"I, um—"

"I'll take his statement." That was Cole, appearing like magic again, only this time more peacefully. The other deputy walked away, and Cole set a hand on Everett's shoulder. "Are you okay to talk right now?"

Everett managed a smile. "You're not going to offer me a bagel this time?"

"Bagels are for homicides. We didn't have one today." He let out a long breath. "Luckily."

"I've been enough trouble that I'd think you'd be glad to be rid of me."

Cole's expression turned serious. "No. Look, I need to hear what just happened here. But when we're done with that, there's something—"

"What the hell is going on here?" Charlotte, who'd somehow managed to bully her way past a phalanx of law enforcement and into the house, rushed at them at full speed. If Everett hadn't known that she loved him, it would have been a terrifying sight. Cole, on the other hand, flinched before holding up a hand to stop her.

"Ms. Tabor, everything's all right. We had an incident, but the perpetrator is in custody and your brother is fine."

"My brother is bleeding!"

Everett frowned, then followed her gaze to his left calf. A red stain was spreading from a small tear in his jeans.

"Huh," he said. "I guess I am." And fainted dead away.

CHAPTER THIRTY-THREE

"'Tis only a flesh wound," Everett said to the EMT, who was probably too young to catch the Monty Python reference and simply looked confused.

"Sir, you lost consciousness, so I strongly recommend that you get further medical attention. We can take you to the hospital in Jackson and they can check you out."

Everett, who was sitting on the rental-house couch with emergency personnel surrounding him like supplicants, thought about how much that little trip would likely cost him. His medical insurance had lapsed after he quit the law firm, and he'd never quite managed to sign on with anyone else.

"I'm noting your advice and absolving you of responsibility. It really is only a scratch." In fact, Ron Tosto's thistles had inflicted damage almost as severe as Willow's bullet. The bullet had barely grazed him. Some disinfectant and a bandage had taken care of things, and his worst injury was to his pride after fainting in front of Cole.

However, Cole clearly had other problems to deal with. As soon as Charlotte learned that Everett was mostly unscathed, she'd turned to Cole and started ripping him a new one for not noticing that Everett had been shot. Poor Cole looked as chastened as a schoolboy who'd forgotten his homework.

"He told me he was all right," Cole repeated for the third or fourth time. "He's an adult, and I assumed he was capable of assessing himself."

"Not if he's in shock!"

"I wasn't in shock," Everett added from the couch. Not really, according to the EMT, who'd decided that Everett had experienced something called vasovagal syncope, which probably wasn't serious under the circumstances. And although the poor guy insisted that Everett should get checked out anyway, *probably wasn't serious* was good enough for Everett.

Cole shot him what might have been a grateful look, Charlotte ignored him, and the EMT stood and shook his head. "All right, dude. But see your doctor for some antibiotics. Keep the wound clean. And promise me that if you have any adverse symptoms—any at all—you'll seek medical help immediately."

"Fine. And thank you."

"You've had quite a morning. If I were you, I'd keep that leg elevated and get some rest."

"Noted."

A few cops were still collecting evidence, but the space around Everett was clear until Cole and Charlotte walked over. They crowded close, Charlotte scowling fiercely. "Seriously, Everett?"

He lay back against the cushions. "Go ahead. Hit me with the I told you sos. I've earned them."

She opened her mouth, closed it, then sighed while shaking her head. "What would be the point? I doubt you'll change your behavior as a result of this mess." Her expression softened into a small smile. "I'm really glad you're okay. Or as okay as you ever are, I guess."

"Thanks, sis," he said sincerely. "How did you end up here anyway?" Everett turned to Cole. "For that matter, how did you end up here? And just in the nick of time."

"That was Ms. Tabor, actually. And also the Rollins-Rosses. They got worried because you didn't show up on time, which they figured wasn't like you, and you didn't answer their calls or texts. So they called Ms. Tabor, and—"

"And you hadn't answered my text either. Ev, did you make sure that Warren's appointment was with Dr. Kelly and not Dr. Hardesty?"

He chuckled. "Yes, dear sister."

Cole was clearly eager to continue his story. "So Ms. Tabor called me. Her concerns, combined with the text you sent me, well, I thought it would be a good idea to talk to you pronto. I was just about to knock on your door when I heard a gunshot."

"And you entered without a warrant, which is okay under the exigent circumstances doctrine." Everett frowned. "I forget the case name. It's been a long time since I took my constitutional law class."

"Are you sure you're all right?" Cole asked doubtfully.

"I'm dandy."

And... he was. Because it occurred to him that he was alive and, for the most part, unhurt. That the case was solved. That people here—not just his family—cared about him. That for the foreseeable future, when he was in a fantasizing mood, he was going to replay mental footage of a hot, uniformed deputy sheriff rushing to his aid. And that even now, that very same hot deputy was going to sit beside him on the couch and listen to Everett tell how he'd nearly cracked the case and how he'd stood brave—mostly—when facing death.

He felt dandy indeed.

CHAPTER THIRTY-FOUR

"I've heard quite a lot about you."

Dr. Kelly's lovely Jamaican accent gave some context to the tropical prints on the exam-room walls. She had a warm smile and a gentle touch as she examined Warren. For his part, Warren was purring up a storm, clearly pleased to be admired by this nice person. If he only knew what was coming next.

"I swear I don't normally get myself shot at," said Everett.

"I hope not. But I was referring more to your handyman work. Ron Tosto told me you finished clearing his front yard last week despite your injury."

"That makes me sound a lot tougher than I am. I was barely scraped. I ended up in more pain from the yard work than from the bullet."

After checking Warren's teeth, she looked into one of his ears while rubbing the other. "Are you available for additional jobs? I have sloped ceilings in the bedroom and I'd like to expand my closet space into the eaves. Carpentry is not within my skillset."

He trotted out his now standard disclaimer. "I'm not licensed, bonded, or insured. But that sort of project is within *my* skillset. And

I'm available. In fact, if you'd like to do it in trade for veterinary services, that would be great."

"Excellent! I'll text you some details this evening." During the conversation, she had palpated Warren's joints and then his belly. Now she chucked him under the chin. "I'm happy to say that your young man seems to be in fine condition."

Everett was surprised by the relief he felt at hearing this news. Dr. Kelly had informed him that Warren was about a year old and that although he had been neutered, he wasn't microchipped. She'd also congratulated him for adopting a stray and for responsible ownership, which had made him so pleased with himself that he didn't feel the compulsion to make his usual claim that this wasn't his cat.

Then he remembered one of the reasons he was here. "What about his weird behavior? My sister thinks there's something wrong with him."

"What sort of behavior?"

Warren certainly wasn't acting as if he was distressed right now. In fact, he'd collapsed sideways on the exam table, still rumbling like a motorcycle, and headbutted Dr. Kelly's hand if she stopped petting him.

"Um, pacing near the windows and front door of her shop but refusing to go out. Walking up to employees and meowing loudly even when his food and water dishes are full. She said sometimes he also meows while he walks between the bookshelves."

"Have you witnessed him do these things?"

"No, but I believe Char," said Everett. "When I'm there he seems fine. I mean, he's always right in the middle of whatever I'm trying to do, but I guess that's a pretty normal cat thing."

Dr. Kelly looked amused. "I think Warren is just fine. When he seems restless, he's simply searching for his favorite human."

Everett frowned. "Who's his fav—" Then it dawned on him. "Me?"

"Sounds that way."

"But I'm not a cat person."

She chuckled. "Apparently Warren is an Everett Vaughn cat."

Well, that was.... Everett wanted to say it was ridiculous. But actually, it was kind of nice. He'd never been the Chosen One before. He grinned. "Fair enough. He sort of very indirectly saved my life."

"How did he do that?" Dr. Kelly gave Warren a two-handed neck rub.

"I texted my sister to tell her I'd made a vet appointment for him. Char messaged back to, uh, remind me of something. When I didn't respond, she got worried. Combined with other things, that led her to call the cops."

"And what was her reminder about?" There was a sparkle in her eyes.

"Uh, to make the appointment with you instead of Dr. Hardesty." Well, that was awkward, considering they were colleagues.

"Why is that?"

"Um. She said that Dr. Hardesty, uh...."

"Has all the charm of a rabid raccoon?" Dr. Kelly smiled.

"Something like that. Is she really that bad?"

"Worse, if she hasn't had her coffee yet. Or if I keep her up past ten o'clock at night." In response to Everett's gape, her smile widened. "She's my wife. She is an outstanding veterinarian, especially with large animals, and she has a kind heart hidden under some very thick and prickly spikes."

Everett felt his face go deep red. "Oh, man, I am so sorry. I didn't mean—"

She waved his apology away. "I encouraged you. It's fine. Honestly, I think she delights in the impression she makes on people. When I first met her, I thought she was horrible." She winked. "I came around."

She looked down at Warren and said, "Sorry, son, but it's time for the pokey bits." Even though Everett knew the shots were for Warren's own good, he turned his head away and focused on the tropical photos.

The receptionist, Beau, brightened when Everett and Warren emerged from the exam room. It had turned out that Beau was in his early thirties, bearded and beefy and wearing a set of scrubs depicting rainbow-hued astronaut cats. His voice was even more swoon-worthy in person.

"Dr. Kelly said this will be a trade account, so there's no charge for today," Beau said. "Warren may be a little off his game after his shots, maybe for a day or two, but then he should be fine. We'll plan to see him once a year, but just give us a call if you have any worries before then."

"If something comes up, I'd be happy to call."

Their eyes locked, at which point Everett realized they might be flirting, an action he hadn't engaged in for well over a decade. It was not like riding a bicycle, but maybe he'd improve with some practice.

"Talk to you soon," said Beau with an eyebrow waggle.

Everett blushed for the second time in five minutes, mumbled something, and fled.

Sierra Pride Animal Clinic was less than a mile from downtown, but because Warren was moderately heavy and not happy about being stuffed into a carrier, Everett had driven. Now he got them back into Janet, patted her dashboard, and drove to the bookstore, where— although not yet officially open for the day—Jessica unlocked the door and took Warren's carrier. After a quick debriefing on the vet visit, Everett headed home.

He'd already cleaned up the mess from Willow's attack, including patching a small hole in the wall where the bullet had lodged after grazing him. It was still odd to think that he'd very nearly lost his life here. The only things that had saved him were the fact that Willow's gun—an antique Smith & Wesson that was apparently a family heirloom—had misfired the first time and then jammed as she tried to get off a second shot. And, of course, Cole McBeth had showed up just in the nick of time.

In a way, Everett was grateful to Willow. His experience with her had done a lot to straighten out the mess in his head. Nearly dying was an effective, if terrifying, way to evaluate your life and get your priorities in order. Everett still might not be certain what he wanted to do with the rest of his life, but he'd made some comfortable decisions about his near future.

Smiling, he collected a stack of papers from the tray of the printer he'd bought on Saturday. He slid them into a messenger bag, shrugged into his blue-checked shirt jacket, and headed to Main Street.

There was a short line at Rising Times, but the pastry selection was still good. "You're later than usual this morning," said Xochi as she handed him the bag containing his cheesecake brownie.

"I had to take Warren to the vet."

"Oh no! Is he okay?"

"Just a check-up. And, uh...." He mimed an injection with his fingers.

"Aw, poor thing. Tomorrow I'll bake him some salmon treats to help him recover."

"He'll love that." Everett set the pastry bag onto the counter, pulled a paper from his messenger bag, and handed it to her. "Would you consider putting this on your door for a while?"

She read it quickly and smiled. "Sure thing."

"Thanks!" He collected his coffee and brownie, greeted Sanjeev Patel as he came in the door, and then headed outside himself.

Main Street was quiet this early on a Monday, with only a few locals heading to work or out for breakfast. Tom Rollins-Ross, taking advantage of a closed day to refresh the window display at the Olive Branch, waved from inside the store. Everett would drop off one of his printed pages later. Granocchio Cellars had a hastily scrawled *Closed until further notice* sign in the window, which made Everett feel a little bad. It wasn't Willow's family's fault that she was a wee bit homicidal. He hoped they came out of this okay.

He arrived at Pages & Pastries shortly after Charlotte unlocked the door. Jessica gave a wave from her place at the whirring espresso machine, which had already filled the building with the delicious aroma of fresh coffee. Today she was resplendent in a lilac-colored maxi dress with a lime-green duster and sparkly sky-blue eyeshadow.

Charlotte, on the other hand, wore jeans and a gray sweatshirt imprinted with the store logo. She was busily swearing at her point-of-sale tablet. "The ghost's been busy again," she said by way of explanation. "Every time I try to enter something, it defaults to a book about poisons. A title that we don't even carry."

"Sounds like you need a tech person to check it out."

"Deja convinced me to give it another day. They intend to conduct a séance tonight to see what the ghost wants."

"Good luck with that," said Everett.

Still staring at the screen, she nodded absently.

"Hey, I've been thinking about having Warren stay at my place for a couple of days. Just to give him a change of scene and so I can keep an eye on him after his shots. I was thinking of picking him up sometime late this afternoon."

Char was smiling at him, and to hide his slight embarrassment he handed her one of his papers. "For your door, please."

She read it and then nodded. "Looks good."

"I'm going to ask other stores to hang it up too. Maybe even at Miner's Stake. I know it's hardly ever open, and it sounds as if the owner's a total curmudgeon, but I think I saw someone moving around in there when I walked by."

Charlotte shrugged. "Good luck with that."

"So, anything you need from me today?"

"I haven't been very happy with the lighting in the children's section. Can you sit down with me later and help me choose something else? Oh, and I'm going to be carrying a range of bookmarks handmade by a local artist. Gifty stuff. I'll need some kind of display rack."

"On it," he replied happily. He hefted his messenger bag. "After I finish my rounds."

He turned and had taken only two steps toward the door when Sophie and Cole entered. She was covered in several layers of goth-lite clothing, as if she'd been raiding the sale bins at Hot Topic. He was out of uniform, in jeans and a plaid button-up, as if he'd just stepped away from the family ranch.

"Sophie is on her way to the orthodontist," Cole announced. "I've promised her a new book by way of compensation."

Charlotte nodded sagely. "An excellent arrangement. And good timing, too. Look what just released. I've been saving you a copy." She pulled a book from under the counter and held it up.

The scowl that Sophie had worn when she entered disappeared, and she squealed. "Oh my God, the new Holly Gold!" She ran over, took the book from Charlotte, and hugged it to her chest. Then, beaming, she turned to her father. "It's about this sixteen-year-old girl who joins the French Resistance during World War Two. Based on a real story! I read the first book and it was amazing, but it kinda ended on a cliffie. This is the sequel." She squealed again.

"That's a review copy," said Charlotte solemnly.

"Thank you," said Cole. "That's an extra few dollars I can put toward someone's very expensive mouth."

Sophie's scowl returned for a moment. "I'm still not happy about braces."

For the first time since he'd entered the store, Cole addressed Everett. "You look fully recovered."

"And nobody's tried to kill me for days. Hey, I never really got a chance to, um, thank you. So... thank you. If you hadn't rushed over—"

"Just doin' my job." Cole, bareheaded, looked as if he wished he were wearing a Stetson so that he could follow his comment with a slight tip of the hat.

"I guess. Hey, you said you wanted to tell me something. I forgot about it in the middle of all the confusion." That was a lie. His curiosity had been killing him, but he hadn't devised an excuse to track Cole down and ask.

Cole looked very much like a deer caught in the headlights. He gave a quick glance at their little audience—Sophie, Charlotte, and Jessica—and cleared his throat. "It was, uh, nothin'. I forget. Not important."

Those statements were somewhat contradictory, a fact that Everett was going to point out, but then Cole pointed at Everett's messenger bag. "What's that for?"

That was probably the worst attempt at changing a subject that Everett had ever seen—and he'd seen a lot. But he decided to cut Cole a break, seeing as Everett owed him his life. So instead of interrogating, he reached into the bag and handed Cole one of the papers.

Cole read it out loud. His voice wasn't as nice as Beau's, but it wasn't bad. "Everett of All Trades. Hauling. Junk removal. Yard work. DIY rescues. Meal prep. Fence repair. Drywall patching. Minor installations." He looked up. "I take it that's your phone number?"

"Yeah. And don't worry, I'm aware of state licensing requirements and will abide by the rules." Getting a contractor's license wasn't easy, but he was considering it.

Cole shrugged. "Enforcement of those is not in my jurisdiction. Just stay away from crime scenes, all right?"

"I'll do my best."

There was an odd expression on Cole's face. He opened his mouth, paused, and closed it again. He stared up at the ceiling. He tapped a booted foot.

It was Sophie who broke the silence. "Does this mean you're planning to stick around?"

Everett smiled at her. "Yep. For a while, anyway." He was eventually going to have to think about housing, when his lease was up. And that contractor's license. And health insurance. And probably a lot more as well. But he was confident he could tackle these issues over time.

"Will you teach me how to cook some stuff?" she asked.

"I'd be delighted."

She shot a look at her father and then back to Everett. "Maybe you could come over for dinner again and, like, do a chef demo."

"Sounds fun."

Cole suddenly waved an arm. "C'mon, Soph. You're going to be late for your appointment."

"My torture, you mean."

They both thanked Charlotte for the book and hurried for the door. But Cole paused before stepping outside and turned back to Everett. "Welcome to Deadman Gulch." A smile played at the corners of his mouth for a moment, and then he was gone.

Everett caught Charlotte and Jessica exchanging a look. But then a family of early-rising tourists appeared, the husband with a baby strapped to his chest and the mother holding the hand of a toddler. Charlotte sailed over to greet them.

Remembering that he still had a cheesecake brownie to eat, Everett exited onto the sidewalk and headed toward City Park, where breakfast al fresco under the autumn-hued trees seemed like a fine idea. Then he would make the rounds with his flyers. That oak ice box was still for sale at Mother Lode Discoveries. Although it was closed today, he might swing by to see if Marian Fisker was around and willing to work out a good deal. Refinished, it would make a nice place to store a few bottles of wine. Later he'd promised to stop by the Olive Branch to discuss this week's menu. He'd already made a mental list of cat supplies: a litter box, litter, dishes, food, a soft bed, some toys, a scratching post, maybe a cardboard house made to look like a sushi restaurant. And hadn't he seen cat harnesses over at the pet supply place? Maybe Warren would enjoy going for walks.

Now, though, the Pony Express rider straightened his bag. He might be old for the job, but he'd braved hundreds of miles of difficult territory—and one hostile local with a gun—to get to his California destination. All that was left was to deliver his important papers... after he had his breakfast.

Grinning and looking forward to his new adventure, Everett sauntered down Main Street.

ACKNOWLEDGMENTS

As always, I owe a debt to many people who helped bring my story to these pages. I'd like to express gratitude to the friends in my critique group, who gave me invaluable guidance and encouragement: Janice, Jay, Jen, Tawnya, Tom, and Rick. My beta readers were also lovely: lyric, Ro, and Thea.

Many thanks to my editorial team, Karen Witzke and Allison Behrens, who work so hard to keep me looking smart. Special thanks to Quinn Behrens, who found the perfect title for this book.

And finally, I so deeply appreciate the readers who come along with me as my muse leads us in all sorts of unexpected directions.

ABOUT THE AUTHOR

Kim Fielding is very pleased every time someone calls her eclectic. Winner of the BookLife Prize for Fiction, a Lambda Award finalist and a Foreword INDIE finalist, she has migrated back and forth across the western two-thirds of the United States and, after a long exile, has returned to Portland, Oregon. She's a university professor who dreams of being able to travel and write full time. She also dreams of having two daughters who fully appreciate her, a husband who isn't obsessed with football, and a house that cleans itself. Some dreams are more easily obtained than others.

Kim can be found on her website: http://kfieldingwrites.com/

Her e-mail is kim@kfieldingwrites.com

facebook.com/kfieldingwrites

ALSO BY KIM FIELDING

Series

Deadman Gulch Mysteries

The Bureau

Greynox to the Sea

Love Can't

Ennek

Bones

Stars from Peril

Chaos and Order (with J. Scott Coatsworth)

Novels

Rook's Time

Crow's Fate

The Taste of Desert Green

Potential Energy

The Muffin Man

Teddy Spenser Isn't Looking for Love

Hallelujah (with F.E. Feeley Jr.)

Blyd and Pearce

A Full Plate

The Little Library

Ante Up

Running Blind (with Venona Keyes)

Staged

Rattlesnake

Astounding!

Motel. Pool.

The Tin Box

Venetian Masks

Brute

Novellas

Peppermint Bark

Shelf-Made Man

Man of His Dreams

Bread Crumbs

Regifted

Bite Me: An Elucidation in Three Acts

Farkas

Ash Believes the Impossible

A Very Genre Christmas

Gravemound

The Solstice Kings

Dei Ex Machina

The Golem of Mala Lubovnya

Refugees

The Dance

Transformation

Summerfield's Angel

The Tale of August Hayling

Phoenix

Grown-Up

The Pillar

The Border

Housekeeping

Night Shift

Speechless

Guarded

The Downs

Short Stories and Collections

Cozy

Happily

Dog Days of December

Firestones

Dreidels and Do-Overs

Get Lit

Christmas Present

Act One and Other Stories

Exit through the Gift Shop

Dear Ruth

Grateful

The Sacrifice and Other Stories

Saint Martin's Day

The Festivus Miracle

Joys R Us

Alaska

A Great Miracle Happened There

Violet's Present

Standby

Anyplace Else